TEMPT ME

A BROTHER'S BEST FRIEND WORKPLACE
STANDALONE ROMANTIC COMEDY

SYNERGY WORKPLACE ROMANCE
BOOK 6

MICHELLE MCCRAW

BN ISBN: 978-1-961373-98-3
D2D ISBN: 9798223989998
IngramSpark ISBN: 978-1-961373-00-6

BOOKS BY MICHELLE MCCRAW

40 and Fabulous

Fashion and Passion

Frenemies and Lovers

Books and Hookups

Conspiracies and Chemistry

Synergy Series

Work with Me

Friend Me

Trip Me Up

Boss Me

Forget Me

Tempt Me

For all the librarians and teachers out there, especially my former teachers Mr. Chehal, Ms. Jackson, Mrs. Helms, and Ms. Berger. Thank you for all you did to encourage me to read, learn, and expand my mind. These are difficult times, and I see you.

1

LARRY'S beady eyes were like my mother's black pearl earrings, round, lustrous, and judgmental.

"Don't look at me like that," I whispered, turning my attention back to Chef Guillaume.

With a genius for multitasking honed in the finest restaurants in France, the instructor flashed me a threatening stare without interrupting the flow of his lesson on shellfish.

Larry blinked, which was weird because I was pretty sure lobsters didn't have eyelids. If they did, Chef Guillaume would've taught us to filet them.

I shifted on my feet, sore from standing in the miserable clogs that mercilessly rubbed the top of my foot. Pulling the kitchen towel from the belt of my apron, I tossed it over Larry where he rested on the cutting board at my workstation. Now I could focus on Chef Guillaume, who'd started a sidebar on shellfish allergies.

Much better.

The towel twitched, and one banded claw waved feebly at me. My chest panged. Chef explained that our local California spiny lobsters were shipped to China at exorbitant prices.

Poor Larry.

A couple of days ago, he'd been hanging out with his lobster buddies in the North Atlantic. Today, he slowly suffocated here in my cooking class at a community college in San Francisco, paling under the unflattering fluorescents, waiting to plunge into the pot of water that had almost reached a boil.

I stared at his immobilized claw. *That makes two of us, buddy.*

Tugging the towel off his head, I tucked it under his reddish-brown body so he wasn't lying on the slippery cutting board. It had to smell like the other poor creatures I'd dispatched in my butchery class.

Did lobsters have noses?

Probably not, thank god. If he did, he'd smell my fear.

We'd started the semester with poultry. They'd come to us deceased with their heads detached, unlike Larry. I'd almost puked at the sight of the pale, featherless bodies, but instead, I imagined what Mother would say if I dropped out of this school too. I'd swallowed and carried on, splitting the parts well enough for a pass from Chef Guillaume.

The next unit had been beef, but that had also come to us face-less. I'd learned to separate the ribs from the loin, and I'd created a standing rolled rib roast Chef hadn't snarled at. He'd called it "not bad," which was as good as an A in any other class. Though I didn't have much experience with As in school, culinary or otherwise.

We'd moved on to fish, and although they had faces, at least they were dead on arrival.

Until Larry.

"Miss Natalie Jones, are you paying attention?" How had Chef Guillaume snuck up on me like that? He scowled at me from the other side of my worktable with his hands on his hips.

"Yes, Chef," I squeaked. I didn't dare look at Larry.

"Then why is your lobster swaddled like un bébé and not cooking in the pot?"

Uh-oh. I glanced to my right, where my neighbor Gregory was wiping down his station. Steam wafted from the cover of his stockpot.

"Waiting for a full boil, Chef," I said, glancing at my pot, where bubbles were starting to break the surface.

"Show me." His lip curled as he stared down at the lobster. "Remove that towel."

"Sorry." Gently, I disentangled my towel from Larry. Poor guy didn't look so good.

Chef's nostrils flared. "Demonstrate for the class how to humanely kill the lobster."

"I...uh." *Humanely kill* sounded like an oxymoron to me. "Could you show me the technique again?"

He reached for Larry.

I leaped to cover the crustacean with my body. "Not him!" I froze. "I mean, I'll do it." It was the least I owed Larry.

Chef raised an eyebrow. "Bon. I will demonstrate, then you repeat."

He whirled and snatched the lobster from Chantal's table. He slapped it onto the cutting board next to Larry. In one smooth movement, he grabbed my knife and buried the tip in the lobster's brain. When it twitched, Larry scrabbled weakly on the cutting board.

"See? Quick and humane." He dropped the dead lobster into Chantal's pot. She murmured her thanks and set the lid on the pot.

"Now you." He held out my knife to me, handle first.

I glanced at my pot. Damn those efficient gas burners. It had reached a full boil. I accepted the handle and turned my attention to Larry. Resigned to his fate, he allowed his antennae to droop.

My heart broke for him.

He'd end up mingled with his friends in a lobster bisque to be served in the school cafeteria or in a lobster roll wrapped to go.

Why should he have to die for some soggy, over-sauced sandwich?

All he wanted to do was live his best lobster life. So what if he hadn't determined what that might be? He deserved another chance to figure out his life.

Wait. Was that Larry or me?

"Miss Jones. May I remind you that we have only thirty minutes left in class?"

Thirty minutes. Chef Guillaume didn't accept late assignments. I'd have to murder poor Larry now if I had any hope of disassembling his carcass in time. The silver lobster pick flashed in the fluorescent lights. The one Chef expected me to use to pull Larry's flesh from his shell.

Larry lifted his claw in farewell, showing me the blue band. Blue like the ocean. Blue like the delicate edges of the shell covering his slender knees, which I'd be expected to tug out with the fork.

I swallowed. *Not today, Larry.*

"Sorry, Chef."

Dropping my knife, I tossed the towel back over Larry and lifted him. He wasn't heavy, only a couple pounds, but his over-sized claws flopped.

"What are you doing, Miss Jones?"

I kept my head down. "I'm leaving, Chef."

The classroom had gone deadly quiet.

"If you walk out that door, you fail my class. It will be difficult to graduate without it."

It would've been difficult to graduate even with a passing grade in his class. Shoving Larry under my arm, I dragged my Louboutin tote from its cubby under my workstation and slung it over my shoulder. "I understand, Chef."

"Do you, Miss Jones?" His gray eyebrow lifted. He must have sensed the pressure that made me return day after day to a class I was failing.

I glanced at my knife roll. I liked the heft of the large chef's knife and the way the handle fit into my hand. It was a shame to leave it here. But I'd have to put down Larry, and if I did that, my short-tempered instructor might chuck him into my pot and boil him alive.

Better to leave it. I nodded at Gregory. He had skills. He

deserved them more than I did. Culinary school was wasted on me, just like college, fashion school, the event-planning internship, and even the flower shop my stepfather bought me.

"Sorry, Chef," I repeated, and with a firm grip on Larry, I turned on my clogs.

I wish I could say I sailed out, but my damn clog caught on the floor and wrenched itself off my foot. I'd always hated them anyway. I stepped out of the other and, in my socks, scuffed out of the classroom.

———

THE UBER DRIVER peeled away from the curb at Rincon Park. I'd gotten used to the fishy odor in the two hours we'd spent in the classroom, but having Larry in the little Mazda was a lot, especially after he'd gotten a little carsick.

Despite the low clouds, the air was fresher at the park, and I strode straight for the pier.

"Don't worry, Larry. I got you. The spiny lobsters might look different, but I'm sure they're nice. You're going to make so many new friends."

He rolled his eyestalks back toward me.

"Seriously, guy. I don't think you'd make it if I shipped you back to Maine or wherever. This is way better than being served in the cafeteria. If you don't like the bay, you can swim right around the peninsula to the ocean."

On second thought, I probably should have taken him to the ocean side of the city, but it was too late for that now. The water was deep here, and there was no commercial fishing in the bay.

When I reached the rail, I propped Larry on it, still swaddled in my kitchen towel. His eyestalks swiveled between me and the water below.

"Look, Larry. I know this is a new place, and you're scared. I've started plenty of new things, and here's what's always worked for me: find a way to help others. That way they need you, whether they like you or not."

Larry wasn't buying it. He rapped the railing with his claw.

"You don't have to take my advice. What do I know, anyway? None of my schools or jobs have stuck, and I'm going to have a heck of a time explaining what happened today to Mother and Charles. But the right thing for me is out there, and the right thing for you is down there."

We both peered into the water. It was deep and blue.

"Find a nice rock and lay low until you get your strength back. Chow down on... What do you guys eat, anyway? Plankton? Seaweed? Little fish? I'm sure it's down there. Maybe you'll meet a nice lady lobster—or a dude, whatever makes you happy—and settle down in a nice, deep part of the ocean, raise some babies together. Okay?" I wiped a bit of ocean spray from my cheek.

He twitched his claws feebly.

"Right. Gotta get those off." I reached into my bag and found the pink Swiss Army knife my brother Jackson gave me when I was twelve. I flicked open the long blade and sliced through the rubber band on his right claw, then his left. Tentatively, he opened and closed his claws.

"Better? Okay, I'm going to drop you in."

But I didn't. I stared into his cloudy eyes.

"This is your second chance, dude. Don't waste it." Who was I to advise him? How many second, third, or fourth chances had I wasted? How many times had Mother given me her narrow-eyed, compressed-lip stare that told me how much I'd disappointed her? How many times had she actually said the words, *Natalie, when are you going to settle down? Why can't you be more like your brothers or your sister?*

I'd never be as successful as my siblings. I should do what Mother had done and marry a guy with potential. She'd introduced me to enough sons of her rich friends that I should've found one I liked by now.

Larry tapped my hand with his claw.

"Right, sorry. This isn't about me. It's about you. Okay, one… two…three." I upended him and dropped him head-first into the water, ten feet below. He sliced in, splashless, like an Olympic diver. He hovered for a second under the water, rocking with the waves that slapped against the pier. It almost looked like he waved at me. Then, with a swish of his tail, he submerged, his brown shell disappearing into the dark water. I waited for a minute, gripping the stinky kitchen towel. Then I let another minute pass. But Larry didn't reappear.

I hoped he'd do better with his second chance than I'd done with mine.

I turned back toward the city. I could get another Uber home, clean up, and figure out how to explain to my parents that I'd dropped out of culinary school two weeks before the end of the term. Or…

I caught sight of the tall building that shaded my brother's shorter building.

He'd gotten his share of second chances. Maybe he could offer me some advice. Or at least more sympathy than I'd get from our mother.

2

WHEN I STEPPED off the elevator to the sixth floor, I realized the flaw in my plan. The dress code at Synergy was casual, but my white coat stained with whatever fluid Larry had puked up on me, baggy chef pants, and the neon-green flip-flops I'd bought from a souvenir stand near the pier couldn't be more different from the designer dresses I usually wore. Everyone gaped at me as I passed.

Channeling my mother, I lifted my chin like I was wearing Hermès and shuffled to my brother's assistant's desk. I missed seeing Marlee there, but since her promotion, she sat downstairs with the other developers.

His new assistant, Paulina, was an older woman from the Caribbean. She took in my appearance and smiled. "Coming straight from school, cariño?"

"Yeah." I kept my wince on the inside. "Is my brother in his office?" I glanced at the glass door behind her.

"No, he's in Mr. Fallon's office."

I sighed. I wanted to see Jackson, but his friend Cooper had taken the express lane to success. Cooper never said anything about my meandering path through life, but he always looked out from under the shelf of his bushy eyebrows and speared me with a glare of disapproval.

I wished I could slink away, but Paulina would tell Jackson I'd been here. I had to carry through with my half-baked plan.

"Thanks, Paulina." I scuffed across the floor to Cooper's office. His assistant wasn't at his desk, but his cousin-slash-security guard, Mateo, stood near the door. He grinned as I approached.

"Natalie! What brings our little Cat Cora here?"

At five-eight, I wasn't little, but compared to Mateo's tall, bulky physique, I must have seemed tiny, especially when I wasn't wearing my heels.

"I wanted to talk to my brother. He's still in with Cooper?"

"They're all in there. Go on in," he said. I pushed the door handle.

It wasn't until my gaze slid off Cooper seated at his desk and my brother leaning against the windowsill to the third person in the room, that I replayed what Mateo had said: *They're all in there.* I realized who he meant by "all."

She was there. My brain stalled out. She wasn't supposed to be in San Francisco at Synergy. She was supposed to be at her office, an hour away, in Silicon Valley.

"Nutter Butter!" Jackson sprang across the room and folded me in his arms. He added a noogie for good measure, disheveling my artfully messy bun.

Why did he have to call me that goofy name? When I was an awkward nine-year-old, I let him call me whatever he wanted because I craved any attention my big brother would give me. Now I was as grown-up as he was. Yet he never failed to point out that adults had jobs and didn't live with their parents.

"Get off of me." I pushed against his overlong arms.

He loosened his hold but kept one arm slung around my shoulders, probably to keep me in noogie range. "What are you doing here?"

"I, uh..." Suddenly, telling my sob story for some sympathy

from my brother seemed like a terrible idea. "I missed my big brother?"

"Aw." He ground his knuckles into my hair again. "Well, you're just in time to laugh at Jamila for what she's done now."

Laugh at Jamila? Not only was she the most gorgeous woman I'd ever met, but she was everything I wished I could be—smart, confident, capable. Like Cooper, she'd never wavered along her march to success.

I'd avoided her for four months since that disastrous party at Billie Woods's place. And now she'd caught me at my lowest point with no designer clothes or makeup to armor me and smelling like the contents of Larry's digestive system.

She sprawled on Cooper's leather sofa, her right leg stretched to the floor, and the left propped on the back of the sofa with her beige stiletto heel dangling from her toes. Her flowy white wide-legged slacks were rucked up, showing the smooth, dark skin that covered her trim ankles and muscular calves. She wore a lilac sleeveless blouse and a pearl choker. The pearls and pastels implied softness, but her sharp words always cut through the illusion.

When she was nineteen, she had an abundant, coiled mane I envied. Now, her hair was cropped close to her head, showcasing her long, elegant neck. Running a billion-dollar software business didn't leave time for curl maintenance.

Flinging one arm across her eyes, she let out a frustrated growl. "I'm telling you, all I did was try to protect my company. That reporter is an asshole."

"That's not how the asshole reporter wrote it in his article," Cooper said dryly.

"What happened?" I asked.

She lifted her arm from her face and gave me a casual wave. "Hey, Nat."

She sounded friendly enough. Maybe four months was enough time for her to forget, though I never would. My voice wavered as I asked, "Is everything okay?"

She huffed out a sigh. "It's nothing for you to worry about, baby. I..."

As usual, my brain shorted out when she called me *baby*. I wished she meant it as a term of endearment, but she'd called me that since she came home with Jackson during spring break their first year of college. Even at nineteen and wearing a cropped Stanford sweatshirt over skinny jeans, Jamila had been impossibly sophisticated in my nine-year-old eyes. She still thought of me as a pigtail-wearing tween, and today I looked like a toddler who'd been playing in the dirt.

"...it's nothing, really."

"Nothing?" Cooper's dark eyebrows shot up. "The *Wall Street Journal* article was particularly unflattering."

"Wait. What?" I asked.

"Keep up, sis." Her nostrils flared, and my face burned hotter. Of course she was sensitive to me tuning her out. Since Billie's party, she must think I was a blond bonehead. Because that's exactly what I'd acted like.

My face burned. "Sorry, I spaced out. Could you tell me again? Please?"

Jamila rolled her eyes. "There's something fishy going on with Moo-Lah. I heard they're launching a product that's a lot like our new app. Every move I make, they seem to be a step ahead of me. I hired a PI to see if one of my folks is talking to them."

"And the press found out," Cooper added. "They called you paranoid."

"Only the paranoid survive," Jamila said. "That's what Andy Grove used to say."

"I agree with Mila," my brother said. "Not about the paranoid bit, but that everyone'll forget. I've done worse things, and I'm a media darling now." He beamed.

"That's because you settled down with Alicia, and she keeps you in line," Jamila said.

I half-expected him to deny it, but he hugged me tighter and said, "She does."

"Don't forget I'm the one who connected you two." Jamila shot him a smug smile.

"Never," he said. "Though I doubt you had marriage in mind when you recommended her as a consultant—and my boss."

If they kept up their best-friend banter, I'd never get to the bottom of Jamila's problem. I pulled away from my brother. "Being called paranoid by the *Wall Street Journal* is kind of a big deal."

"Exactly." Cooper pointed at me. "There were paps at Mila's office today. That doesn't seem like something that's going to die down."

"Like, more than five?" I asked.

"Not more than twenty." Jamila waved an elegant hand. Her nails were short but impeccably manicured and painted a vibrant purple.

"Holy crap," I said. "That's serious." She needed help. I got out my phone and searched for the article. I scanned through it, half-listening to my brother and his friends.

"Take the rest of the day off," Cooper said. "On Monday, I'll send Mateo with you. He'll hold off the paps and get you into your office safely."

She snorted. "I'd look like some damsel in distress trailing your meaty cousin. Everything will settle down over the weekend. I can't afford to take the day off. We're scheduled to release the app in June." She pulled her phone out of her pocket and glanced at it. "Sorry, I gotta take this." She pushed off the sofa and strode from the office.

"This is not good," I said, scrolling through the article. "They've painted her as a paranoid wacko. Who the heck is this PI? Do you think they were the source of the press leaks?"

Jackson shrugged. "Not if they want to keep their business. If Jamila finds out they sold the story, she'll ensure they never work in San Francisco again."

Cooper nodded. "You don't want to be on the other end of Jamila's vengeance."

"That's the problem," I said. "She can't afford to come across as a vindictive nutjob."

"A little preventive aggression never hurt anyone," Jackson said.

"Never hurt anyone?" I scoffed. "Ask Martha Stewart how that worked out. Women can't get away with what men can."

Both men stared at me blankly.

I rolled my eyes. "You wouldn't understand. I think I can help."

"Sure, Nutter Butter." Fortunately, Jackson was out of noogie range.

"I can." I stood as tall as I could in my flip-flops and baggy pants. Raised in the tech world, I'd lived in the spotlight all my life. Even longer than Jamila. "I have some ideas."

Jackson snorted, deep in his throat, the way he always did when I said something he felt was ridiculous. "You're always complaining about how much time culinary school takes. When would you have time to help Jamila?"

I looked down at my feet. The scarlet polish was half gone on my right big toe.

"Oh, no." Jackson's voice dripped with sympathy. "You didn't drop out, did you?"

I'd come here seeking his sympathy, but as it turned out, his sorrowful tone was the worst. "Not exactly."

"Fuck. My perfect little sister got kicked out?"

"Maybe?" I rubbed my toe against the edge of the thick rug. "I, uh, liberated a lobster from my butchery class."

"Really?" He barked out a laugh. "Lobsters are basically overgrown bugs. It's not like it appreciated your help."

I planted my hands on my hips. "Larry *was* appreciative of not being murdered."

"Larry?" Jackson's voice rose with hilarity. "You named someone's dinner?"

Cooper rested his chin on his hand and covered his mouth. Was he laughing?

"Screw you. Cruelty to animals isn't funny."

"You have to admit," my brother said, "getting kicked out of a community college culinary school for stealing a lobster is pretty damn funny. As is thinking you can help Jamila out of her PR slip-up. You might plan a good party, but you have zero public relations experience."

"But—" I shot Cooper a pleading look.

He held up his hands. "Sorry, Natalie. Jay's right. People go to school to learn the ins and outs of public relations. Leave it to the professionals."

"But..." How could I have wanted my brother's sympathy? It was the absolute worst. What I needed from him—or anyone— was a shred of confidence in my abilities. Apparently, the Synergy office was not the place to find it.

"Go home," Jackson said. "Put your feet up. Eat some chocolate. Try some retail therapy. I'll text you tonight to check on you, 'kay?"

I sucked in a breath through my nostrils and sighed it out. He was right. Who was I to help Jamila? I hadn't even graduated from college. I still lived at home with my parents. In a suite with a luxurious, multi-jetted shower that was calling my name. "Okay."

"Did you drive here?" Jackson asked.

"No, I—"

"Ask Paulina to give you a ride home. I'll give her the rest of the day off."

"Thanks. See you, Cooper." I waved and trudged out of the office in my ridiculous flip-flops. Jamila stood on the other side of the door, one arm crossed over her stomach and her other hand wiping a tear from her cheek.

I abandoned all thoughts of a shower.

3

In the fifteen years I'd known her, I'd never seen her cry. Not when Jackson accidentally threw an elbow and smashed her nose on Thanksgiving, not when her app came in fourth place in that contest and she didn't get the funding she deserved, and not after her weird hookup with Cooper, the one I wasn't supposed to know about and (I was pretty sure) Jackson didn't.

But outside my brother's office, moisture glistened in her eyes.

"Oh, hey." She blinked and sniffed, and she was diamond-hard Jamila Jallow again. I'd have thought I'd imagined the tear, but her mascara was the tiniest bit smudged in the corner.

"Are you okay?"

"Never better." She drew herself up. "You going home?"

I hesitated for less than a second. "No. Are you staying here?"

"My admin said the press went away, so I'm going back to the office."

"I'll go with you." The words burst from my mouth like machine-gun fire in one of Jackson's video games.

She scrunched her forehead. "Why would you want to go all the way to Silicon Valley?"

Crap. I'd forgotten she worked down in Mountain View. It'd be a pain to get back home with no car, but it would be worth it to ensure she was okay. "I've never seen your office." That was true. "I'm considering switching programs into software development." That was a lie.

Her gaze pierced me. "From culinary school to programming is a significant change."

"Oh, you know"—I waved a hand airily—"it's in my blood."

"Don't." The word was sharp like a firecracker. "You're smart and capable of doing anything you want. Don't hide your light under a bucket."

She hadn't forgotten about the Christmas party. She'd said almost those exact words then too, and then I'd done something truly idiotic.

"Jamila, I—"

"Why not stay here? Jackson will give you an internship and teach you everything you need to know about coding."

My cheeks heated, and the truth came bubbling out. "I don't want him to give me anything. I want to earn it."

My family had money, but they all made contributions in their own ways. They ranged from my mother's volunteer work to Jackson's multibillion-dollar company.

Except for me. I'd been handed things my whole life. If I wanted respect from my family, and myself, I had to find a way to contribute to society. Jamila could understand that, even if she hadn't grown up in a mansion like I had.

I gazed into her dark-chocolate eyes. I couldn't let her go without helping her in some way.

"I get it," she said. "Let me snag my jacket, and then I'll give you the tour of Jamilow Software's global headquarters." She winked and flung open the door to Jackson's office.

A minute later, she was back, shrugging into her white blazer. I almost laughed at the difference between her spotless blazer and my stained chef's coat, but I had to save my breath for jogging to keep up with her long strides to the elevator.

"Hey, Paulina," I called as we passed her desk. "Jackson said you can have the rest of the day off. Have a great weekend!" That'd serve him right for all the noogies.

Because of the fish stink clinging to my clothes, we lowered the windows of her white Porsche Cayenne on the drive to Mountain View. She dragged the story of Larry and my disastrous day from me. I didn't mind because her musical laugh was my favorite. It wasn't a flute-like titter but a sound clear, bright, and loud like a trumpet. It always made me feel like sunlight landing on my face, and I laughed too.

Once we hit 101, the wind noise kept us from talking much, so I didn't have a chance to ask what had bothered her earlier. I'd figure it out at her office. Then I'd find a way to make it better. That was something I didn't suck at.

She parked her SUV in the CEO's reserved spot. A reporter perched on top of one of the giant planters outside the glass front doors, but Jamila blew past him. Keeping my face averted, I followed in her wake. The last thing she needed was for him to recognize me in my stained outfit and have to explain why the Joneses' socialite daughter was dressed as one of Jamilow's line cooks.

As soon as we were in the lobby, a blond, white guy in his thirties rushed Jamila. He wore an ill-advised combination of raspberry-colored pants that were too loose in the seat and an expensive-looking pair of navy-and-brown brogues. His slim-fit white shirt was rumpled, and his shirtsleeves were rolled up to the middle of his forearms.

"Thank fuck you're here. I've been fielding calls all day. We need to talk—" He scanned me from my windblown hair to my green flip-flops, and looking down his nose, he said, "The entry for the kitchen staff is next to the loading dock."

"It's okay," Jamila said. "Natalie, meet Winslow Keating-Ashworth, my COO. Winslow, this is Natalie Jones. I promised her a tour of the office."

Winslow gave me a longer survey. His red-rimmed blue eyes widened. "Natalie Jones, of the Jasper Joneses?"

My chest tightened every time someone brought up my dad. They all seemed to remember him—know him—better than I did. "Yeah," I said.

"Sorry, I…" He gestured at my stained uniform.

I rolled my eyes. Jamila's number two or not, he should treat staff members better than that even if they worked in the cafeteria.

"Let's walk and talk," Jamila said, gesturing for us to flank her. The security guard tried to stop me, but one steely glare from Jamila had him opening the gate for me to pass through without a badge.

"Cafeteria's through there." Jamila waved toward a set of double doors as she stepped onto the open staircase that led to the second floor. "I'll introduce you to the kitchen manager later if you decide that's still your passion." She winked.

I smiled back, wishing I could catch that wink and lock it away. Had I ever spent this much one-on-one time with Jamila before? My brother was always around to steal her attention with their inside jokes, his similar career, and easy camaraderie. Not today. Today, Jamila was all mine on our private tour. Despite my gross clothes, I was going to treasure every moment she spent with me today.

"Billie's on the warpath," Winslow said. "She's called twice. She wants to know why you didn't consult the board before you hired a PI."

I winced at the reminder of the Christmas party's hostess. Tech heiress Billie Woods was a friend of my mother's who funded startups and sat on several boards, including Jamila's. She had a reputation for being a keen investor. I didn't envy Jamila's being on the receiving end of her wrath. I still felt the burn of her glare as I was carried out of her party.

"She texted me," Jamila said. "I'll give her a call back in a bit and settle her down. You stay away from her. We don't need to get her any more riled up."

Winslow's cheeks matched his trousers. "I've got a meeting scheduled this afternoon with the investor relations folks."

"Why?" Jamila asked as she breezed through a set of glass doors. I was still scuttling up the stairs, and Winslow didn't bother holding the door for me. I caught it just before it closed and hurried through.

So much for my private tour.

We passed a row of offices. Behind the frosted glass doors, most appeared to be occupied even on a Friday afternoon. The labels next to the doors had only names, but I assumed they were upper management from the large windows and the wood furniture I could make out through the glass.

"Do you think we should send a message to the shareholders about the situation?" Winslow asked.

I hadn't liked the dude at first, but he seemed to be doing the right things. Sometimes first impressions were mistaken. Grudgingly, I raised him a notch in my book despite his disastrous fashion choices.

"No," she said. "This whole thing will be forgotten by Monday."

"No, it won't," I said.

She glanced over her shoulder, and her eyes widened like she'd forgotten I was there. "Sure it will."

"You were in the *Wall Street Journal,*" I said. "Mainstream press. Even if they drop it, the tech news outlets won't. They'll be on this story like…like…"

"Like ticks on a dog?" Jamila supplied. She faced forward again, her jaw stony. "It's fine. We handle that all the time. Everything you do is a news story when you're one of only a handful of tech CEOs of color."

"You can spin this to your advantage," I protested. "Why not deal with it proactively like Winslow is suggesting?"

"Because you're both wrong." She sliced a hand down. "I don't spin. I'm a straight shooter. Everyone knows that." She held open the door of a corner office for Winslow and me. "My office, Natalie," she said with a grand flourish.

She had every right to be proud of her office. The view was much more meditative than my brother's office, which looked smack into the high-rise across the street, or Cooper's, which offered a glimpse of the Bay Bridge between two other buildings. Her office window framed a green lawn that ended at a sparkling pond ringed by evergreens.

Inside her office was a sleek, glass-topped desk with a high-backed cream leather chair. When Jamila settled into it, she looked like a queen on her throne. Winslow plopped into one of the club chairs on the other side of her desk while I perched on the other.

"Pop quiz, Nat. What does Jamilow do?" She steepled her fingers.

"You make apps," I said confidently. Everyone knew that.

"Apps that do what?" Jamila asked.

I'd never downloaded one. I winced at my ignorance. "Something about advice?"

She smirked. "Not everyone has access to generations of college education or world-class financial advisers. The Jam-In app started back in the day offering college admissions help targeted toward lower-income students. It ranked schools by affordability, ease of getting financial aid, value, and whatnot."

"But what set it apart," Winslow said, "was the natural-language search that let students type in what they were looking for. The algorithm took that information and provided a list of target schools and suggested scholarships."

"It was my baby," Jamila said with a fond smile. "The analytics told us students were looking for more help, so we expanded into life coaching. Goal setting, accountability, that kind of stuff."

"That's when it really took off," Winslow explained. "We partnered with real-life coaches to provide individual coaching for paid subscribers."

"And"—Jamila wagged a finger—"we recruited some of our former advisees to be mentors and coaches, the Jammers."

"Then we got into financial advising. Now we're expanding to—"

"That's enough of what we do." Jamila cut Winslow off. "We have various partnerships that help get the word out. The combination of artificial intelligence and human help is our secret sauce. No one has been able to replicate it."

"Yet." Winslow raised his eyebrows.

Jamila pursed her lips. "Yet." She and Winslow were using some secret language I didn't understand.

She rapid-fire typed on the keyboard, and a few seconds later, an organizational chart lit the wall-mounted screen behind her. "So, Nat, here's how we work. That's me at the top, and Winslow, finance, marketing, and R&D report to me. You said you're interested in programming, which falls under research and development for our new products or operations for existing products. That's Winslow's team."

Her phone buzzed. She glanced at it, silenced it, and flipped it over.

"Jamila, you can't just—" Winslow began.

"Can't what?" She fixed him with a stare so sharp I was surprised he didn't flinch.

He regarded her steadily. "You can't sweep this under the rug."

"He's right," I said. "You should consider a press conference. Nip this in the bud."

"A press conference?" Uh-oh, now the steely gaze was on me. I felt my shoulders hunch. "There is no bud to nip here. It's as dead as my Christmas poinsettia. There was one sad reporter out there today. By Monday, they'll have moved on to whatever the Kardashians are doing."

"Those reporters aren't even on the same beat!" I protested. Why was she refusing to see the problem here?

She stared past me and raised her hand, beckoning someone in.

The woman started talking before she was fully in the office. "Jamila, you need to take care of this shit."

I turned to look at her. She was curvy and petite with a mass of dark curly hair and tan skin. Her combination of unlined skin and world-weary brown eyes made it hard for me to tell her age; she could have been anywhere from thirty-five to a well-preserved fifty. Though her business-casual blue golf shirt and khaki slacks could've come straight out of a '90s Best Buy commercial.

"What shit, Ree?" Jamila asked.

"I got a call from not one but two journalists asking about this PI bullshit. And I do not have the spoons to be dealing with it. Not since you've pulled in the launch date by two weeks."

Jamila's nostrils flared. "Journalists shouldn't be calling you."

"Well, they sure as hell are." Ree folded her arms and raised an eyebrow.

"I'll put Felicia on your phone. She'll take care of it."

"And who'll answer your phone?" Ree bobbed her chin.

Ooh, I liked her.

"I will." Jamila's words hung in the air as the black phone on her desk rang. She lifted the handset and immediately set it back in the cradle, silencing it. "See?"

"Hmph." Ree shifted on her feet. "We have a bigger problem. QA found a bug. My team says it'll take a week to fix it."

"A week? We don't have any slack in the schedule."

"Exactly. We're going to have to push the launch."

"We're not pushing the launch," Jamila growled.

"Get me more developers."

"Sure." Jamila's eyes danced over to me, and her lips curled up at the corners. "Meet Natalie Jones. She's expressed interest in joining our team as a developer. Natalie, this is Rhiannon Verlaine, head of development."

I stood to shake Ree's—Rhiannon's—hand. Jamila couldn't be serious. I could probably remember some of what Jackson had tried to teach me one spring break when he was bored. I'd been twelve and bratty, and I hadn't learned much. But if Jamila needed my help, I'd take a learn-to-code-in-a-day course and use my genius brother as my lifeline.

Rhiannon's hand was warm and dry to my cold and clammy hand. "Absolutely not. Sorry, sis. Let me clarify. I need *capable* developers, not children."

I felt my smile freeze. A child? I was twenty-six. Maybe I looked younger with my makeup melted off my face from the lobster steam. Still, she couldn't tell by looking at me that I was incapable of helping. I'd been wrong earlier: I didn't like Rhiannon Verlaine at all.

"Then go hire some capable developers," Jamila said smoothly.

Rhiannon threw up her hands. "Like I have time to hire anybody."

"Sounds like you'll need to work with what you've got because we're keeping to the schedule. We can't afford to be a day late. If Moo-Lah beats us to the market, we're done."

I knew Moo-Lah. Everyone had the cash app on their phone. Their annoying mooing cow ads had interrupted my pursuit of gems about a thousand times in the game I played on my phone when I was bored.

"We're done?" Rhiannon's eyes widened.

Jamila pursed her lips like she hadn't meant to say it. "Not done-done, but we'll have lost first-to-market advantage. It'll be harder to regain that market share. I need you to hit your dates, Ree."

I glanced up at the organization chart still displayed behind Jamila. Everyone in this building reported to her. That was a lot of weight on Jamila's narrow shoulders. The words *I need you* showed a rare vulnerability in her.

I wished she'd said it to me.

Rhiannon sighed through her nose. "Fine. I'll see what we can do. It's going to take a lot of pizzas."

"Do it," Jamila said. "Get the team rides home after hours. And if you need me to get my hands dirty…" She cracked her knuckles.

Rhiannon snorted. "Keep your dirty hands out of my code. The last time you programmed a module, no one could figure out what you'd done. We had to toss it because we couldn't maintain it. Save your hands for dealing with that nonsense." She pointed out the window that faced the road where a news van trundled toward the building.

"Oh, shit," was Winslow's helpful contribution.

Rhiannon spun on the toe of her Chucks and walked out.

"Listen, Jamila," I said. "Let me help. I might not be a qualified developer, but I can set up a press conference for you. We'll handle this proactively before it gets out of hand."

Winslow disguised a laugh with a cough.

Jamila was kinder. "I appreciate the offer, baby girl, but leave it for the…for us. We'll handle it."

Had she almost said, *Leave it for the grown-ups?* I was nine years old again, wearing pigtails, and she was patting me on the head. I wilted into the club chair.

"Sorry, I don't have time for the rest of that tour," she said. "Felicia sits right outside, and she'll call you a car home. Okay? Good seeing you, Nat."

As if I hadn't been humiliated enough for one day, she'd dismissed me. Winslow didn't even wait for me to leave the office before he started talking to her about run rates and burndowns. I slunk out, closing the door gently behind me, and let Felicia call me a town car. Unlike my Uber driver, he didn't say a word about my fish stink.

Jamila needed help. I had to figure out a way to offer it so she'd accept it. So on the drive back to the city, I phoned a friend. Or a friend of my mother's.

She answered on the first ring. "Lippman PR. Della Lippman speaking."

"Hey, Della. It's Natalie Jones."

"Natalie! How are you? How's your mother?"

"We're fine. Mother's working on a book ban project right now, in Texas, I think. She hates those."

"I'd hate to be a book banner with Audrey Jones on the case."

"Me too." I shuddered. I hoped that when I got home, Mother was too fired up about racists to be bothered by what I'd done with Larry. "Hey, I need a favor."

"Uh-oh. No one ever calls me for a favor because they have joyful news to share with the world."

"Because you're the best crisis communications consultant on the West Coast."

"That I am." I could hear the smile in her voice.

"So, a friend of mine, Jamila Jallow—"

"Oh, no."

I winced. "You heard."

"She's put her foot in it with that PI stuff."

"She thinks it's going to go away, but—"

"It's not," Della said.

"I know, right? So you'll help her?"

"I'm sorry, honey. That job's going to take a lot of work, and I just took on a major project for—for someone else. I wish I could help."

"Oh." I sank back into the leather seat, too disappointed to even dig for who that "someone else" with a "major project" might be. "Can you recommend anyone? All I need is a consult. I'd like to do most of the work myself."

She was silent for a minute. "You know, I think you could. You've seen me in action. Your mother too. And you've got a cool head. That's what you need in situations like these. Stay on message. Tell as much of the truth as you can, and don't let anyone goad you into saying more. I have a niece, Hannah, who just graduated with a degree in communications. She's looking for a job. I think she can help. She's a little on the shy side, but I think you two could make a good team."

Someone with an actual degree might not want to take direction from someone who'd poured thousands of her parents' dollars into three aborted degrees and who—I sniffed—*still* smelled like fish. But communications-major Hannah was my best chance at helping Jamila.

"Will you send me her info, please?"

"Absolutely. Good luck."

I was going to need it.

4

SUNDAY at 11:00 a.m. sharp, I opened the door of my parents' Presidio Heights mansion to find Jamila Jallow holding a plastic container.

"Wh—" was my brainy response.

"Morning." Her smile dazzled me. Then the corners of her mouth drooped. "Mind if I come in?"

"Sorry." Stepping aside, I took in her wide-leg jeans and butter-yellow blazer. I wished I'd worn something understated and elegant too. My bubblegum-pink Alexander McQueen flared minidress was too reminiscent of the ruffled dresses I wore when she used to tower over me. Wishing I could melt into the floor, I said, "Mother didn't mention you were coming today."

"Probably because she didn't invite me. Charles did."

"Jamila darling, you're always welcome." Mother brushed past me to kiss Jamila's cheek. "You never need an invitation."

"Thanks, Mrs. H. I brought lemon squares."

"How lovely."

Jamila might have missed Mother's eye twitch, but I didn't. My mother loved Jamila but not her Southern ways. Hostess gifts of food disrupted her carefully planned meals.

Taking the container, Mother linked her arm with Jamila's.

"Come chat with Charles. Natalie, Jackson is coming up the walk. Let them in, would you? And stop slouching."

I shot my shoulders back and turned away from the view of Jamila's butt in those jeans to open the door for my noisy brother and his family.

After I'd hugged my brother and sister-in-law and bumped my teenage nephew's fist, I rested sleepy baby Valentine on my hip—though I should stop thinking of her as a baby now that she was a walking, talking toddler—and followed her family into the dining room. Needing a minute to compose my face, I kissed Valentine's soft cheek, breathing in the scent of baby shampoo.

She grabbed my hand and smiled at my ruby ring like she always did. "Pitty."

"Pretty," I murmured. "That was your great-great-grandmother's ring. Someday, it'll be yours."

I sneaked a glance at Jamila. Why had my teenage crush roared back like this? Jamila joined us for brunch several times a year, and I'd been able to act like a normal person around her since I'd learned to mask my emotions in high school.

Maybe the fluttering in my stomach wasn't a crush after all but guilt over how I'd acted at that awful Christmas party. I'd feel better if I apologized. But how could I do that with Charles leaning close to talk to Jamila and my brother and his wife bounding over to hug her?

Maybe not right now but soon, I'd make it right. I led the kids into the powder room to wash our hands.

FIFTEEN MINUTES LATER, I was shoving pancakes around my plate, and Jamila was the center of attention as my stepfather grilled her. How many times had she sat at our table for brunch, soaking up wisdom from one of the few Black executives in the Bay Area? Now she was one herself, and Charles's mentoring sessions had grown into conversations between equals.

"Not one word." She mimed zipping her lips. "The launch is a secret."

"I hear it has something to do with financial services."

She frowned, then lifted her cup of coffee to her lips. A smudge of her purple lipstick marked the rim. "We added financial advising as a beta earlier this year."

"AI financial advising," Charles said. "I heard you're adding human advising."

"Huh. I guess it's not a secret, then." She speared a strawberry with her fork and closed her lush mouth around it, setting off an eruption of flutters in my stomach. Quietly, I laid down my fork.

"The question is," he mused, "who? I doubt you'll let your amateur coaches advise their peers about money."

"The peer-coaching model has been very popular for our life coaching service," Jamila said. "And the AI has gotten great feedback."

"Don't try to change the subject on me." Charles wagged his finger. "Why didn't you come to me? I run a bank. I know a thing or two about financial advising. Andrew's bank could help you too."

"Where is Andrew?" Jamila glanced around the table for my other brother.

I bit my lip, unwilling to mention the sensitive topic. Mother pursed her lips, but she said, "I have a complicated relationship with the woman he's dating. They grace us with their presence about once a month."

"Mother's working on it, though," I said.

"Back to your financial partner," Charles said. "Why didn't you come to us?"

Jamila's smile wavered. "I appreciate all you've done for me over the years, both of you." She glanced at Mother at the other end of the table. "Winslow had a connection, and we used it. Besides, the AI is the real gem."

Charles set down his fork. "Come on, now. No AI is going to

be better than an experienced human adviser. What do you think, Jackson, Alicia?"

They didn't hear. Valentine had knocked over her dad's coffee, and there was a flurry of napkins at that end of the table while Mother consoled the wailing toddler.

Jamila shocked me by asking, "Natalie, what do you think? Are human financial advisers better than AI?"

It was a second or two before I realized my mouth was hanging open. I snapped it shut. "Me?"

"You said you were interested in programming," Jamila said. "Surely you have opinions about artificial intelligence."

"I..." I didn't. Other than some halfhearted messing around with the latest chatbot app, I hadn't given it any thought at all. But I had thoughts about public opinions. "What does your market research say? Are your customers willing to trust a machine to tell them what to do with their money?"

Charles chuckled. "Smart girl, our Natalie."

I sat up straighter.

"Because of confidentiality concerns," Jamila said, "we limited our market research. It was inconclusive. I'm sure it'll follow the same model as our other apps."

I grimaced. "You're launching an app on limited market research and gut feeling? What if one of your customers loses a ton of money and blames it on your AI?"

"That could happen with human advisers, too. Besides"— Jamila waved a hand—"the beta's gone great. Our user satisfaction scores are high."

"There's a big difference between friendly beta users and the general public," I said. "Does your marketing team have the messaging down? Do they have a task team ready to go if there's a negative response?"

Jamila shook her head. "Don't worry about it, Nat. It's under control."

I pursed my lips. Was it? Jamila's attitude was wrong. All it would take was another flare of her temper to turn her launch into a major disaster.

"Natalie, dear," Mother said from her now-calm end of the table, "aren't you going to try the bacon? Telma made it with the maple coating you like."

I stared at the platter of bacon in front of me. It smelled delicious, but I remembered Larry waving his antennae, pleading with me not to drop him into that pot. His face wasn't even cute, but he had a face, and feelings too. And that bacon had once had feelings.

"No, thanks." I passed the platter to my nephew, Noah.

He snatched two pieces. "Are you a vegetarian now? My friend Lakshmi doesn't eat bacon, either."

"I think I am."

"No bacon? Is vegetarianism your new thing, Nutter Butter?" Jackson asked.

"If programming doesn't work out," Jamila said, "you could work for PETA."

I gave my brother and Jamila a wide-eyed shake of my head. I'd lucked out all weekend. Charles and Mother had been at some cocktail party Friday evening when I'd dragged myself home from Silicon Valley. Saturday, Mother had gone to an all-day function, and Charles had played golf and spent time in the garden with his prized roses. I'd kept to myself in my room reading everything I could find online about crisis communications. So I hadn't told them yet about culinary school.

"Don't be ridiculous, you two," Mother said. "Cooking is Natalie's passion. She's even taking a class about meat this term. What's it called?"

"Butchery," Charles said.

"Yes." Mother shuddered. "I don't think I could do it."

Jackson barked out a laugh. "Neither could Nat."

His wife, Alicia, had caught my headshake. She put a hand on his shoulder and whispered something in his ear. He had the good grace to look sorry and rolled his lips between his teeth. Jamila stilled.

But it was too late.

"What's this, Natalie?" Mother asked

Crap. I wished I didn't have to have this conversation in front of my brother, his family, and Jamila. I wished Andrew was here to act as a buffer like he always did. It was my fault for delaying. Mother would've figured it out anyway when I didn't go to school on Monday.

"I, uh." I glanced at Noah, who watched me like I was the latest video game. I wished I didn't have to admit my failure, especially in front of him. What kind of example was I, flitting from school to school, career to career?

I knew which kind—a terrible one.

"I quit the culinary program." I looked down at my blueberry pancake. Surely sensing a problem from the way I'd picked at my dinner Friday night, our cook, Telma, had made my favorite brunch dish. She was one of the reasons I'd thought cooking school was a good idea. Telma could make anything better with food.

But not this.

"You didn't, Natalie." Mother's voice was imperious.

Even Charles couldn't resist a comment. "But you loved cooking school."

I glanced at him and had to blink away a tear at his kind expression. "I didn't. Not really. I didn't like the pressure, the rushing."

"Or the fashion," Jackson joked. My big brother could never resist a dig. Thank goodness he was out of noogie range.

"What do you think you might try next?" Alicia asked. That was my sister-in-law. Always focused on the future.

"Maybe…" Glancing at Jamila, I took a deep breath. "Maybe public relations."

"Nat." Jackson shook his head. "Jamila doesn't need your help."

"She does!" I flapped a hand at her. "She needs someone's help." Why was I the only one who saw it?

It was the wrong thing to say. Jamila's expression went as cold and hard as Mother's china.

"What's going on, Jamila?" Charles asked.

"Nothing y'all need to worry about," she said, but Charles dragged the story out of her.

When she finished, he grimaced. "Maybe you do need some help."

"It was quieting down Friday afternoon," she said. "They'll forget by Tuesday."

"We should call Della," Mother said.

"I already did," I said. "She can't take it on."

Mother hummed.

"I can help," I said. "I've done a ton of research, and I called Della's niece. She's a communications consultant." That was a stretch. She seemed almost as clueless as I was, but we'd scheduled a coffee on Monday to strategize. Paying her, even in coffee, made her a consultant.

The silence around the table told me what Jamila and my family thought of that idea. Even Charles, who was usually my ally, sipped his coffee.

"Jamila, darling, you'll need to watch that temper of yours if you're working with a financial services company," Mother said. "They're notoriously risk averse."

"It'll be fine, Mrs. H. I've got it under control."

That was a lie if I'd ever heard one. Just as I was about to call her on it, she shot me a calculating look. "So, Nat, who are you dating lately?"

Even baby Valentine stopped her babbling.

"N-no one," I said, glaring at her. She'd been a part of our family for so long that she knew exactly which levers to use.

"We met a nice young man on Friday, didn't we, Charles?" Mother set down her fork.

Charles hummed into his coffee and didn't meet my eyes.

"Augusto Moretti."

"Sounds like one of Jackson's cars," I muttered.

"He's from an exceptional family. They're one of the top wine distributors in Italy."

I made a noncommittal noise in my throat and rotated my pancake on my plate.

"Since you're suddenly free, why don't you show him around the city?" She produced a business card from her skirt pocket and handed it to Noah, who set it next to my plate.

I'd been ambushed.

Jamila stood. "More coffee, Charles?" Without waiting for his answer, she snatched his cup from the saucer and took it to the kitchen. I hoped she'd chipped a nail throwing me under the bus. I glanced at the card. It had grapes embossed in the corners. I could think of at least three ways to make it less cheesy.

"I don't know," I said. "I've got a project I want to work on this week."

Jackson snorted. "If Jamila's your 'project,' give it up now. She doesn't want your help. She's just too nice to say it."

Alicia shot him a sharp look. "What Jackson means to say is that she probably needs more…experienced help. Maybe you could help her find someone?" She handed the baby to Jackson and walked into the kitchen.

"Alicia's right, darling," Mother said. "Leave PR to the professionals. I'll call Della and ask her for a referral. Go out with Augusto. Have fun."

"No." I didn't stand up to her often, but with Jamila in the house, I couldn't put on my socialite act. Not again.

"Fine." Her icy blue eyes glinted. "Then you'll spend time with Sam when she comes to stay. It's been a while since you two spent time together. She's made such a good connection with Niall. Maybe she can introduce you to one of his friends."

"Sam's staying here? But she has a place downtown." My older sister split her time between her fiancé's Ohio farmhouse and San Francisco, where she'd started up a gaming division within Jackson's company.

"They're doing renovations to the building, and Niall's under a deadline. Since she'll be alone this month, she's staying here. Didn't I tell you?" She looked down at her plate, having the good grace to blush. My relationship with my nerdy, accomplished sister was prickly at best.

"It'll be good for both of you," Charles said. "You won't be lonely while your mother and I spend our anniversary in Paris."

"Right." They'd told me about that. "I'm sure Sam will be busy while she's here. We'll hardly see each other." I hoped.

"You two can reconnect now that you won't be at school." He gave me what was probably meant to be an encouraging smile. "Take some time off. You'll figure it out, kiddo."

And that was that. They'd banished me to the kids' table with a box of crayons. Not even my family had confidence in me. My plans to help Jamila were delusions of grandeur. And I'd get to spend a couple of weeks watching my sister accomplish her dreams. Maybe Mother was right, and the best plan for me was to make a good connection through some man. I twisted the ruby ring on my finger.

I didn't want some man. I wanted what I could never have. At least, not while she saw me as nothing but Jackson's little sister like they all did. Just pat me on the head and send me toddling off in my fancy dress, armed with small talk and a platinum credit card.

The memory of how I'd acted at that Christmas party, and what I'd said to Jamila, burned in my belly. Maybe if I acted like an adult and explained, then apologized, she might see me as a grown-up and let me help her. But confessing to my family about dropping out of culinary school had been hard enough. There was no way I'd attempt my apology in front of them.

I'd have to take it to her turf.

5

WHAT BETTER WAY TO drive home the message that I was basically a child, far too young to be interesting to someone as brilliant and worldly as Jamila Jallow, than to roll up in my mother's stodgy Benz in front of Jamila's home in Menlo Park?

Because that's exactly what I did.

I sat for a minute in the car. As I drove through the established neighborhood of midcentury bungalows, I'd thought it was another of Jackson's practical jokes. Surely a billionaire like Jamila lived in a mansion. But when I pulled up to the address he'd given me, the clean lines of the gray house along with its black shutters, fresh white trim, Texas-yellow rosebushes bracketing the front-facing two-car garage, and the bold stylized *J* hanging on the violet door told me Jamila Jallow lived here.

Straightening the chain of my pink faux-fur Roger Vivier bag on my shoulder, I clacked up the driveway and the front walk in my pink gladiator-style heels and my dress from brunch and rang the bell.

I waited a full minute, long enough to doubt she'd come home after brunch. Had she gone to work? Or a bar? My sister Sam wasn't a big drinker, but her fiancé told me that she sometimes needed a drink after spending time with our mother. I rang the bell again and examined the pot of blue-purple African daisies on the stoop. Not a single dead leaf was past its prime to mar their perfection.

"Hey!" A voice called from the neighboring porch. "You coming to see Jamila?"

I turned to face the petite woman in a tracksuit, her salt-and-pepper hair tied in a ponytail.

"Yes?"

"Tell her to come over and pick a basket of avocados. And tell her to be sure to get the ones off the top branches. I can't reach those."

I blinked. "Yes, ma'am."

She looked me up and down. "I suppose you can have some too."

"Um…thank you?" Telma got our avocados from the market. Although I'd lived in California all my life, I'd never picked an avocado off an actual tree. Maybe I should consider a career in fruit picking. I'd tried everything else.

She harrumphed and went back inside her house.

A second later, I heard pounding, then scrabbling by the threshold. What was coming through the door? I took a step back.

When Jamila opened the door, all thoughts of fruit and trees fled my brain. Her feet were bare, showing toenails painted a shimmery amethyst. She wore black leggings under an oversized gray Jamilow T-shirt with the neck cut out. It hung off one shoulder, displaying the wide strap of a royal-blue sports bra. Her makeup was gone, and only a shadow of her purple lipstick remained. Sweat glistened at her hairline.

She held something in her hand, pressing it against her shirt. Something that…moved?

"What are you doing here? Is everything okay?" Her eyes widened. "Is Jackson okay? Your mom?"

"Yes, everyone's fine."

"Did I forget something at your house?"

"No, um…not that I know of. Sorry, I—can I come in?"

She glanced down at her bare feet and then back up. "Sure."

As I stepped over the threshold, I remembered the messy bun I'd put my hair into while I'd been talking over PR strategy with my new consultant, Hannah. Quickly, I pulled the clip out of my hair, shook it out, and combed my fingers through it.

Jamila stared at me.

"What?" My cheeks heated. I'd forgotten to check my appearance before I got out of the car. Had my eyeliner smudged? I shoved the clip into my purse.

"No, you're fine," she said. She turned and led me from the small foyer into the living room. The ceilings were lower than I was used to, but huge windows overlooked meticulous landscaping and a small pool in the back. The open floor plan and minimal, low-slung furniture felt open and airy.

"Your home is beautiful," I said.

"You've never been here before?"

"No."

"Huh."

When she didn't offer to give me a tour—not that there could be much to see in such a small home—I settled onto the gray upholstered sofa, straightening my dress over my knees. Jamila took a seat on the curved loveseat across the coffee table.

"What's that?" I asked, pointing to the hand she cupped against her shoulder.

Without hesitation, she unfurled her long arm toward me. Curled up on its back in her palm was a hamster. No, not a hamster. It was light brown with a dark snout. Sharp spines poked out of its brown back. "This is Quill. Short for Quill.i.am." Her cheeks darkened. Was she blushing?

"It's a hedgehog?"

"Yeah." She stroked a finger between his eyes and onto his forehead. He seemed to smile in his sleep.

Despite my mother's no-pet policy, my sister Sam's dog, Bilbo Baggins, had his own spot under the table at family brunch. When I babysat for Jackson and Alicia, their cat, Tigger, usually made an appearance. I'd never known anyone with a pet hedgehog. The novelty must have been what made my brain slip a gear, so the most ridiculous question popped out of my mouth. "Does he sleep in your bed?"

"No. He's nocturnal. He has a habitat in the second bedroom."

"Is that why he's sleeping now?" His little pink feet stuck up from his fluffy, white belly. He was adorable. And a lot quieter than Bilbo.

"Um." She looked down at him and stroked his forehead again. "No, he's tired. When you rang the bell, we were—" She sat up straighter. "We were dancing."

It was all I could do to keep my mouth from falling open in shock. "Dancing? Like on *Dancing with the Stars?*"

"I guess. If he's the star, and if it's always hip-hop night."

I let my gaze wander from her glowing face to her bare shoulder. It reminded me of that old movie I'd watched with one of my nannies, *Flashdance.* "And only you wear the costumes."

"We left his in the gym. The sequins make him itch."

I widened my eyes. "Seriously?"

"Nah, I'm pulling your leg, baby."

"Oh." I tugged the hem of my skirt over my knees.

"So if your family's okay, why are you here? You're not already shilling for Jackson's foundation, are you? I donated last year. Wait." She winced. "Are you mad about the PETA comment? I didn't know you hadn't told them you'd dropped out of culinary school."

"No, it's fine." Twisting my ring, I said, "I was going to tell them. I just hadn't gotten around to it yet."

"They aren't mad, are they?"

"They're disappointed I've quit. If I don't find something else soon, Mother will start pushing me to marry someone suitable. But that's not why I'm here." I took a deep breath. "I want to talk to you about your PR situation."

Lifting her chin to stare at the ceiling, Jamila sighed. "That again? I thought you were interested in programming. I could help you with that."

"You've got programmers." With a heroic effort, I kept from curling my lip at the memory of Rhiannon's dismissal. "Public relations is what you need help with."

"Did you have to fight any paps to get into my neighborhood?"

"No."

"Were they staked out on my lawn?"

"No."

"Because that's what happened when my neighbor the next street over got caught insider trading. My 'PR situation'"—she made air quotes—"is already over. They've moved on."

"I'm not sure that's true." I'd been following the story in the *Journal*, and it had a ton of comments (and racial and misogynistic slurs), but I wasn't about to tell her about those.

"Natalie." She lasered me with her glare. "I've been in this industry longer than you. I know the kind of shit that makes the news and the kind that doesn't. This is the kind of thing that pops up on a slow news day, then the next week, everyone is back on their bullshit chasing actual corporate miscreants."

"But what if Monday is a slow news day too? What if you're the closest thing to a corporate miscreant they have to chase?"

"Chasing requires a runner. I'm not doing that. I'm going to walk into my office tomorrow and do my work. Nothing to see here." She held up the hand that wasn't cradling Quill.i.am.

"I think you should let Mateo drive you to work tomorrow. Just in case."

"Not happening. I'm driving myself to work like the grown-ass woman I am."

I shook my head. Jamila was stubborn. It was one of the reasons she was so successful. The word *quit* wasn't in her vocabulary.

I leaned forward. "Still, I think you should designate a response team. It'll keep you out of the spotlight and allow you to focus on your work. If you don't want me involved, you can probably loop in Winslow and some folks from your marketing team. They should be able to handle it." The response team was key, according to what Della had told Hannah and me. Jamila might pretend the whole thing didn't bother her, but she was too emotionally involved to handle the situation rationally.

"I don't need a response team because there's nothing to respond to. This whole situation is ridiculous."

"You might see it that way, but you can't control what everyone else thinks or says."

She raised her sculpted, dark eyebrows. "Can't I?"

"No!"

"So why do you think a response team can help me? The whole thing is pointless. When I don't play their little games, they'll go away and find someone else to fight with."

I should've known better than to argue with someone as brilliant as Jamila. "But—"

"No, Nat. I'm not giving this nonsense one more minute of my very valuable attention. End of story."

"What about this financial services partner of yours? What will they think?"

I knew I'd touched a nerve from the tightening of her mouth. "I can handle them too."

"Can you? Most finance people are pretty risk averse. Every time I go visit Charles at work, I feel like I'm in a black-and-white movie."

She lifted her nose. "There you go again, focusing on appearances. You don't have to put on a show on my account. Not like you did at Billie Woods's party."

The blood drained from my face. "I—"

"You know I'd never hurt you, right? Not even by association. I value my relationship with—with your family, especially Jackson and Alicia."

"No, I..." My head spun. Hurt me? I'd been the one who'd

offended her with my drunken confession. "I'm sorry, Jamila. I got nervous, and I drank too much. I didn't mean to…"

"To tell me you loved me?" She snorted. "You know I didn't take you seriously."

I cringed. I'd been one hundred percent serious. I'd crushed on her for so long it felt like love. Especially when I'd had too much wine. "You were so nice to me. You said I didn't have to hide my true self." That's when the word *love* had tumbled out of my mouth.

"I meant it," she said. "And then you went all in with the airhead act."

I shut my eyes, but that was a mistake because the whole scene played out in my memory. She'd shrugged my arms off her shoulders and told me to play at love with someone else. And that's exactly what I'd done. I fluttered over to my friend Daniel and loudly and expressively confessed my love for him too. He laughed it off, but since I didn't love him, it hadn't hurt the way Jamila's laughter had.

"Why'd you get so drunk that night?"

I pressed my lips together. I'd accepted the glass of champagne because I could nurse a glass of the disgusting stuff all night. But that night, with Jamila's full attention on me, I didn't know what to do with my hands or any other part of me. I drank what was in my glass, and Billie's waiters kept refilling it. When I was drunk, I acted like a brainless trust funder, which was exactly what everyone expected me to do.

"It was an accident."

She glared at me. "I suppose it was also an accident that you went home with Daniel what's-his-biscuit."

"Daniel van der Poel is my friend. My platonic friend."

"It looked platonic when you kissed him."

My cheeks burned. Daniel and I had gone to so many events and parties together that pretending to be dating was second nature. After Jamila's dismissal, he'd gone along with my sloppy kiss, but when I'd tried to sell it with my tongue in his mouth, he'd hoisted me up in his arms and carried me out of the party, loudly proclaiming that I couldn't hold my liquor.

Daniel was a good friend. Another guy might've taken advantage of me, but he held my hair while I puked in Billie's hydrangeas.

But Jamila wasn't even my friend. "Why do you care who I kiss?"

She jutted out her jaw. "I don't. I just hate it when you undervalue yourself."

Undervalue myself? I was a rich girl who didn't have enough brains to settle down in a career. My only asset was my looks. Everyone knew it, including my family. Jamila thought it that night too. I crossed my arms.

"Anyway," she said, "I don't need or want your help. I've got everything handled, so you don't need to worry about me."

Another protest rose to my lips, but I swallowed it down. She was right. I wasn't qualified to help her. Nothing I said would change her mind.

She stood. "Thanks for coming by."

I rose from the couch. "Anytime." I really meant it.

She led me to the door. "Tell your family I said thanks again for brunch. And, um, maybe don't come back here. I wouldn't want your family to think I invited you. You, of all people, understand the importance of appearances."

Reeling, I barely registered the slamming door.

It wasn't until I was back on her porch that I remembered the message from her neighbor. It served Jamila right to miss out on a basket of avocados. I stared at the pot of daisies, wanting to rip them out of the pot and shred them right there on her porch. Then stomp on them in my Valentino Garavanis.

That was childish, and I didn't need to give Jamila any more proof that I was young and foolish. She'd witnessed the aftermath of my culinary school disgrace. My deplorable behavior at the

Christmas party. Not to mention the whole acne-and-braces phase, and before that, my pigtails.

So I walked slowly and gracefully down the front steps as if she was interested enough to watch me go.

6

I COULDN'T HAVE MISSED the news of Jamila's fall if I'd tried.

With no school to go to Monday, I was still in bed as I grabbed my phone to check what was going on in the world. Jamila was the first video on my TikTok page. It had half a million views. By the time I'd refreshed it for the third time, it had two million.

I recognized the front of Jamila's building from my visit two days ago. Only one photographer was outside. She could have easily sidestepped him the way we'd done on Friday.

The video was edited to start after the journalist asked his question, so I didn't know what he'd asked that made her get up in his face. Her dark eyes flashed, and her shiny red lips curled into a snarl. "You sonovabitch. Say that again." I couldn't decipher what he said, and the closed caption was nonsense. But Jamila's words were crystal clear, and the text printed at the bottom of the video assaulted my eyes.

"You think you know me? You know fuck-all about my community or me or my goddamned business. You can kiss my paranoid ass."

By the third viewing, I couldn't tell if she'd intended to give him the bird or an uppercut. Her arm swung up, and he reared back, making the video swing wildly as an arm in a long-sleeved chambray shirt came around Jamila's waist and pulled her away, cursing.

The comments blew up. A few said, "I support you, Jamila!" but most denounced her as paranoid, insane, too loud, too crass, or simply not the icon people wanted their daughters to emulate. Some questioned the value of a company led by someone so clearly unprofessional.

It was a disaster.

Groaning, I dragged myself out of bed, showered, pulled my hair back into a bun, and put on a black business suit with a red floral blouse. I found Mother puttering in the conservatory. Kissing her cheek, I told her not to expect me for dinner and caught a rideshare to Mountain View.

———

WITH THE SECURITY guard mobbed by journalists, it wasn't difficult for me to catch a Jamilow employee outside Jamila's building, flirt with him for a minute, lie about having forgotten my badge, and tailgate him into the secure area. After I promised to find him at the next happy hour, I climbed the stairs to the second floor and caught the door to the executive suite as a harried-looking man scuttled out clutching a fistful of papers in one hand and his laptop in the other.

Every office I passed was lit up, and people paced behind the frosted glass doors. In the open part of the floor with cubicles, employees gathered in clumps, whispering. Some groups clustered around phones, probably watching the TikTok or reading the comments.

So much for productivity before their big launch.

Striding unchallenged to Jamila's office, I smiled at Felicia, who glanced up for only a second before she dropped her forehead back to her hand and rubbed while she pressed the phone to her ear. Channeling all the confidence I could muster, I sailed into Jamila's office.

The CEO wore the fabulous oyster-pink pantsuit from the video, but she'd taken off the jacket, revealing a sleeveless ivory shell and a string of pink pearls. She leaned back in her chair, almost flat, with her hand flung over her eyes.

Winslow leaned against the windowsill staring through the glass at the news vans parked beside the road that led to the building. He looked like he wanted to jump through it. His pants were lime-green today. They didn't look any better with the two-tone brogues than the pink ones had. The back of his white shirt was rumpled like he'd sweated in it.

A couple of employees clutched their laptops to their chests and shifted their feet on the plush tan rug in the center of the room. After glancing at me, their focus darted between Jamila, Winslow, and the two people seated in front of Jamila.

A man and a woman I didn't know faced her. Staring at her phone, the woman barked about the stock valuation, so she must have been the chief financial officer. The man stared at Jamila's glass desk.

"Can you not do that, Hope? Please." Jamila moaned without lifting her forearm from her eyes. "It's giving me a headache."

"Sorry," CFO Hope muttered. "I find comfort in numbers when I'm stressed."

"Maybe you can watch the numbers more quietly," Jamila said. "What I need right now is—"

The man sitting next to her leaped to his feet. "You know what? I quit."

Jamila lifted her arm and stared at him. "You what?"

"I quit. This isn't what I signed up for."

Jamila leveled a glare at him. "You're the chief marketing officer. I'm not asking you to do anything but market the goddamn apps."

His pitch rose. "How can I sell apps in this environment?" He waved an arm at the news vans. "This job has completely unbalanced my chakras. I need to go home and watch a nature video." He turned on the toe of his Italian loafer and stormed out of the office. The two employees in the middle of the room scuttled out after him.

The CFO stood.

"Not you too," Jamila said in a low voice.

Hope snorted. "You think I'd quit over this? I started my career at Enron. This is a walk in the park compared to that shit-show. I'll be more useful to you in my office. I'll send you a summary of the financial coverage and its impact on the stock price by the end of the day."

"Great," Jamila sighed.

As Hope walked out, Rhiannon walked in wearing khakis and another blue shirt, this one long-sleeved. She strode behind Jamila's desk, crossed her arms, and cocked her hip. "I need your approval on that job requisition I sent you an hour ago."

Jamila shoved her computer mouse, which sent it skidding across the desk. "How the fuck am I supposed to keep up with email? Look at that shit." She gestured at her screen.

Rhiannon pursed her lips. "That's why you're paid the big bucks, boss." Bending over the desk, she scrolled and clicked. "That's the one. Approve, please."

Jamila winced as she stared blearily at the screen. "Two contract developers? You really think that'll help right now?"

"With this much distraction, we need all the help we can get. We won't make our date without them. I've got grunt work they can do to free up other folks." She straightened the cuffs of her chambray shirt.

The video came blasting back in my memory.

"You were the one who kept her from throwing that punch!"

"What the fuck are you doing here, Natalie?" Jamila blinked liked I was an apparition come to haunt her on her worst day. "I wouldn't have punched that asshat. He wasn't worth ruining my manicure." She held out a hand and examined her short, shimmery blue nails.

I caught Rhiannon's eye. "Thanks for that."

"Someone needed to do something," Rhiannon said. "Hey, you

should pay me to do PR. I don't need some designer suit to save you from those jackals—or yourself."

The hairs rose on the back of my neck, and my nails dug into my palms.

"I told you," Jamila said, "I didn't need saving. I had it under control."

Rhiannon snorted. "Looked like you did. Where was Miss Fancy Suit when you went off on that guy?" She tossed her curly hair.

I straightened my suit coat. I didn't care if she had saved Jamila from an even bigger PR disaster. Rhiannon was not a nice person.

"I came to help," I said.

"Help? You?" Rhiannon scanned my outfit until I started to rethink the bold red blouse. "Be careful, you might chip a nail."

I flexed my hands. "I'm capable of helping. I have a plan."

"Oh, yeah?" Rhiannon crossed her arms and cocked a hip. "Let's hear it."

"Ree." Jamila muttered something I couldn't hear, but it made Rhiannon curl her lip at me and stride out of the office.

When Jamila lifted her eyes to me, they were bloodshot and puffy. Was that from today? Had she slept last night? I opened my mouth to ask, but she spoke first.

"Nat, today is not the day for you to come flouncing in here to try out your hobby of the week. Go on home. We'll talk next week after this is all over."

Just like that, I was fifteen again, and my brother, Cooper, and Jamila were telling me to go away because the grown-ups were talking business. I twisted my ring.

But I wasn't fifteen anymore. I was twenty-six. Maybe I didn't have a degree, but I'd spent all my life in the spotlight. As the youngest Jones, I'd observed plenty of my siblings' mistakes. So I gathered my shredded pride and my last ounce of courage. "This isn't going to be over next week. This is serious, Jamila. I bet Hope told you that you've already lost customers."

She shrugged. "We don't need customers who are afraid of a little cussing."

"What about your financial services partner?" I asked. "What do they think of all this?"

Winslow whirled from the window. "You told her about the partnership with FA?"

"No, I didn't. You just did," she said wearily.

"Your financial partner is First Arbiter? But they're so…stuffy." They made Charles's bank look libertine.

"Billie has a connection there," Jamila said. "She and Winslow."

"Not Kenneth Royal," I said.

"Yes, in fact, I do know Kenneth," Winslow sniffed. "We're in the same golf club."

I grimaced. FA's CEO was the most rigid man I'd ever met. I couldn't get him to crack a smile even with my party antics. He famously demanded all of his employees—men and women—wear the same gray suit and blue tie.

"He won't be our partner for long," he said. "Not if they invoke the morals clause of our agreement."

"We'll sweet-talk them the way we did when your divorce went public," Jamila said.

His cheeks went blotchy red. "My divorce isn't as public as this."

"If this makes FA show their henhouse ways, we don't need 'em." The snap was back in Jamila's voice. "We'll find someone else."

"But don't you need them?" I asked. "You've come so far, and the launch is only…how far away?"

"Less than six weeks," Jamila muttered.

We'd be lucky if we could clean up this mess by then. "I think you could save it if you helped them understand what happened. What did that guy say to you?"

"Nothing I couldn't handle." She jutted out her chin as if she were daring me to punch it.

Winslow sighed. "What do those guys always say? Something about being a Black woman in tech. It's her trigger, and everyone knows it."

"Fuck off." Jamila waved her hand.

"Was that it?" I pressed.

"It?" Jamila raised her eyebrows. "Would you like it if someone questioned your credentials because of the color of your skin or because you don't piss standing up?"

"No." My face heated. "I didn't mean, 'Is that it,' as in, 'Is that all?' I meant, is that what he said?"

"More or less."

I wanted to dig deeper into what the reporter said to make her lash out like that, but it didn't seem productive. Talking about it was making Jamila curl up like…like Quill.i.am.

I propped my hands on my hips. "You need a crisis communications team, and I'm here to head it up."

Jamila rolled her eyes.

"Wait," Winslow said, sizing me up. "Maybe this isn't a terrible idea. Distract the media with PR Barbie."

"Hey! I'm right here!" I interjected.

Winslow carried on like I hadn't said anything. "She's a Jones. People respect their name, their brand. People will listen to her."

Jamila wrinkled her nose. "I don't need a crisis communications team."

"Maybe you don't," he said. "But maybe you do. At least this way, you'll have someone to direct all the calls and emails to, so you can focus on your work." He nodded at her computer monitors.

She sighed. Then she stood and stretched her arms up over her head. The move made her neck impossibly long, and all I could think about was running a finger down it.

Her next word snapped me back into reality. "Fine."

"Fine? Really? You'll let me head up your crisis communications?" I held my breath.

"Yes. Do what you need to do. Please, try to keep the demands on my time minimal, and do something about all that bullshit." She waved at the news vans outside.

"Absolutely. I'll need access to Felicia and anyone trained in corporate communications."

Her nostrils flared. "You don't ask for much, do you?"

"Only what we need to do this right."

"Okay. But no more than ten percent of anyone's time. Including mine."

I bit my lip. I'd definitely need more than four hours a week of Jamila's time. Considering she probably worked more like sixty or eighty hours a week, maybe I could get ten percent of that. If I used a longer time horizon, I could front-load the demands so that it averaged out to be ten percent over the next six months. I'd put the problem to bed long before then.

"I'll need an assistant," I said. "Don't worry, I know just the person to bring on."

"Bring on?" She rolled her eyes. "Should have figured you'd take over. You're a Jones. One more thing." She paused to look me in the eye. "Ignore what Winslow said. I don't want any of that Barbie bullshit. Be on your A game for this. You know what I mean."

She was talking about that Christmas party. I nodded, not trusting my voice not to waver.

"Okay, then," she said. "You can tell Felicia, and she'll make it happen."

Bubbly happiness overflowed in my heart. If I made Jamila's PR problems go away, she'd forget about that awful party and finally see me as an adult.

I skipped behind her desk and threw my arms around her. "You won't regret it, I promise."

When my hands touched her bare shoulders, she froze as if I'd shocked her. My skin buzzed. After a second, she relaxed, and her hands landed lightly on my back to pull me closer.

The perfume at her neck was sensual and floral like jasmine. With the coconut scent of her hair, she smelled like the tropics, like the time our family vacationed in Bali and the night air carried the delicate scent of jasmine and faded sunscreen. I closed my eyes and imagined reclining on a beach, warm sand between my toes, and Jamila beside me.

Gently, she pulled away and dropped her hands from my shoulders. "Get to work. Remember, ten percent."

I collected myself enough to grin at her. "You got it, boss."

Already composing a text to Hannah, I pushed out of Jamila's office and pulled up a chair to the other side of Felicia's desk.

"Looks like I'm your new PR consultant."

7

LATER THAT AFTERNOON, I poked my head into Jamila's office. Alone, she mirrored Winslow's position from earlier, leaning a shoulder against the window frame and staring through the glass. Although it was after six, the late-April sun was still high in the sky, and it glinted off the cars as they snaked along the road on their way to homes, pets, families. Maybe Jamila wished she could go home, put on her comfortable clothes, and snuggle up with Quill.i.am. But as she'd shown me on that organizational chart, she was at the top, and every one of those cars, homes, and family dinners was paid for by the work she directed. She'd always be the last one out.

"Did you eat today?"

She whipped her head around at my voice and took a beat to narrow her eyes. "Yes. Felicia makes sure I eat lunch."

"Good." I crossed my arms. Jamila was so slender I wondered if lunch was the only meal she ate regularly.

"Figured you'd have gone home by now," she said.

I shrugged. "Lots to do today."

"You made a dent in the news vans." She chuckled. "Not literally, like I'd have done. I meant some of them left."

I closed the door, fearing her response to what I had to say next. "I promised them a press conference tomorrow."

"They went away because you said you'd talk to them?" She squinted one eye at me.

"Come sit down." I walked toward the seating area, lowered myself onto the loveseat, and set the mug on the low coffee table. "That's for you."

Her eyes brightened. "Coffee?"

"It's after five. It's herbal tea."

She curled her lip. "I may be older than you, but I'm not some grandma who drinks herbal fucking tea."

"Wow, okay. Then don't drink it." Maybe she was hangry. I should've brought some cookies too. "Come sit." I patted the cushion beside me.

Jamila chose the chair instead and peered at the golden-brown tea. "Smells like grass."

I chuckled. "You drink matcha. That stuff looks like grass."

"Matcha is what the cool kids drink. Chamomile—or whatever that is—is not."

"It is chamomile. Try a sip. It's relaxing."

She pushed it away. "No, thanks. So, what did you want to talk about?"

Next time, I'd bring her a cup of decaf. I already knew she drank her coffee black, like her mood.

"The press conference tomorrow. You'll say a few words and then answer some questions. I drafted a speech for you." I held out a tablet with the speech pulled up.

She took it from me and scanned the document. "I'm not apologizing to that douchebag." I hadn't thought she would, but it was worth a try.

Slowly, I nodded. "We can revise that. Would you be willing to apologize to the shareholders and employees who were negatively impacted by your actions?"

Her lips thinned as she considered it. "Can I use a word like 'regret' instead of 'apologize'?"

I winced. "'Regret' sounds insincere. 'Apologize' or 'sorry' are more direct, and that's on brand for you. We need to convey the message that you understand what you did was wrong and that it won't happen again."

Her shoulders crept lower, away from her ears. "I can do that."

Relief flooded through me as she read the document more slowly this time. When she finished, she looked up. "It's not bad. You even managed to make it sound like something I'd say."

"Thanks." I looked down at my lap to hide my blush.

"Need me to memorize it?"

"Just be familiar enough with it that you can look up from it to make eye contact. I'll email you a copy." I took the tablet back, deleted the apology to the reporter, and sent off the document.

"Talk for two minutes and answer a few questions? No problem." As she leaned back in the chair, the lines under her eyes told me how exhausted she was.

I wished I could let her go home, but we weren't done yet.

"We need to practice the questions and answers."

"Practice? You don't trust me?"

"Everyone performs better after practice."

"I've been performing for the media since you were watching cartoons and playing with dolls." Her lips went even thinner. "I've learned a thing or two over the years. I made my millions from nothing but the brain in my head, not a trust fund. I don't need you to teach me how to speak to journalists."

I took a deep breath. I knew how many advantages I'd had growing up. I needed to prove to Jamila that it hadn't come with a sense of entitlement. "I'm not trying to teach you anything. I only want you to be ready to answer whatever questions they fire at you and for you to remain calm and professional."

"Calm and professional?" She leaped out of the chair and paced on the carpet. "I am *nothing* but calm and professional. I put on my mask and smile at the investors and the press and whoever else I have to so I can run my goddamn company, and they'll leave me the fuck alone!" She stopped and whirled on me. "You should know, with that empty-headed pretense you put on at that Christmas party. At every party. You're playing by their rules, just like me."

Pain sliced through me at the direct hit.

This wasn't about me. It was about making the bad PR go away so Jamila could focus on running her company. I shoved down the hurt and leaped to her side, but she shrugged off the hand I put on her shoulder. "I'm sorry. I didn't mean to imply you were anything less than professional."

She rubbed her thumb between her eyes. "I'm tired. It's been a long day."

"I know. I wish I didn't have to ask you to do this, but I want to be sure you do the excellent job I know you're capable of, and that you're ready for whatever ridiculous questions they might throw at you."

She glanced at me sidelong. "Isn't it your job to fill the room with people who *won't* ask ridiculous questions?"

"I've tried to fill it with as many friendlies as possible. However, hope for the best, prepare for the worst is my motto."

She grunted. "Fair."

"Come sit down," I said. "I think we can knock it out in less than an hour."

"Won't I be standing at a podium tomorrow?"

"That's the plan."

"Then I'll stand." She planted her feet on the carpet and rolled back her shoulders. "You play like you practice. Isn't that what they say?"

"I..." I was too distracted by the column of her neck rising above the shoulders of her jacket and the glimpse of her collarbones over the scooped neck of her blouse to think clearly.

"Hit me." She lifted her chin.

Right. I was here to help her practice, not to ogle that neck I'd wanted to kiss since I'd hugged her earlier. She didn't want that from me. The insults she'd thrown at me earlier—cartoons, dolls, trust funds, and masks—still stung. She'd never see me as anything but Jackson's annoying, privileged little sister. Never as an equal, as someone she wanted to kiss.

Though if she thought I was annoying, I could use that to help our practice.

"So, Jamila," I said, looking down at my tablet like it was a reporter's notebook, "why'd you try to punch my colleague yesterday?"

"I did not—" She stopped when her shout bounced off the office walls and rang back into her ears. She cleared her throat. "I think the video will show that I did not, in fact, punch anyone."

"That was okay," I said. "Though I think the talking points for questions like those are, one, the reporter said something offensive that made you angry. Care to share what it was?"

She pressed her lips together and shook her head.

"It's probably best to focus on your response. Two, you responded informally—"

"Informally? That's what we're calling it?"

"I think 'informally' is better than 'crudely.' Three, you recognize that your response was ill-advised, and you're sorry for its impact on your shareholders and employees. Let's try again. Jamila, why did you try to punch my colleague yesterday?"

She inhaled and exhaled before responding. "I think the video shows that I did not punch anyone. However, I apologize for the negative impact that my informal word choice had on Jamilow's shareholders and employees. Better?"

"Perfect."

After forty-five minutes of practice, Jamila's responses were press conference ready despite her surly expression.

I grabbed the tablet and stood. "Great job. Go home and rest. I'll see you in the large conference room downstairs at nine a.m. Wear that white suit with a pastel blouse."

"Now you're telling me what to wear? You think I'm incapable of dressing myself?" she growled.

"I'm trying to take one more decision off your list," I said coolly. "Successful people limit decisions about small things so they have more mental energy for important decisions. Like Steve Jobs' black turtleneck and New Balance sneakers or President Obama's closet full of blue and gray suits."

I thought I saw Jamila relax her jaw a fraction as I sailed past her.

"See you tomorrow," she mumbled.

I could help her through this situation without being tempted to act on my crush. Because that's all it was: a juvenile crush, left over from when I was a kid.

Now I was grown-up. The last thing I needed was attraction for someone as brilliant—and prickly—as Jamila Jallow. Someone who'd never see me as an equal.

8

"WELL, THAT'S OVER," I said, trying to smile when all I wanted to do was scream. The only good part of the whole press conference fiasco was that it was done. I jogged upstairs to the second floor, risking breaking my neck to get ahead of Jamila's long strides.

"You did fantastic," Winslow said, loping alongside her.

I shot him a wide-eyed stare. Had we been watching the same press conference?

"You think so?" Jamila smoothed down her blouse.

"Absolutely," Winslow said. It was awfully early to be taking edibles, but that was the only thing that could explain his chill attitude.

I had my own badge now, so I swiped it at the door to the executive suite. I held open the door for Jamila and Winslow. But instead of heading for the back corner, I turned right and ushered the executives into the windowless office I'd been camping out in. It was smaller than Jamila's and just large enough for two desks, one of which was occupied.

Hannah jumped when we entered and brushed at her skirt. Her medium-brown hair was pulled away from her pale face into a ponytail, and her black skirt suit and white blouse screamed, *entry-level professional.* A couple years younger than me but with a degree I didn't have, Hannah was the help I needed, especially after today's press conference.

"Hey, Hannah. Meet Jamila Jallow and Winslow Keating-Ashworth. Jamila and Winslow, Hannah is our new PR assistant."

Jamila shook her hand. "I don't recall hiring an assistant or authorizing a PR budget."

Hannah's brown eyes widened behind her glasses. She looked like a deer frozen in the middle of the road with an eighteen-wheeler bearing down on her.

I waved a hand. "Felicia and I took care of it. Now sit, and we can debrief."

Jamila plopped into the sturdier of our two guest chairs. I rounded the other desk to sit behind it, which left Winslow with the wobbly backless chair I'd found in a storage room. After glancing around for another option, he perched on it gingerly.

"Hannah," I said, "what are the early responses?"

"Somebody live-tweeted it. They thought it was…" She looked up from her monitor.

"Go on," I said.

"They thought it was a bit of a snooze."

"Exactly what we were going for," I said, relieved. "Professional, predictable, nothing to see here."

"Until…" She winced.

"Let's hear it." I knew what would come next.

"The, uh, candid moment."

"The what, now?" Jamila asked.

"Next time," I said, "if you're going to call someone out, wait until after the press conference is over."

Jamila laughed. "Okay, sure."

I squinted at her. She glared back at me. Winslow picked at lint on his butter-yellow trousers. He was either too nice or too much of a coward to help.

"Seriously," I said. "You can't go off on someone during a press conference."

She dipped her chin and her eyebrows. "I can if they're out of line."

"That may be okay in your boardroom or in your office, but it's not okay at a press conference." I wished I could add, "we talked through this," but I couldn't. Foolishly, I hadn't dreamed anyone would ask such an off-base question. Even more foolishly, I'd never expected Jamila to jump down their throat.

"I want her banned from the premises," Jamila added.

"Okay, but next time, take a beat. Try one of those breathing techniques we talked about. Then, when you feel calm, answer the question or say, 'no comment.'"

"'No comment?'" She jumped out of the chair and tried to pace, but the small space boxed her in. She cursed as she bumped a shin on the side of my desk. "Is that what Mark Zuckerberg would say? Oh, no, never mind, he's a *man*. No one would ever toss a question like that at him!"

Winslow looked up at that. "They do ask men who they're seeing."

"Not at a fucking *apology press conference!*"

"How bad is it?" I asked Hannah.

She winced. "Not great. They're using the P-word again."

"The P-word?" Jamila demanded, hands on her hips.

"Paranoid," Hannah said, almost too low to hear.

"It'll be fine," I said with more confidence than I felt. "We'll try another few tactics, and we'll practice our breathing techniques." I shot Jamila a pointed look. "It will go away eventually."

"You said it'd go away if I did this press conference."

I stood so fast my chair spun and thumped into the wall behind me. "That was before you threatened a reporter for the second time in two days."

"Maybe we need a distraction," Winslow said.

"Great idea." I leaned on my desk. "Something positive for the media to focus on."

"You could go do something with that charity you run in Austin," Winslow said.

"I can't just turn the camp on and off," Jamila said testily. "They have a schedule."

Ignoring her protest, I said, "That's an excellent idea, Winslow. Jamila, tell me more about the camp."

I could almost see the spines rising on her like Quill.i.am's. "I don't want to involve the camp. I don't have time for this. I need to focus on our launch."

As if on cue, there was a knock at the door, and Rhiannon marched in clutching a laptop. Today, she was back to another golf shirt. This one was greenish-blue like Jamila's mermaid fingernails. "There you are, standing around like we don't have a crisis."

Heat bubbled in my chest. She paraded around like her work was so much more important than mine. I straightened. "That's exactly what we're doing. We're dealing with a crisis."

Rhiannon snorted. "Some song and dance in the conference room? You think that's a crisis? We've got an actual problem right here." She tapped her laptop.

"What kind of problem?" Jamila spun around to stare at her employee.

"Security flaw."

Jamila threw up her hands. "But InfoSec reviewed everything. They documented the security acceptance criteria!"

"Which we failed in their review. Someone used some open-source code, and it introduced a vulnerability."

Jamila rubbed between her eyebrows. "What's the damage?"

"This sets us back at least a week," Rhiannon said. "Maybe two."

"That's unacceptable," Jamila snarled. "I want all hands on deck to fix this."

"We're already operating in all-hands mode. A week was my optimistic estimate."

"One week. No more. We can't let Moo-Lah beat us to market."

I didn't understand everything Rhiannon had said about the

security problem with the app, but a chilling thought struck me: had Rhiannon herself introduced the flaw? Was she sabotaging the app, delaying the release so Moo-Lah had the advantage? She was supremely positioned to do it. No. Jamila trusted her. Rhiannon had to have earned that trust. As little as I liked Rhiannon, I had no reason to doubt her loyalty.

Jamila was at the threshold before I registered that she was walking out.

"Wait! We're not done here," I said.

"Yes, we are. I have more important things to deal with."

"No, you don't. If we don't turn the message around, no one is going to buy the app regardless of if you release on time."

"Turning the message around is your job," Jamila said. "Mine is to launch this product." She strode out the door. Rhiannon shot me a smug look before she followed her boss and slammed the door.

Winslow carefully stood, shooting a resentful glare at the backless chair. "I've been asking her to focus more on strategy for years. But in times of crisis, she can't resist the call of the code."

Jamila said her job was the products, and mine was PR. I had to focus on that. "Hannah, do you think we could direct some attention to Jamila's charitable activities?"

"I think that's a fantastic idea," she said.

"Winslow, can you tell me more about this camp?"

"She started it when she made her first million. It's a foundation that runs coding camps for girls in Austin, her hometown. They're so popular they fill up within hours of opening registration."

"Is there information on the Jamilow website?" Hannah asked.

"It has a separate website. She wants to keep the focus on the kids, not on herself." He rattled off the address, and Hannah typed it into her phone.

Yet, I couldn't let go of my new suspicion. It roiled in my gut like bad sushi. I checked that the door was shut. "One more thing. How long has Rhiannon worked here?"

He blew out a breath. "Almost since the beginning. We hired her after our second round of funding. She was a senior developer then. Now she leads the development team."

"Has there always been this much…friction between her and Jamila?"

He chuckled. "Always. They both have strong opinions."

"Do you think she'd do anything to hurt Jamila?"

He shot me a sharp look. "Like sabotage the development?"

"Exactly."

"Maybe." He brushed at a wrinkle on his preppy pants. "She's been complaining a lot lately about being overworked."

Had Moo-Lah offered her money? Early retirement must sound nice to someone like Rhiannon after over a decade working at a startup's pace. I hated to jump to conclusions, but Jamila had suspected corporate espionage when she hired the PI.

"Thanks for your honesty," I said.

"Sure. I should follow her lead and get my hands dirty." He cracked his knuckles.

"You code too?" He gave off more of an MBA vibe than a coder vibe. I'd never met a programmer with his taste in fashion.

He chuckled. "Jamila and I met in the computer science program at Stanford. I was a couple of years behind her, and we partnered up on the first app."

"You were her first hire?"

I thought a sour expression flitted across his face, but it was gone before I was sure I'd seen it. "I was. I'm still her number one. Our code has my fingerprints all over it."

I shot him a grateful smile. "I'm sure she appreciates your help. And so do I."

Without a word, he left and shut the door. What did he care about thanks from someone who was only here because I hadn't let Jamila push me out?

I'd prove to him and Jamila, too, that I could help. While they managed the code, I'd manage their reputation. Then they'd have to recognize me.

———

AS CHAOTIC AS Jamilow had been that day, home was worse.

Charles stood inside the front door, arms crossed, a mulish expression on his face. "We're not leaving without them."

My mother jammed her fists on her hips. An errant lock of hair escaped her bun and floated next to her face. Her cheeks and chest were red. "I'm more likely to have a heart attack from being late to the airport than from missing an ACE inhibitor or two. It's not like they don't have them in Paris."

He shook his head. "We're not going to Paris without your pills."

"Are any of these the right ones?" Sam appeared behind Mother. She'd come down the stairs as silently as a cat and held out a fistful of orange bottles.

"No, I looked through those already," Mother said. "I must have run out."

I peered at her flushed face. "When was the last time you took one?"

"This morning? I don't remember." She flapped a hand. "We need to leave for the airport. Our flight is in three hours."

"Then we'll pick up your prescription at the pharmacy on the way to the airport," Charles said.

While they argued about whether the pharmacy was or was not on the way, I motioned to my sister to show me the pill bottles. One of them was pain meds from her heart surgery; I pocketed the expired pills to toss out later. One was a hormone replacement, but one was her ACE inhibitor for hypertension. I plucked it out of Sam's hand and checked it. At least a dozen pills remained.

"Here it is, Charles." I handed it to him. "Stop being a grumpy bear and go to the airport."

He kissed my cheek. "What would we do without you, Natty Bumppo?"

I didn't hate that nickname nearly as much as what Jackson

called me. "Have fun on your trip. Mother, dial back the diva, okay?" I hugged her.

"I'm not a diva," she muttered. "Thank you for saving the day."

"Go on." I opened the front door.

Charles lifted her Gucci carry-on and hugged Sam. "Have fun, girls."

"Fun?" Sam lifted an eyebrow. "I'm here to work."

That was my big sister. Serious and dull. I couldn't remember her ever playing with me when we were kids. She'd always been too busy messing around with computers with Jackson.

"Then do good work, darling." Mother awkwardly patted her shoulder. "And don't let Bilbo chew the Aubusson."

"He's here?" I scanned the room for the little demon.

No one heard me in the bustle of Charles guiding my mother out the door. It closed behind them, leaving us in silence for a moment, before it opened again, my mother's torso poking through the opening to grab her handbag off the table by the door. "Goodbye, girls. See you in two and a half weeks!"

I let my gaze rest on my sister.

Since she'd started her company, she'd upgraded her wardrobe marginally. It was still all black, but now instead of army surplus pants, she wore a pair of soft-looking work pants she'd probably bought from an online ad. Her shapeless cardigan was gone, replaced with a sweater that was only one size too big for her petite frame. The sleeves covered all but her unpolished fingertips.

There was a jingle, and her little dog appeared at the top of the stairs, something furry and pink in his mouth.

My stomach turned to ice. "Is that a chew toy?"

"No, I only brought his brown horse. What's that, Bilbo Baggins? Bring it here."

Wagging his tail, he galloped down the stairs. My stomach shrank in on itself with each jaunty step. He dropped his prize on the floor at Sam's feet.

"Oh, no." My Roger Vivier faux-fur bag was almost unrecognizable. The fur was matted with dog slobber, it was missing its jeweled clasp, and its strap was gnawed through. She picked it up and held it by a corner. "Is this yours? I hope it wasn't a favorite."

I rubbed my temple. "Does it matter? It's ruined now."

"Can I pay you for it?"

"Doubtful. It cost two thousand dollars new. You're still in startup mode, and I'm sure you pay yourself last. Your trust fund could've covered it, but, oops, you gave it away."

She went even paler than usual, her freckles standing out across her nose and cheeks. "I'm really sorry. He doesn't usually destroy things. He must be nervous. I-I…could pay you in installments?"

I rolled my eyes. "Don't worry about it. I can't wear something like that to my new job."

"New job?" Her dark eyebrows winged up, making her deep blue eyes look otherworldly.

"I'm working for Jamila as her PR consultant."

She grimaced. "I hope it wasn't you that let her say those things."

My face heated. "No one *lets* Jamila say anything. She does what she wants. But I'm working on it."

She huffed an almost-laugh. "Good luck."

"Do you know anything about Moo-Lah, the company?"

She scrunched her nose. "A little. I've met the CEO, Pavel Thakor, a few times."

"Jamila thinks they're spying on her. Do you think they're also capable of sabotage?"

"Whoa. That's a serious allegation."

"I know." I bit my lip. "Jamila thinks it's normal coding challenges, but I'm starting to think someone's working against her from the inside, paid for by Moo-Lah."

"I don't know, Nat. Most tech companies are too busy with work to mess with someone else's."

"But everything's going wrong for her right now."

"Sometimes that happens." My sister shrugged. "Software development is creative work, and it doesn't always go smoothly. Part of it is Jamila herself. If she kept a lower profile, she wouldn't get in as much trouble."

The heat spread from my face down into my belly. How dare she imply that any of this was Jamila's fault. "Not everyone wants to disappear into the background like you, Sam. Jamila wants to stay relevant and top of mind. She'd never hide who she is."

Sam scooped up her dog and buried her face in his black fur. When she lifted her head, her eyes were glossy. "I'm going to bed. It's been a long day."

I huffed. What did she have to be upset about? "I've had a long day too."

"Goodnight then. See you tomorrow…maybe." She trudged toward the back of the house, her Doc Martens creaking. Her little dog grinned maliciously at me over her shoulder, a clump of pink fluff dangling from one tiny fang.

My sister thought Jamila should be quieter? Hide her light? Absolutely not. I bet Pavel Thakor thought that too. Maybe he was trying to force her to step back so Moo-Lah could rule uncontested.

Sam reminded me of Rhiannon. They both wanted to keep their heads down and do their work. They thought PR was a waste of time. Rhiannon probably chafed under Jamila's assertive personality. Maybe Moo-Lah had offered her something more—a cushy management job or a kickback to fund an early retirement.

I'd figure it out, and they'd all realize I'd been right. Sam, Jackson, everyone who thought I was playing dress-up. When I found the leak, when I proved Rhiannon had spilled the information and was actively sabotaging Jamilow, Jamila would be grateful.

Maybe then she'd see me as a grown-up, someone valuable.

9

AFTER THAT, I avoided my sister and kept my bedroom door closed to keep her destructive rat of a dog out of my room. The good thing about my parents being away was that I didn't have to Uber back and forth to the office, but driving Mother's boxy Benz made me feel a hundred years old. I found myself wearing neutral colors and checking for crow's feet in the rearview mirror.

One benefit: the black suits made me appear less conspicuous as my plan came together.

On Monday afternoon, Mateo's blue eyes sparkled as he rubbed his hands together like a cartoon villain. "Do I have a backstory?"

"A what?" I polished the lenses of the high-tech glasses with the recording device embedded in the endpiece and handed them to him. We were camped out in the small conference room on the first floor of the Jamilow building. The sun sent low rays piercing through the front windows of the building.

"You asked me to play a role in your diabolical plan," he said. "Actors have backstories. Motivation. What's my motivation?"

I rolled my eyes. "You're an agent of Moo-Lah, hired to offer Rhiannon cash for secrets. Specifically, you want the name of Synergy's financial services partner."

His face scrunched. "But we know the name of their partner. It's—"

"Moo-Lah doesn't know. At least, I don't think they do. Remember, you're playing a role." How had my smart friend Mimi fallen for such a himbo?

"Money could be my motivation," he mused. "My abuela is sick, and I need to pay the hospital bill."

"Sure. Whatever works. Now try on the glasses."

He put them on and looked at me. Whoa. How did the dorky black frames make him look even hotter? Mateo was handsome in a burly way that didn't usually turn me on, but the glasses took his good looks to the next level. But these days I didn't find anyone, of any gender, attractive unless they were a tall, beautiful genius who talked about code all day.

I glanced at my phone and saw the top of my head. I needed to refresh my highlights. Shaking out my hair, I looked back at Mateo. "Now say something."

"Something," he said. The word came tinnily from my phone.

"Cute." My response came back too, slightly fainter. "You'll have to stand close to her when you make the offer."

"What's her motivation?" he asked.

"Also money. She's looking to stop toiling under Jamila and retire to some beach."

He frowned. "That doesn't sound like a very good motivation."

"I don't know. Maybe her cat is sick. Or she has a grandma."

"Her grandma would be pretty old."

"So she probably has medical bills too. You can bond over the high price of hearing aids or walkers."

"Natalie. You're in the point oh-oh-oh-oh-one percent. What would you know about medical expenses? Or the national disaster that is this country's healthcare system?"

"That's beside the point. Argue with me about healthcare later. Now I need you to make the offer to Rhiannon."

"You said this would be fun. It doesn't seem fun so far."

"Of course it's fun. You get to wear a costume. You've got your motivation, and you're going to chat with a stranger. It's like… improv. Pretend this is an acting class."

"I've never enjoyed acting. Now, dancing…"

A sneaker squeaked behind me. I peered around the corner. Rhiannon strode toward the door with a backpack slung over her shoulder.

"Here she comes. Go, go, go." I gave him a little push, but Mateo was a mountain. It must have felt like the brush of a gnat's wings to him.

Fortunately, he took the hint and jogged after her. "Hey, Rhiannon!"

I cringed at how loudly his voice echoed in the lobby, then I ducked behind the wall. On my phone's screen, Rhiannon's face turned up toward the camera. I shoved the earbud into my ear, and her voice came faintly to me. With a tiny stab of guilt, I hit the record button.

She scowled. "Do I know you?"

"No, but I think we have mutual interests," Mateo said smoothly.

He was good.

"And what would those be?"

I held my breath. *Please don't talk about your fake abuela and her lumbago.*

"I'm looking for some information."

"What kind of information?"

"All I need is a name. Who's Jamilow partnering with on the new app? I can pay you well for that knowledge."

I held my breath.

"How well?" She narrowed her eyes.

Ooh! We had her!

"Very well. Insulin money."

"Insulin?" She scrunched her nose.

"Or beach money. You'd be able to buy your own villa."

"Beach villa money, huh? For a name?"

I held my breath.

"Exactly. Tell me a sum. One that would make you comfortable in your retirement."

Another scowl. "Good thing I'm not retiring, then. I like my boss too much. Hey. Bruno." She turned her head toward the security guard who was as beefy as Mateo and definitely meaner, if his expression was any indication.

"This guy bothering you?"

"Nah. But I would like to know how he got in here. He's not a Jamilow employee."

Crap, crap, crap. Should I blow my cover to save Mateo? From the panicked expression on his face, probably. But he was a big guy. He could handle whatever Bruno threw at him.

I hoped.

Bruno stepped between Mateo and Rhiannon. "Where's your badge, man?"

Mateo fumbled in his pocket and pulled out the visitor badge I'd gotten from the previous guard. Nuts, I'd signed for him! The security log would betray me. How would I get Mateo and myself out of this mess?

"Hey, amigo, we're good." Mateo held out his hands in a stop gesture. "Keep the badge. I'm leaving." He took two steps toward the exit, then he turned. "No name?"

Aw. This was why Mimi had fallen for him. He was persistent and charming.

Rhiannon's lips thinned. "No name. Get your sorry ass out of this building."

I didn't have to see any more. I stopped the recording and hit the button to blank my phone's screen.

Rhiannon and Bruno muttered for a few minutes before I heard the squeak of her sneaker. I peeked around the corner as she pushed through the glass door of the exit. I waited five more minutes for her to get into her car and leave before I fluffed my hair to conceal my face and strode toward the exit, head down.

"Have a good night," Bruno called, sounding friendly and not at all menacing.

"Night," I mumbled.

Outside, I slunk to Mateo's Jeep and slid into the passenger seat. "Well, that was a colossal failure."

"Sorry, Nat. I tried."

"I know. You did your best."

"I don't think she's the leak."

"That's going a bit far, don't you think? Just because she didn't fall for your offer doesn't mean she's not on the take. Maybe she's a loyal snitch, and she only talks to her contact at Moo-Lah."

"I don't know, Nat. She seemed pretty protective of Jamila."

He was right. She did. But that didn't mean she wasn't the source of the leak.

"Let's go," I said.

When Mateo turned on the car, the headlights illuminated a tiny woman wearing a blue shirt, khakis, and a furious expression.

I screamed.

Mateo yelled.

She scowled, then circled around to my side of the car and made a cranking gesture.

Wincing, I rolled down the window. "Hey, Rhiannon."

"Don't you 'hey, Rhiannon,' me. You should be ashamed of yourself. You too." She jabbed a finger at Mateo.

"It was all me," I said. "He was just doing me a favor. I was trying to protect Jamila."

"With entrapment? Really?" Her scowl was world-class. "You trying to Catherine Zeta-Jones me?"

"Do what now?"

"I've been loyal to Jamila longer than you've been alive, girlie."

"I don't think that's—"

"I would never, ever betray her. Don't be messing with me."

"No, ma'am," I mumbled.

Holding her head high, she turned on her heel and left.

"¡Mierda! I would *not* want to be you at work tomorrow." Mateo clucked his tongue.

"Me either."

———

THE NEXT MORNING, I stopped at the coffee shop in Mountain View Jamila liked and ordered four coffees. Black for Jamila, a vanilla latte for Felicia—she was the key to Jamila's calendar, and I needed to keep her happy—and two iced caramel macchiatos, one for Hannah and one for me. As I tapped my credit card on the pad, I squashed down the foreboding that weighed on my chest all night.

The barista, a woman in her sixties, tore off the receipt. "Need this for your expense report?"

"No, thanks. This one's on me."

She raised her eyebrows, taking in my ecru suit and pale pink blouse. "Dressed up for someone special?"

"Just work."

Her eyebrows shot up. "In that getup? Everyone in Silicon Valley wears jeans and ball caps to work."

I straightened the sleeve of my blazer. "My boss doesn't. And you know what they say, dress for the job you want, not the one you have." Not that I wanted Jamila's job. That sounded more horrific than crustacean murderer.

"Actually," I confessed, "I did something bad last night. I need some armor to feel brave enough to go back." The ball of dread was back, filling up my stomach. Maybe I could give my coffee to Rhiannon. No, she'd probably think it was another bribe.

"I never thought of a designer suit as armor, but you do you." She leaned over the counter. "Go get 'em, hon."

"Thanks. Have a great day."

When the coffees were ready, I took them out to the Benz and nestled the carrier into the console.

At the Jamilow building, I dropped two cups with Felicia. Jamila was already in her Tuesday-morning developers' meeting, but Felicia inhaled hers with a grateful smile.

Point scored.

My good luck continued as Hannah and I huddled in our office all morning fielding calls from journalists and strategizing about next steps. I had a list of ways for Jamila to build positive buzz on my tablet when we walked down the hall to our daily meeting with Jamila.

The coding teams held daily stand-up meetings, and I'd copied the concept for our updates. We literally stood—so no one felt comfortable enough to get long-winded—and provided rapid-fire updates on our progress and the day's focus. As little as Jamila liked talking about PR, she could take it in these small doses. We had ten minutes of the lunch hour Felicia so ferociously guarded.

But today, there was an extra person in Jamila's office.

Rhiannon.

"Oh, hey, are we early?" I asked.

We were not early. We were exactly on time, the way Jamila liked it.

Jamila glanced at her phone. "No, I was wrapping up with Ree."

I let out a small sigh of relief. She was leaving.

"I'd like to stay today," Rhiannon said, malice lighting up her whisky-brown eyes. "See how the PR efforts are going."

My heart dropped into my stomach. I was so screwed.

"Really?" Jamila asked.

"It's going to be really dull," I said. "Just talking about how we can raise Jamila's profile in the community."

"I think we need to talk about last night's PR activity," Rhiannon said, a smirk pulling her lips up.

"The press conference?" Jamila asked. "That was days ago. We've already done a postmortem. I know I'm not allowed to threaten the press. Make sure that's on your list, Nat." She winked.

Rhiannon said, "Why don't you tell Jamila what you and that lunkhead did after work last night, Natalie?"

"A lunkhead?" Jamila raised her perfect eyebrows. "Did you have a date, Nat?"

"N-no." I wished a trapdoor would open in Jamila's office and suck me down into a dungeon. At least I'd be safe from Jamila's sharp eyes.

But there was no escape for me. I had only eight minutes before Felicia ejected us all.

"I...I was trying to find the leak. So, I set a trap."

"A trap?" Jamila asked. "For who?"

I glanced at Rhiannon, but she only folded her arms across her light-blue polo shirt.

"For Rhiannon." I huffed out a sigh. "I thought she might be the leak."

Beside me, Hannah gasped.

"Me," Rhiannon said. "One of your longest-tenured employees. I left a solid job with a 401(k) and unlimited vacation to come here. Remember the couple of months when we didn't get paid on time?"

Jamila nodded, a blank expression on her face.

"I didn't take time off for the first three years. Not one sick day because I believed in Jamila when hardly anyone else did. Sometimes it was just Winslow and me. And, sure, I could've retired a couple years ago if I sold my stock options, but I stayed. Didn't even want a promotion up here to the executive floor—"

"You refused it," Jamila interrupted.

"Damn straight," Rhiannon said. "All I want is to make great software. I don't want a villa on the beach. Not yet. But when I do, believe me, I'll be fine. As long as Jamilow's shares don't tank."

I closed my eyes. Why hadn't I thought of that? Like Winslow's and Jamila's, Rhiannon's wealth was tied up in Jamilow. She had zero incentive to sabotage the company.

"I'm really sorry," I said. "It was wrong of me to try to bribe you."

"You tried to bribe Rhiannon?" Jamila's voice was loud enough to hear in the next ZIP code.

"I did. I'm sorry. I won't doubt you again, Rhiannon."

Rhiannon said nothing. I was not forgiven.

"I let you talk me into doing this PR bullshit. Don't make me regret it." Jamila's voice was icicle sharp. "Stay in your lane, Natalie. Only public relations. Leave my employees alone."

"I...I..." *I was only trying to help.* "I understand."

"Natalie's heart is in the right place," Hannah said in a voice almost too soft to hear. I blinked at her. She never said anything in front of Jamila. Jamila terrified her.

"I don't care where Natalie's heart is. I need her to keep her goddamn nose in her own business. Got it?" Jamila barked the last two words at me, but Hannah cowered.

"Got it. Sorry. Again. Now, we have a list of ideas—"

The office door swung open, and Felicia stood in the doorway, hands on her hips. "Time's up. Everybody out. Jamila needs some peace and quiet."

"But—"

"Email it," Felicia said.

My shoulders slumped under the weight of my disappointment. I'd screwed up my chance to help Jamila.

Rhiannon sailed out, chin held high. "See you later, Jamila."

Hannah scuttled out, and I slunk behind her. After Felicia shut the door, I lingered at her desk. "Any chance I could get five minutes with her later?"

"No. She's leaving for a trip this afternoon."

"A trip? Where?"

"Austin. They're kicking off the coding camps this week. She never misses the first day."

"Wait. She's going down to Austin and hanging out with girls who code at a camp she founded?"

"Uh-huh." Felicia opened her drawer and pulled out her

purse. She slung it over her shoulder, a clear signal it was time for me to leave so she could go to lunch.

"That's perfect! We'll snap some photos and feed them to the media. Everyone will know how amazing she is."

Felicia pursed her lips. "I don't know how excited Jamila will be about all that. She's not one to exploit teenage girls."

"It's not exploiting the girls. It's drawing attention to the good Jamila is doing. Don't you want people to focus on that rather than on her media missteps?"

"Of course I do. I'm not sure Jamila will see it that way, though."

"Send me her flight info, and I'll go with her. We'll keep it low-key. I'll take some photos and post them on social media. No journalists. I'll even book my travel. Okay?"

"I guess that would be all right. I'll email you her itinerary after lunch."

I shimmied with excitement. "Perfect. Thank you so much!" I hugged her.

She pressed her lips together and brushed imaginary wrinkles out of her blouse. "We'll see if you're thanking me when Jamila finds out you're tagging along. Good luck."

"Enjoy your lunch!"

I practically skipped down the hallway to my office. I'd found the perfect way to help Jamila and make her forget my mistake.

10

DESPITE THE COCKTAIL sitting on the bar in front of her, Jamila's expression soured when I sat next to her in the first-class lounge at the airport.

"Didn't Felicia tell you I was coming along?" I hung my tote on the hook under the bar.

"Yeah, but don't expect me to be happy about it."

Signaling the bartender, I said, "I know you're angry with me. I get it. But I couldn't pass up this opportunity. We'll get some great traction on social media, and, hopefully, that'll push out the negative attention."

"I don't fund the camps for social media." She lifted the glass to her lips, took a healthy swallow, and set it down. "I do it because I wish I'd had a coding camp to go to when I was younger, so I could've met other girls like me. And so I could see an example of a Black woman who'd made it in tech."

I rubbed the goosebumps that popped up on my arms. "I know. I don't want to disrupt what you're doing. All I want is to show everyone the good you're doing. Expand your reach. Maybe other girls will see what you're doing and seek out something like it in their towns or resolve to reach a hand back to help someone else once they've made it."

"Made it," she scoffed. "Is that even a thing? Is there ever a platform you can stand on where you think, 'That's enough. I've made it'? If there is, I've never seen it."

I took a measured sip of my wine. "I think some people are like that. Jackson, for example. He's happy right where he is, coding and living his best life with his family. But you're more like my mother, always striving for the next success." I didn't say, *Never satisfied with what she has.* How could she be satisfied with a daughter who couldn't seem to figure out her life?

"You're like that too." She scanned my face. "You could be a socialite, wearing fancy clothes and hosting parties. And sometimes you play that part." I blushed, remembering the disastrous party at Billie's. "But you're not satisfied to do that. You're always trying to better yourself with all those programs and careers."

"Huh." Was she right? Could I not settle on a career because I was always striving for the next thing? The answer didn't sit right inside me. "I don't think that's it. I think I need to find the thing I enjoy doing. And once I do, I'll be satisfied. Happy."

She tilted her head. "When you do, tell me what it's like."

"I will." I lifted my drink. "To happiness."

She clinked her glass against mine. "To happiness."

———

THE CAMP TOOK place at a residence hall on the University of Texas campus. Felicia told me Jamila stayed in the dorm like the campers, but I'd booked a hotel room nearby. I was half afraid Jamila would kick me out as an uninvited guest and half grossed out by dorm rooms. There was a reason I'd stayed at college only a year.

Inside the beige brick building, I flapped my notebook at my face, thankful for the air conditioning. It was only nine in the morning, but May in Austin was already heating up. I wished I hadn't thought a silk blouse, blazer, and jeans were an appropriate outfit for a coding camp.

I eased off my jacket and folded it over the back of a chair at the edge of the dining hall where I could watch the girls. They ranged in age from twelve to eighteen, with every shade of skin. At the center of each round dining table, a snarl of power cords from their laptops converged at a surge protector.

I realized my mistake as soon as I spotted Jamila onstage. The clacking of keys and the buzz of conversation halted as soon as she stepped onto the raised platform opposite the cafeteria doors.

My mistake? Thinking I could come to Austin and be unaffected by Jamila's casual confidence as she sauntered onstage. She wore cutoff jean shorts and a T-shirt with the camp's logo across her chest. Her toned legs were endless in those shorts. I had to bite my tongue to keep it from rolling out of my mouth like a cartoon wolf.

"Welcome to coding camp!" Jamila's voice boomed through the speakers to the back of the room. The girls cheered and clapped. When they quieted down, Jamila continued, "It wasn't that long ago that I was sitting in my room in my grandma's house teaching myself to code. Back then, I had a thick paperback I'd checked out from the library and a secondhand desktop computer I'd bought with money I'd earned from babysitting and walking dogs. I shared the room with my two little brothers, who teased me for being a nerd. Raise your hand if someone has called you that."

Many hands went up around the room.

"Well, nerds, let's embrace our passion and be proud. Let's take back the word *nerd* and celebrate ourselves. Let's keep on doing what we love and believe in ourselves despite the naysayers who think girls can't code. Let's prove them wrong this week." Her "What do you say?" was drowned out by cheering.

I'd never wanted to be a programmer like my siblings, but that day, I wished I had. I wished I'd found something that would set me on fire like the hundred girls in that room.

The camp director, an energetic Latina about my age, took Jamila's place on stage and spoke for a few minutes about the week's coding assignment. Then the girls got to work. The counselors moved among the tables, answering questions. I snapped photo after photo, trying to capture the joy in the girls' movements and expressions. Jamila strode toward one of the younger girls, who scowled at her laptop's screen, arms folded. I jogged over to witness the interaction.

"What's the matter"—Jamila read the girl's nametag—"Ana Maria?"

The girl tossed her heavy black braid over her shoulder. "My program does the first thing, but then it hangs. It won't do the second thing even though I told it to in the code."

"That happens to me all the time." But instead of telling Ana Maria how to fix it, Jamila asked her questions about how she could approach the problem. As they talked, the scowl melted off the girl's face. I snapped pictures as quickly as I could.

After a few minutes, Ana Maria's eyes brightened. "That's it! That's what I did wrong!" She peered at the screen, positioned her cursor, and typed in a few commands. A second later, she shouted, "It worked!"

Jamila held out a fist, and Ana Maria bumped it. "Way to go!"

"Thanks, Jamila." Ana Maria turned her attention back to the screen, and Jamila moved on.

I scored a seat next to her at lunchtime.

She glanced at me. "What, you're not going to document lunch too?"

"Nope. You can eat your sandwich in peace." I nodded at her plate. "I promised Felicia."

She chuckled. "Felicia thinks I don't eat enough."

"I bet you'd forget if she didn't remind you."

"Maybe. Sometimes I forget on the weekends."

"You need a weekend Felicia."

"No, thanks." She crunched into a chip. "I like to have my weekends to myself. No one telling me what to do."

"Oh, come on. You're the CEO of your company. No one can make you do anything you don't want to do."

"Really? That's what you think?" Jamila sipped her water. "Everyone tells me what to do. The board, Felicia, my management team, Kenneth Royal, and even you, Miss Bossy Pants. I can't even get away for a couple of days without you following me and nagging me to smile for the camera."

"I did not nag you." I set down my fork with a clatter that was swallowed up by the noise in the dining room. "I took candid shots. I never said a word."

"Hmph. Well, I was always conscious of you with that phone. You might as well have been nagging me."

"Sorry." I hated that I'd ruined her enjoyment of the camp. "Would you like me to stop for the rest of the day?"

"Nah. It's fine. I know you're trying to help."

My chest swelled. "I promise, you're going to love the posts. I got some great shots. You're doing so much for these girls."

"Thanks." She lifted her sandwich and took a bite.

"I noticed you're staying another night. Are you going to see your grandmother?"

Her lips turned down as she chewed. She swallowed with difficulty. "Nah."

"Oh. Is she—"

"She died." She blotted her lips with her napkin. "Ten years ago."

"Oh." My hands felt too big, so I folded them in my lap. "I'm sorry."

"It's fine. We weren't that close."

"But you—"

"We were different, okay? She never got me, and I sure as hell never understood her."

I grimaced. Suddenly, the air conditioning was too much. I shivered. "Sorry."

"Don't worry about it. It was a long time ago." She returned to her sandwich. The camper on the other side of her asked her a question, so I asked the counselor sitting beside me how she'd gotten involved in the camp. Before I knew it, lunchtime was over.

The afternoon was more of the same, more coding time, then a few of the girls shared their programs with the group. Dinner was scheduled to be a picnic on the lawn, and I hoped to get more photos of Jamila interacting with the girls in the early evening light. The shadows loved to play in Jamila's bone structure, accentuating her strong cheekbones and her full lower lip. I couldn't wait to capture it in hi-res on my phone.

As I trailed the last girls out of the hall, I spotted Jamila with two giant men. They wore jeans and golf shirts, one in maroon and the other burnt orange. One of them pushed her shoulder, and the other one caught her roughly.

What the heck?

I sprinted to help her.

11

"HEY! STOP IT! LET HER GO!" I shouted.

The two men were built like linebackers, but I was too fired up to be afraid. I raced up to the guy holding Jamila and pummeled his shoulder. There was zero give to the muscle under his maroon shirt, but he looked down.

"What's this?" He caught my hand, but at least that made him release Jamila. She stepped away, breathless.

"Run! Get help!" I shouted.

"Oh, I like her," the one in orange said. "Feisty."

"Let her go, Jevin," Jamila said.

"But she's assaulting me," he said. "From the looks of her clothes, that could be a very lucrative lawsuit."

"Like you're hurting for funds," she scoffed. "If you don't let her go, she's liable to punch you. Then she'll sue *you* when she breaks her hand."

"I know how to punch so I won't break my hand," I snapped.

At the same time, he said, "Sue *me?* Unlikely." He released my hand and stepped back, shrugging.

"Are you okay?" The other guy asked. "Need me to look at your hand?"

"No. Thank you." What kind of assailants were these? "Jamila, are you okay?"

"I'm fine." She rolled her eyes. "Natalie, meet my brothers, Jevin and Jaleel Jallow. Guys, meet Natalie Jones. She's doing some PR work for me."

"Call me J.J." The orange-shirted one stuck his hand out. His shake was surprisingly gentle.

"Wait. You're all J.J.—all three of you."

When he grinned, his teeth were brilliant white against his full, dark lips. The family resemblance hit me. Why hadn't I seen it as sibling horseplay and kept my nose out of it?

"She's a girl. No one would give her a nickname like that. She's Mila. I got J.J. because I'm the older one, and he's just Jevin."

"*Just* Jevin? I'm the good-lookin' one." His grin was equally sparkly. In fact—

"You're twins?" I glanced between them. Jevin carried himself more casually, and J.J. stood straight like a redwood, but otherwise, they were identical.

"They are," Jamila said. "Total nightmare."

"We were only getting you back for all the abuse you gave us when you were bigger than us," Jevin said. "One hundred percent fair."

"Ah." I remembered her speech from earlier. "These were the brothers who called you a nerd."

"We were snot-nosed kids," J.J. said. "Of course we were going to call our studious big sister a nerd. Anything to make her pull her face out of the computer screen and notice us."

"The question is, what are you doing here?" Jamila asked. "I distinctly remember *not* texting you."

"We know you always come for the first day." Jevin shrugged. "We wanted to see you."

"What if I was busy?"

"Busy?" He glanced at me, then he did a double take. "Oh, I see."

Jamila whacked his beefy arm. "Not like that. I meant that I'm busy with the camp."

Not like that. Of course it wasn't. I only wished it were.

"Too busy for your brothers to take you to dinner?" Jevin did a superior impression of a puppy-dog-eyes emoji.

She put her hands on her hips. "You're not going to stick me with the check?"

"You're a billionaire," J.J. said.

"You do fine," she said. "And who paid for your school?"

"You did." When he looked down at his sneaker, I caught an echo of what he must have been like when he was smaller than Jamila. J.J. was the quiet one.

"We're buying," Jevin said. "Now come on. You, too, Natalie. I want to hear about this PR work."

But on the ride to the restaurant, there were no PR questions for me. I sat in the backseat of Jevin's black Escalade next to J.J. while Jamila and Jevin argued in the front seat about where we were going, Jevin's driving, and whether the air conditioning should be on or the windows open. Finally, he pulled into a gravel parking lot next to a shack.

A literal shack.

A haphazard array of picnic tables dotted the scrubby grass, and all types of people occupied them, most dressed casually but a few wearing business suits with jackets folded beside them on the benches.

When I didn't move to get out, J.J. stuck his head back into the car. "You coming, Natalie?"

"Wait, I...I thought it was another joke. We're actually eating here?"

"Texans don't joke about barbecue," he said. "This is the best barbecue spot in Austin."

I slid out of the SUV.

"Find us a table, Mila," he said. "We'll get in line."

I only noticed the line as J.J. mentioned it. It extended almost to the parking lot. While the two men sauntered to the end of it, several women watched them. A few shook their heads in appreciation.

"Come on." Jamila grabbed my hand like I was six and towed me to a table where a group of guys in battered jeans and boots had just stood. "Y'all all done?" she asked in a sweet-tea voice.

"Yep." One tall man plunked a straw cowboy hat on his head and swiped at a spot of sauce on the table. The neatness of his movement, along with his sandy-blond hair and blue eyes, reminded me of Cooper Fallon. "It's all yours." He winked.

"Thanks, cowboy." She grinned.

My cheeks burning, I tried to shake my hand loose so she could properly flirt back, but she held on tight.

He snagged a beer bottle from the table and held it up in a toast. "Y'all have a pleasant night."

"Thanks. Y'all too." She sat on the bench and scooted over so I could sit beside her.

But I didn't sit. I snatched some paper towels off the roll in the center of the table and started wiping it down. "You don't have to stay here with me," I muttered. "You can…you can chat with him if you like." I scrubbed at a stain, but it was so old it was part of the wood.

"Chat with who?"

"That cowboy." I nodded at him. He and his friends strolled toward the parking lot.

"Why would I do that?"

"He…you…you two were flirting. He's your type. Don't you want his number?"

"Flirting? We were being friendly. It's how people are down here. We don't mean anything by it."

"Oh?" I wiped another invisible spot.

"And I don't have a type," she said. "Except for people who are smart and interesting."

Two words that, for sure, didn't describe me. I wadded up the paper towel and looked for a trash can.

"Your cheeks are red. Are you sunburned?" She peered at my face.

I wanted to hide, but the outdoor dining area had zero shelter. "I don't know. Maybe." I spotted a trash bin and strode to it to dump the wad of paper towels. I took a breath to try to cool my blush, but the air was anything but cool. Even with the sun hovering just above the distant trees by the river, it was hot and sticky.

"I forget how much stronger the sun is down here," Jamila said when I returned to the table. "Sit with your back to the sun. Wouldn't want to ruin your pretty skin with a burn."

"You think my skin is pretty?" Sinking onto the bench opposite her, I touched my cheeks, which flamed at the compliment.

"Course I do." She rolled her eyes. "It's like peaches and cream."

"Your skin is gorgeous," I blurted out. Then I closed my eyes to block out her face. *What a ridiculous thing to say!*

But she said, "Thank you." When I opened my eyes, she smiled at me, her eyes crinkling at the corners and the apples of her cheeks shining in the early evening sunlight.

I'd have done something silly like reach across the table to touch her glowing face if her brothers hadn't lumbered up at that moment clutching beer bottles.

"Food'll be a minute, but we got these," J.J. said.

He tried to pass me a brown bottle, but I held up a hand. "No, thanks, I don't like beer."

"No beer? What else can I get you?"

I couldn't imagine the shack had a decent wine list. "Water will be fine."

"I know just the thing," Jevin said. He winked and returned to the shack.

A minute later, he was back with a red Solo cup, a lime wedge balanced on the edge. "Ranch water with an actual water chaser." He plunked down a bottle of water.

I sniffed the fizzy drink. The smell of alcohol and citrus rose from it. I took a cautious sip. It tasted pleasantly bubbly and limey with a bite of booze. "What is it?"

"Sparkling mineral water, tequila, and a squeeze of lime. It's what all the skinny girls drink."

I took another sip. "I don't usually drink tequila, but this is good."

He grinned, then cocked his head at the garbled voice that came from the speaker hanging from the shack's gutter. "That's us. Come on, J.J."

The two men returned a minute later, each clutching two aluminum platters. The parchment-lined rectangle J.J. plunked in front of me held a paper boat full of thinly sliced beef, a square of cornbread, a smaller boat of something stewed and green, and a cup of soupy beans.

"This is for us to share, right?" I reached for a packet of wet wipes from the center of the table and scrubbed my hands.

"That's all for you. If you'd like to trade some collards for some of my fried okra, I wouldn't fight you."

"Sure, and you can take the meat."

"You're a vegetarian?" J.J. asked, scooping up the boat of meat and dropping it on his tray.

"Yeah."

"Sorry about that. Mila, you should've told us."

She narrowed her eyes. "You passed on the bacon at brunch, but I didn't think it was a forever thing."

My cheeks heated again. Of course she didn't think I'd stick with it. I never stuck with anything.

"How long have you been a vegetarian?" Jevin asked.

"Since my butchery class in culinary school. I had to drop out."

"Ah. That'd do it," J.J. said. "I went off meat for a while after my gross anatomy lab."

"Your...what?" I asked. In his stretched-tight polo shirt, J.J. looked more like a pro athlete than a brainiac who took anatomy.

"We dissected cadavers in med school."

"Med school? You guys aren't defensive linemen?"

J.J. chuckled. "You think Mila got all the brains in the family? Sure, we played in college, but I'm an oncologist, and Jevin is an attorney."

"Here," Jamila said, removing a dollop of creamy potato salad before depositing the boat on my tray. "You still eat dairy, right?"

"Sure." Fried okra, mashed potatoes, and macaroni and cheese landed on my tray. "Wait. There's no way I can eat all this."

"Eat what you want. My brother and I can pack away anything you don't." Jevin patted his flat belly.

I sampled each dish. They were all amazing. I had to hand the mac and cheese back to Jevin or I'd have eaten the entire carbolicious mountain of calories.

At some point, Jamila brought me a second cup of ranch water and switched seats with J.J. to sit next to me. Between the funny stories, inside jokes, the sunshine on my back, and the warm smell of barbecue spice in the air, everything took on a rose-colored quality.

Maybe it was the sun melting into the horizon that colored everything pink. Maybe it was the tequila. Or maybe it was Jamila's hand, planted on the bench between us, her pinky finger pointed toward me. All I had to do was extend my pinky to touch hers.

I snuck a glance at her. She was listening to a story Jevin was telling about his client, whose divorce had been cut and dried until the wife refused to split up their two dogs. They'd had to hire a pet psychologist for an opinion on whether separating the dogs would result in pain and suffering to one or the other.

I didn't care about the couple or their pets. All I cared about was the long column of her arm, gilded on the back by the setting sun. Her shoulders and triceps were slender but defined, and her skin looked like silk. The back of her hand glowed golden, and I imagined if I touched it, it'd feel like a river rock, smooth and warm.

It had to be the tequila that made me stretch out my pinky to stroke hers. It was just as satiny warm as I'd imagined. She didn't twitch or even look down, but her smile broadened. I took that as a sign to curl my pinky around hers, the sides of our hands nestled together. I was holding Jamila's hand.

Kind of.

But it didn't last long.

She tugged her hand from mine to stretch both arms over her head. Her T-shirt rode up, showing me a peek of her flat stomach that I wanted to kiss.

"Curfew's at nine," she said, "and camp starts early tomorrow."

J.J. narrowed his eyes. "You're not going to pay your respects to Nana?"

That woke me from the happy haze I'd drifted into. This trip had peeled back Jamila's layers for me. Austin was where she kept her brothers and memories of her Nana.

"Is that why you kidnapped us? You wanted to drag me to the cemetery?"

"You haven't been since the funeral." He shrugged. "I imagine you two have things to say to each other."

"She's dead, J.J. We can't talk anymore. If we could, she'd probably yell at me. The week before she died, she left me a voice mail that near peeled the skin off my ear. Can't imagine what she'd have to say now."

"About your PR situation?" Jevin glanced at me.

"Yeah." Jamila rolled her eyes to the cloudless sky. "She's probably up there telling everyone what a fuck up I am."

J.J. winced. "You know she loved you—"

"All she cared about was that I didn't inconvenience her. You remember."

"Don't be like that," J.J. said. "She loved us in her own way. She gave us a home—"

"A begrudging home. One I was delighted to leave when I went to college. One I'm thankful I never needed to go back to.

Now, are you two going to take us back to campus, or are we calling a rideshare?"

"Nah, we'll take you back." Jevin rose.

J.J. stood. "I really think—"

Jevin put a hand on his twin's shoulder. "That's enough, man. She always did walk her own path."

J.J. nodded, but he didn't look happy. Neither did Jamila. She grabbed my tray, clanked it against hers, and stormed off toward the trash bin.

When I stood, the world tilted around me. I tried to swing my leg over the bench and wobbled. I grabbed the table to steady myself.

"Hold up, baby girl." Jamila grasped my elbow. How had she gotten there so fast? Did she have superhuman speed, too, as well as intelligence? "You okay?"

"How much tequila was in those drinks?"

From my other side, J.J.'s arm curled around my waist to support my spaghetti legs. "Folks round here like a strong drink. That second one was probably a bad idea, considering your body weight."

"She was eating, though," Jamila said like I wasn't there. "She shouldn't be this drunk."

"She's probably not much of a drinker. Nurses a glass of wine all night?"

"Goddammit. What am I going to tell her brother?"

I snapped my head up, whacking J.J. in the chin. "Don't tell Jackson."

J.J. swore and rubbed his chin. "Dang, girl. That's gonna leave a mark."

"How's your head, baby girl?" Jamila put her hands on my head and felt for a lump.

I imagined she was running her hands through my hair. "Feels nice." Then she touched a spot that sent searing pain through my foggy brain. "Ouch!"

"Aw. You're a mess tonight, aren't you?"

Our faces were close enough that I could've leaned forward and kissed her. But she didn't want to kiss someone as sloppy and childish as I was proving myself to be tonight.

"Yeah," I said. As if I hadn't already embarrassed myself enough, a tear slipped down my cheek.

She tilted up my chin and wiped away the wetness. "Let's get you back to your hotel."

"My rental's on campus," I mumbled.

"She can't drive," J.J. protested.

"Take us back to campus," Jamila said. "I'll drive her to her hotel, then pick her up in the morning before camp."

Jamila sat in the back of the SUV with me. Normally, I'd have enjoyed her nearness, but after embarrassing myself getting drunk off two drinks, I slumped in the seat and leaned toward the open window, the humid air blowing in my face to keep nausea at bay.

When they dropped us at my rented Buick, Jamila's brothers hugged me. They gave Jamila longer hugs and murmured with her for a few minutes. I was too busy berating myself to listen. I'd come here to help Jamila, yet here I was, forcing her to take care of me.

After her brothers left, Jamila drove me the short distance to my hotel. She pulled into a ten-minute parking space in front.

"Need help getting to your room?"

"No, I'm okay." Digestion and the fresh air had done their job, and I felt steadier. All I wanted was to hide in my room for the next eight hours. Heck, maybe I'd hide for the rest of my life. Jamila would never forget how ridiculous I'd been tonight.

"Hey, baby girl." Jamila slipped a finger under my chin and tilted it up. Her brown eyes pierced into mine. "You sure you're okay? I don't think I've ever seen you this quiet."

"I'm fine," I mumbled.

She didn't take her finger away, and her gaze dropped lower.

She was about a foot away from me. Her flowery scent bloomed around me in the compact car. Most of her burgundy lipstick had come off during dinner, but a faint stain remained on her cushiony lips. Her tongue darted out to lick them, and her glossy lower lip gleamed in the hotel's security lights. It called to me, and I couldn't resist.

I leaned in and brushed my mouth over hers.

Once. Twice. My drier lips tugged against hers like my skin didn't want to release her. None of me wanted to release her. My hands lifted as if I could cradle her face.

"Natalie," she whispered, breaking the spell. I reared back, bumping against the passenger-side door.

Jesus. I'd just kissed Jamila Jallow. Against her will. That whisper was not an I-want-you whisper. It was a stop-now whisper.

"Sorry," I wailed, struggling with the seatbelt latch.

"Hey, it's o—"

I finally got the belt off and shoved through the door, then ran like a coward into the hotel lobby.

I didn't even wave goodbye.

12

THE SUN WAS STILL UP—BARELY—BUT it felt like midnight when I slammed the Hyundai's door and waved off the rideshare driver in front of my house. The combination of battling my hangover through a full day of coding camp, the flight from Texas, and the extra effort of avoiding Jamila as much as possible weighed my body down.

All day, I'd looked forward to a long soak in my tub with the limited-edition, celebrity-endorsed bath bomb I'd been saving for a special occasion. Even through the packaging, it smelled like honey and promised herbal relaxation.

I unlocked the door and shuffled in, bumping my roller carry-on over the threshold. But instead of the blissful silence of an empty house, yapping met my ears. Bilbo Baggins skidded across the tiles. When he'd regained his footing, he danced around my feet. I froze, not wanting to step on him mid-whirl.

Sam leaned on the doorframe of the hall that led to the living room. "It's Natalie," she called.

"Of course it's me," I growled. "I live here, unlike you."

My sister shoved her hands into her pockets. "It wasn't me who was worried."

A mass of curly, dark hair filled my vision before a set of arms cinched me. "There you are. I was so worried when you didn't show up to drinks."

"Drinks? Nuts." With the last-minute trip, I'd completely forgotten about my standing Thursday-night happy hour with Mimi. Obsessed with bargain booze and munchies, she'd found us a bar that offered a selection of margaritas for half price, plus all-you-can-eat chips and salsa. Though I wasn't sure I'd ever be able to drink tequila again after the ranch-water disaster—or look Jamila in the eye.

"I'm sorry I missed it." I dropped the handle of my suitcase and hugged Mimi. It wasn't quite as good as a CBD-infused bath bomb, but she gave wonderful hugs, and I melted into her softness.

"It's okay. I'm glad you're not missing." She released me and leaned back to scan my face. "Where were you? Not working, I hope."

"Let's sit down. I'm exhausted." I tugged Mimi into the living room and sank into the sofa. Mimi sat next to me, and Sam inexplicably followed and sat in Charles's favorite armchair. Bilbo leaped into the chair and curled up in her lap.

"I'm sorry for skipping drinks," I said. "I hope you didn't wait for me long."

"It was okay. Mateo met me when I texted him you hadn't showed, then he dropped me off here on his way to work. He's on nights this week at tía Rosa's."

"How's Mateo? He's not mad about what I asked him to do at Jamilow, is he?" I shot a guilty look at Sam. I hadn't told her what Mateo and I had done last Monday night. My successful sister never would have stooped to entrapment.

She remained silent, watching us with those otherworldly blue eyes of hers.

Mimi chuckled. "He had the best time playing your little spy game, even if you got caught. That night, he came home and..." Her cheeks blazed red.

"You guys did *not* roleplay spies!" I laughed at the guilty expression on her face, and suddenly, I wasn't so tired anymore.

"Turns out, he has a *Mr. and Mrs. Smith* kink. He may have tied me to a chair at one point." Now her entire face was crimson.

"Wow." I fanned my face. "Happy to have been of service."

"Any leads on the leak?" she asked.

"None." I frowned. "But Jamila's coding camp was PR gold. That's why I missed happy hour. We went to Austin so she could be there for the first day. I took a million pictures, and after I've blurred out the girls' faces, I'll post so many that everyone will forget her little slip-up." Or maybe I'd send them to Hannah so she could post them. I wasn't sure I could ever go back to Jamilow after my own slip-up.

"Hang on. You went on an overnight trip with Jamila?" Mimi's brown eyes widened.

"It wasn't like that."

"What was it like, then?" Mimi asked.

"Well, I started to understand her a little more, like why she runs the camps, and I even met her brothers. Did you know she had brothers?"

Mimi shook her head.

"They're funny and amazing just like Jamila. We went out for barbecue, and I had this drink, and…and I may have gotten a little drunk and kissed her." I whispered the last part.

But Mimi didn't whisper. "You kissed Jamila? Finally!" She pumped her fist. "Was it incredible?"

I flung myself back against the sofa cushions and slapped my hands onto my face to hide my blush. "Incredibly humiliating. She practically booted me out of the car. I spent all of today hiding from her. I even waited in those horrible plastic seats at the airport instead of hanging in the first-class lounge. I don't think I can go back."

"Oh, no." Mimi pulled one of my hands off my face and stroked the back of it. "Office romances are the worst. When things go wrong, there's no escape. I had to quit my job when my ex and I broke up."

"*Office romance* is overstating things a bit since the attraction is completely one-sided."

"Completely?" Sam asked. "Are you certain?"

I'd forgotten she was in the room. And that she hadn't known I had a huge crush on my boss or that I was bisexual—and neither did our mother.

"It's nothing," I said. "Just a crush."

My sister frowned. "Why would you think that?"

"Because…because she's *Jamila Jallow,* and she's brilliant and so much more put together than I am."

"You're brilliant and put together," Sam said.

"I'm not as smart as you or Jackson or Jamila. I only pretend to have it all together. I don't run a startup like you or manage a foundation like Mimi."

"Hell, I don't have my shit together," Mimi said. "I don't know what I'm doing. I was an accountant before I took the job at the foundation. I spend half the day googling how to run a foundation and the other half doing it."

"I've never run a company before," Sam said. "I meet with Cooper once a week for coaching."

"But…but you two are amazing at your jobs!"

"Some days yes, and other days definitely not," Mimi said.

"I've never known you not to go for what you want," Sam said. "You made up a job at Jamilow and convinced Jamila to let you do it. Why couldn't you apply that to a relationship with Jamila?"

"Um…because it's inappropriate? She's my boss even if I'm not actually a paid employee. Plus, she's not interested in me."

"Did she kiss you back?" Mimi asked.

I thought back on it, but everything was tequila-hazed. "I thought so at the time, but maybe not? I'd been drinking."

"You should talk to her," Sam said.

"That's fine for you to say," I said testily. "You don't have to face her."

"No, but you can do it," Sam said. "You're the brave one."

"Am not!" I tossed a throw pillow at her.

She tossed it back. "Are too."

"Stop it, you two. You'll wake up Bilbo." Mimi snatched the pillow from my fist. "Nat, you're gorgeous and smart. Jamila would be a fool not to want you. You're going to march into the office tomorrow and talk to her about that kiss."

I crossed my arms. "It'd be a lot easier to quit."

"But then Jamila wouldn't have her PR consultant to save her from this mess," Sam said gently. "She needs you, and you need to clear the air so you can work together."

"And *work* together, if you know what I mean." Mimi poked my side.

"You two are the worst," I said, but I didn't mean it. I meant the opposite. They'd given me enough hope to go back to Jamila.

No, not to Jamila. I meant go back to Jamilow—back to my job.

13

"GOOD NEWS." I forced a smile onto my face as I leaned in the doorway to Jamila's office. I'd canceled our daily PR stand-up meetings. I'd said it was because of the goodwill we'd earned with the posts about the coding camp, but the truth was, I was still too embarrassed to be in the same room with her.

"Yeah?" Her eyes lingered for a second on her screen before she turned her full attention to me.

"Yeah. I scored you a feature in *Buzz Bizz*. They want an interview and some photos."

"Great. Have them send me the questions, and I'll fire off some responses. Felicia has my headshot." She looked back at her screen and resumed typing.

I cleared my throat. "No. I mean an actual interview. Like, sitting in a hotel suite talking to a journalist followed by a photo shoot."

The keyboard went quiet. "I thought you said this was *good* news. That sounds like I'm going to have to make time in my schedule to talk to someone, have them misrepresent what I say, and end up in a worse spot than before. Plus, photos. Sitting still for too long gives me a crick in my neck."

She made it sound terrible, but looking at the bright side was one of my superpowers. "The best news is that you don't have to negotiate the schedule. I've already done it for you. The interview is tomorrow, Saturday, followed by the photo shoot. We're just waiting on a location."

"You scheduled me on a Saturday." Her eyebrows shot up. "Pretty high-handed of you. What if I have plans?"

I winced. Maybe she had a date. "Do you?"

"No. Other than a dance party with Quill.i.am."

"He won't mind postponing. This is a perfect chance for you to tell your story, to get people to focus on the good you do and on Jamilow. Not the mistake you made."

"Believe me, it wasn't a mistake. That guy deserved it."

"Then tell them what he said." I still wondered what a journalist could say to make Jamila lose her cool.

"No, thanks. I don't want to give him one more minute of anyone's attention, including mine."

"I'll email them that the incident is off the table for the interview."

"Just tell them when we show up," she said.

We? "You want me there?"

"You're my PR specialist. Of course I want you there."

Warmth bubbled in my chest, and I slapped the doorframe to distract from my blush. She wanted *me.* "Okay."

JAMILA DID us all a favor and found a location for the interview and photo shoot. Unfortunately, it was a place I was uncomfortably familiar with, Billie Woods's mansion in Atherton. Although it was the next town over from Jamila's, Billie's neighborhood couldn't have been more different. It was the type of place I'd expected Jamila to live: an enormous house with an expansive lawn and all of it meticulously maintained. The homes were set far from the winding street, which would make porch-to-porch conversations about avocados impossible. There were no bicycles lying in the driveways or dogs playing fetch in the yard. A stately black Rolls-Royce cruised by on the street. Not a Ford or Toyota was in sight.

Like the night of the party, there was a sticky note above the doorbell instructing me to come in. But when I pushed open the door, I had to step back outside and double-check the address.

The house was empty. The furniture was gone, as were the books on the shelves. Even the rugs had been rolled up and removed. When I'd come to the party, a hundred people had filled the open-plan space with their chatter and laughter. Now it was silent.

"Hello?" I called.

"Back here." The voice floated from the back of the house.

I followed the voice, my heels clicking on the tile and echoing off the hard, empty surfaces.

I found myself on a grandiose enclosed porch. It was as large as the living room with glass garage-style doors that could be lifted to open the room to the outdoor pool area. The elegant furniture had been removed here too, and mismatched pieces had been brought in, including a white chaise and a few industrial-looking chairs. Gauzy white curtains danced in the breeze from the open windows.

When I saw the photographer's equipment already set up and the makeup artist adjusting the light at a folding table, my stomach muscles relaxed. Everything looked ready for Jamila. I wouldn't waste any more of her precious Saturday than necessary.

I checked in with the photographer's assistant about the plans for the shoot. He showed me the nearby sitting room he'd designated as a changing room for Jamila. A rack of clothing stood beside a screen. While he lowered the blinds over the exterior windows, I checked that Jamila's outfits had made it there safely. She'd sent a couple of suits and a sheath dress. I'd added a pair of jeans, a T-shirt from her coding camp, and a buffalo-plaid shirt to layer over it to bring out her human side.

Everything was in order.

One side of the room was set up for photos. On the other side was a seating area for the interview. Two tan couches faced each other across a coffee table. A pair of dark-brown wingback chairs anchored the sides. The vase of African daisies I'd ordered was the only color in the space. I hoped they were similar enough to the ones I'd seen on her porch to make Jamila feel more at home.

I introduced myself to the journalist, Nita D'Alessio. I'd read her pieces before. Although she had a definite anti-capitalist slant, her articles were usually fair, and they presented the tech titans she interviewed as human beings.

"Remember, Jamila has stipulated that we won't be discussing the TikTok incident," I said. "She's asked me to cut off any questions regarding that topic."

"That's what everyone wants to know." Nita touched a finger to her chin. "The readers would be more sympathetic if they knew what set her off."

Exactly what I'd thought. "She doesn't want to give that guy any more attention than he's already received."

"Fair. He's an asshole."

"Really? You know him?"

"Sure. He's the one you stay away from at parties, if you know what I mean."

I curled my lip. "Gross."

"Exactly. What about her COO, Winslow Keating-Ashworth? Is he off-limits?" She glanced out at the pool. "It must have been an interesting divorce."

Interesting? I'd heard it mentioned a couple of times, but I couldn't imagine that anything about Winslow was as fascinating as Jamila. "Let's keep it focused on Jamila. She's the star of Jamilow."

"Okay." Nita shrugged. "You can sit on this couch." She pointed at the one that didn't have the camera pointed at it. "Jamila will sit on the other one. I'll be in the wingback chair."

"Got it. We need to approve any video from the interview before it's posted."

"Sure. It's mostly for transcription purposes, but we'll let you know if we'd like to release any of it. I'll send you the file. You'll have sign-off, of course."

"Perfect."

The hairs rose on the back of my neck a second before Nita said, "Ah, here she is."

When I turned, I had to fight to keep my face from doing anything weird. Jamila strode toward us like she owned the place dressed in weekend-casual denim trousers—I dared anyone to call the pressed straight-leg pants she wore jeans—a tan suede jacket, soft eggshell blouse, and kitten heels. No one, not even me, rocked business attire the way Jamila did. She made it look effortless, like she'd come out of the womb wearing pinstripes.

I wanted to bask in her reflected glow.

I shook myself and pasted on a smile. "Jamila, this is Nita D'Alessio. Nita, meet Jamila Jallow."

As the women shook hands, Nita sized her up. When Jamila performed her own scan of the journalist, jealousy stabbed my gut. I wished Jamila paid that much attention to me.

We settled into our seats while the tech performed the audio check. When that was done, Nita started with a few questions about Jamilow's upcoming launch that Jamila handled with ease, her eyes sparkling as she talked about her team's brilliance and teased about the product, carefully avoiding spilling any real details about what it did or the partnership that made it possible.

Switching topics, Nita said, "Tell me how you started Jamilow."

"Everyone knows that." Jamila waved a hand dismissively.

Nita leaned forward. "Indulge me."

I wished I had the courage to do that. To speak as suggestively as Nita had, to give Jamila a peek at her cleavage though—I glanced down—I didn't have that much cleavage to show off. I crossed my legs and kept my mouth shut.

"I started it at Stanford." Jamila settled back against the sofa cushions. "Well, I guess I started the app on my breaks from Stanford. When I was home during winter break my freshman year, I went to a party with my high school friends. As you do." She winked.

Nita nodded and scribbled on her notepad.

"Some of the younger kids were there, and they asked me questions. Not about Stanford so much as about going to college in general. The process was overwhelming to them. I realized some of them didn't have any family who'd gone to college." Jamila leaned forward, her elbows on her knees. "My nana went to college. She was a teacher. She did all she could to push me. So I told them a little about how I'd done it and gave them my number.

"Then when I got back to my grandmother's place and was talking with my brothers, I realized they were pretty clueless too. They played football, and they'd get recruited, but they didn't understand how to weigh their options. Or what they would do academically once they got there. After talking with them, I realized I could provide a service to kids like them. Kids like my friends."

I'd heard the story before, but now that I'd met her brothers, I understood how Jamila's advice might have led to their success. I tilted my head, eager to catch every word and examine it in that new light.

"So I programmed an app to answer most of the questions my friends had about going to college." A fire blazed in Jamila's eyes. "Standardized testing, grades, financial aid, applications and forms, scholarships. I only meant it to be useful to kids back in my old school. But then, talking to some of my classmates like Winslow, who had all the advantages I didn't, I realized it wasn't only kids like my high-school friends who could benefit. Anyone could. So I made it bigger. I gave it an AI interface so it could take info from the kids and provide a customized plan and advice."

"You partnered with Winslow Keating-Ashworth," Nita said.

"Yeah. He wasn't as good at coding as I was, but he had ideas for the business side of things. Connections, too. He was the one who said we should nudge the app toward life coaching. Easy stuff like a morning routine, making lists, putting your phone away at night, or advocating for yourself with professors."

"And the human coaches?" Nita prompted.

Jamila chuckled. "I took a psychology class and learned people can be way more complicated than artificial intelligence can handle. So we planned to augment the AI with access to therapists, but we needed funding for that. That's when we entered the app into a contest. We didn't win, but we got the interest of one of the judges, and she gave us our initial backing."

"And you bought her out a few years later?" Nita said.

I frowned. I hadn't known that.

"I didn't want anyone else calling the shots. I never wanted…" Jamila stared out the window at the sparkling pool for a moment.

"What didn't you want?" Nita prodded.

Jamila shook her head and finally directed her gaze at me. "I didn't want to tell my life story to some reporter. I'd rather focus on my business."

I wished I could release her from the interview. It was unfair that some jerk could goad her into making an unguarded, unwise comment, and only Jamila paid the penance for it. But that was life as a woman in tech. Jamila had signed up for it. Though she never could have predicted that fifteen years later, she'd be here, in someone's empty mansion, sharing uncomfortable details of her life. I shot her a sympathetic smile.

"But you haven't shied away from other partnerships," Nita said. "You've partnered with coaches, therapists, and college-prep services, so whom are you collaborating with next?"

Jamila smiled, smug. "Now, Nita, you know I can't comment on that."

Heat prickled along my skin. Witnessing Jamila's and Nita's chemistry made me feel like a voyeur. Was the cameraman uncomfortable too? I glanced up at the ceiling fan, wishing I could turn it on through sheer force of will.

"The article won't be printed until after your launch," Nita said. "Are you sure you don't want to talk about it?"

"Call me after the launch." Jamila winked. "I'd be delighted to talk about it then."

"Great. I'll get your number when we're done."

I wanted to run outside and jump into the cool depths of the pool. Where I wouldn't have to watch Jamila seduce the woman I'd brought in to rescue her reputation.

14

I SAT silent while Nita and Jamila ignored me.

I had no right to be jealous, I reminded myself bitterly. Jamila didn't care about me, at least, not like that. I'd kissed her without bothering to get her permission, which she surely would've denied me. She had every right to flirt with whomever she wanted, wherever she wanted.

Nita asked another question I didn't hear, and I let my gaze trail over the journalist. She was curvy in a way neither Jamila nor I was. Maybe Jamila liked women with more flesh on their bones. Like me, she had long, thick hair, but hers was chocolate brown, not blond. Her skin had an olive tone to it, not pale like mine. Her dark eyes were sharp, showing an intelligence that clearly intrigued Jamila.

Plus, she was confident in a way I only pretended to be. I knew from my research she'd been a journalist for more than ten years, writing for increasingly impressive publications. And now she had a feature article for *Buzz Bizz* with a custom photo shoot. She was so sure of what she wanted out of life. Her career was rising, and I couldn't pick a field, much less succeed at one.

Nita was everything I wasn't. No wonder Jamila liked her.

Jamila shifted to cross her legs, which alerted me something was wrong. Normally, she took up as much space as possible, but now she seemed to hunker down. Shaking off my introspection, I tuned back into the conversation.

"Everyone knows that Jamila Jallow was a star at Stanford and had a million-dollar app less than a year after graduation. But few know you grew up modestly in Texas."

"I don't usually talk about it." She cut her gaze to me.

I took it as a signal for help. "You don't have to talk about anything you don't want to."

"Your work with your coding camps got a lot of buzz recently on social media," Nita pressed her. "What's behind your interest in offering free camps to underprivileged girls?"

Jamila flashed her a dangerous smile. "I want to give back to the community in Austin and offer kids the opportunities I wish I'd had."

"Opportunities you wish you'd had? Did you not have coding classes in your school?"

Jamila barked out a laugh. "No. My high school didn't even offer AP classes. I got a summer job to afford the tuition at a local community college so I could take the advanced math and science my school didn't offer."

"Would you consider your family economically disadvantaged?"

"I wouldn't." Jamila crossed her arms. "We had enough to eat and a supportive family and community. We had everything we needed."

"Let's focus on the present, on what Jamila does to give back," I said before Nita could ask a follow-up question. "Jamila, can you talk more about the camps? How long have you run them?"

Jamila's shoulders relaxed as she launched into the history of the camps. But like Nita, I wondered about Jamila's life before Stanford. She'd burst into my life fully formed as a driven college student. She and her brothers were successful now, and she claimed they'd had enough growing up. She'd mentioned her fraught relationship with her grandmother, but she hadn't said a word about her parents. What *was* Jamila's story?

Clearly, she didn't want to tell it, and Nita stopped pushing for it. After another half hour, they were done, the phone number exchange was made, and Nita sashayed off, leaving the techs to pack up. The photographer called Jamila over. He snapped a few test shots, adjusted the lighting, and tested again. When he was satisfied, he sent Jamila off to change.

She emerged from the changing room in a buttery yellow Alexander McQueen suit. The jacket was long and lean. I nearly swallowed my tongue when I realized she wore it shirtless. The single button was right at the base of her ribs, giving me—I mean, the photographer and the flipping world—a long V-shaped view of her satiny skin.

"What do you think, Nat?" She lifted her arms and twirled, Wonder Woman–style, to show me how the jacket flared in the back just above her shapely rear end in her slim-fit pants.

"Whoa." I gripped the arm of the chair I'd pulled over to watch. "You look…you look fantastic," I said, loud enough to hear over the throbbing beat of the dance-club music the photographer had turned on.

"Think so? I couldn't tell from your expression." She smirked at me over her shoulder.

Darn her, she knew exactly how much I liked that suit.

The makeup artist touched her up, then the photographer beckoned. He directed Jamila to sprawl across the white chaise. After snapping a dozen photos, he asked her to perch on the chair with her elbows on her wide-spread knees and gaze directly into the camera with the same smirk she'd given me. Her expression dared anyone to underestimate her.

I certainly didn't. Jamila was powerful, confident. She wouldn't hesitate to act if she felt her company was threatened. And that's why she'd hired the investigator. She wasn't paranoid. She knew something was up, and she'd never let a leak endanger her company.

"Nat."

When I looked up, Jamila towered over me. She'd snuck up on me like a ninja.

"Hey." I blinked a dozen times to organize my thoughts. "What's up?"

"I'm putting on a dress next. Can you help me with the zipper?"

"Oh, uh…" Alone with Jamila, I'd be tempted to do something ridiculous again, something I shouldn't. Like kiss her. I glanced around for someone else to help. But my traitorous knees lifted me to standing. I supposed I'd do anything she asked me. "Of course."

I followed her into the dressing room. She grabbed the sheath dress from the garment rack and headed behind the screen in the corner. After a minute of awkward hovering on the other side, I flipped through the other outfits on the rack to distract myself.

"You always did like clothes, didn't you?"

I glanced over my shoulder. Jamila peered around the edge of the screen. The yellow blazer and pants were slung over the top of it. Was she naked?

I cleared my throat. "I still love clothes. Let me hang those for you."

I stepped to the center of the screen to avoid being tempted to peek. After lifting the suit, still warm from her body, I resisted planting my nose in it and inhaling her scent. I stuck a hand over. "Hanger?"

The wood hanger pressed into my palm, and I busied myself arranging the suit.

"Ready." She emerged from behind the screen, pressing one hand to her chest to keep the dress from sagging off her.

The pencil sheath dress was a rich poppy red with a high front slit. The split boatneck bodice barely clung to her shoulders and revealed a vee of skin between her breasts. Professional yet alluring, the dress would draw every eye in any room Jamila entered. I couldn't keep mine off her slim silhouette.

She turned. "Zip, please."

The opening scooped low in the back, below her shoulder blades. The zipper started at her tailbone, giving me a peek of the lacy petal pink waistband of her panties. She hadn't tried to zip it at all. She also wasn't wearing a bra.

"You okay there, Nat?" She glanced over her shoulder again and smirked at whatever foolish expression I was making.

"Um, yeah." I launched myself toward her and tried to keep my sweaty palms off the wool-silk blend. The photographer would fuss if I left a handprint. I pinched the fabric at the bottom of the zipper, and with my other hand, I slowly drew the pull up her back.

"You know," she said, "if I didn't know better, I'd think you were into me."

My fingers slipped off the zipper. "What—what makes you think that?"

"Oh, I don't know, just the way you can't stop staring at me today. Then there was that kiss the other night when you were drunk, or do you not remember that?"

She was giving me an out. It'd be so easy to claim I didn't remember. To blame it all on the tequila. But that wasn't who I was. Maybe I'd conceal the truth for a while, like I'd done with my parents when I'd dropped out of culinary school and when I'd lost my car, but I wasn't a liar.

"I remember. And I'm sorry."

"You're sorry?" She waited until I'd pulled the zipper all the way up, then she rotated as gracefully as a ballerina to face me.

"Yeah. I, uh, didn't ask first. Plus, I know you're not into me."

"You do, huh?" Her eyebrows lifted. "You know that for a fact."

"I...yes?" How the heck did she expect me to answer that?

"Are you sure you're into me?" In her beige heels, she towered over me. She parked her hands on her hips. "You're not just bi-curious?"

I stood as tall and straight as I could, and I still came up only to her chin. "I'm bi for sure. I have some experience." I'd kissed a girl in college, and in the immortal words of Katy Perry, I'd liked it. So I'd kissed a few more.

"You do?" Her gaze zeroed in on my lips. I licked them. She wore a shiny, kissable burgundy lipstick, and I swayed forward. "Interesting."

Dropping one hand to her side as the other stayed propped on her hip, she sauntered out of the room, hips swaying.

I stood gaping at the doorway. What the heck had just happened? Did that mean Jamila Jallow was interested in me? Was she teasing me? I replayed the conversation. She'd never actually said she liked me. Or that she wanted to kiss me.

Did she?

Like a zombie, I stumbled out of the changing room and sank into a chair to watch the shoot. Was I reading too much into the fierce stare that occasionally wandered to me? Or the exaggerated swing in her hips as she turned at the photographer's direction? At the cheeky wink she tossed my way when she caught me staring, open-mouthed?

When the photographer finally released her, she beckoned. I followed her into the ersatz dressing room. She turned her back to me without a word, and I lowered the zipper, pausing at the bottom. I let my index finger hover over the waistband of her panties, wishing I dared to ask if I could touch her.

But I didn't.

"I think we should celebrate," she said, stepping back behind the screen.

"Celebrate?"

"That this ridiculous thing is over. Here, catch." The red dress floated up in an arc over the screen, and I caught it.

It smelled like her floral perfume, and it was all I could do not to bury my face in it. Carefully, I slipped it onto a hanger and clicked it onto the rack.

She emerged wearing the trousers and blazer she'd worn before. "Celebratory dinner? My treat."

"Um, sure." Although it was foolish of me to torture myself by spending even more time with her, I couldn't resist.

She snorted. "Don't sound so excited about it."

"I'm excited," I protested. "Where do you want to go?"

"Mind if we do takeout at my place? I'm ready to get out of these heels and wash my face."

Good lord.

15

THAT EVENING, I sprawled on Jamila's sofa. Decimated Chinese food containers were scattered across the coffee table, and Quill.i.am nosed a crinkly cat ball inside his habitat. A classic episode of *Star Trek* played on the television.

She froze Patrick Stewart on the screen, zapping my false sense of security.

"So…you're into me." She sat on the floor, her back against her sofa. Tonight's leggings were a soft pink that reminded me uncomfortably of the peek I'd gotten at her panties.

I put both feet on the floor and looked toward Quill. He pointed his tiny pink nose in the air, listening.

"I think you know I am," I said testily.

"Interesting."

"You've said that." I still didn't know what it meant.

"Is that why you're helping me with PR?"

"No!" I rotated to face her. "I'm helping you because you need help. Liking you…that's separate."

"Did you start liking me when you came to work at Jamilow?"

"Why do you get to ask all the questions? Maybe I have questions."

"Maybe you do. But I think we both know how this works, baby girl."

I looked down at my lap. Of course I knew how it worked. Jamila was always in charge. It was one of the things that revved my engine.

"How long?" Her voice was soft, but the compulsion in it was steel.

"Since I was, like, fourteen. Actually, that was only when I realized I liked you the same way I liked Harry Styles. It probably started earlier than that."

"Wait. You haven't actually dated Harry Styles, have you?"

"O.M.G., I wish. Though I'd hate to date someone with better hair than me."

"No worries there." She ran a hand across her short curls. I wished I could lean over and follow her hand with mine to show her how much I liked it.

"That long?" She stared at me with her dark eyes. The light from the television highlighted her cheekbones.

"Yeah, I figured out then that I was bi. I thought it was just an inconvenient part of my personality, though. One I could ignore. So I've only ever dated guys. Because of Mother." I crinkled my nose.

"And what would Audrey say if she knew you'd kissed me?"

I snorted. "You know Mother. She only thinks I'm worth anything when I'm playing the perfect little socialite. She's given up on me finding a career and wants me to settle down and give her more grandkids. The PR work I'm doing for you is the only thing keeping her from pushing some rich guy at me. Maybe a rich woman would be just as good?" I peeked at her out of the side of my eye.

She laughed, loud and brash. "Maybe. Though they're harder to come by. Fucking patriarchy. I'm not into long-term. Sorry, baby."

Of course she wasn't into forever and certainly not with me. She saw me as some ridiculous girl with stars in her eyes. I should get my purse and go before I humiliated myself more than I'd already done.

"Tell me about the experience you mentioned earlier. You only date guys, but…" She raised her eyebrows.

My cheeks flamed. "I, uh. I had some study dates in college, with girls. We kissed and touched a little."

"Got off?" she demanded.

"Sometimes. Then, after—"

"When you were in fashion school, or when you had the florist shop?"

"I didn't know you'd followed my career so closely." I chuckled. "Neither. When I worked that internship at the event-planning company."

"You hooked up with a bridesmaid?" Her eyes went wide.

"No. Guests were off-limits."

"And you always follow the rules."

"Mostly." Freeing Larry had been the exception. "Anyway, sometimes the team would go out after events, and a few times, I hooked up with someone I met at the bar. Sometimes a guy. Sometimes a girl. What about you? I've seen you date both men and women." In fact, she'd gone to a lot of events with Cooper Fallon. That was before he'd gotten engaged to his former assistant.

"Yeah, I've always known I was bi. I dated more girls than guys in high school. I liked sex—a lot—but the last thing I wanted was to wind up pregnant and miss my chance of going to college. Girls were safer."

"Were they?" I asked. She'd said it with unexpected bitterness.

"Well, except for my popularity. I was the lesbian nerd in high school. That was fun."

I tried to imagine a nerdy Jamila in high school but failed. She was so confident, so elegant. I bit my lip. I'd gotten a taste of her history in Austin, then another one today. I wanted more.

"In Austin, you talked about living with your grandmother and your brothers. What was that like?"

She rubbed a hand over her face. "Thanks for putting up with my brothers, by the way. I know they can be a lot."

I grinned. "They're fun. And they idolize you." *Just like I do.*

She snorted. "I don't know about that, but we've always been close. Our daddy was a trucker, and he'd be gone for a week at a time. Mama worked part time, and she'd leave us with the neighbor who wasn't too nice. I realize now that taking care of three rambunctious kids was a lot to ask, but it was kind of us against them, you know? I tried to keep the boys out of trouble, and I defended them when I couldn't."

She looked away. "Anyway, Daddy died when I was six and the twins were three."

I laid a hand on her shoulder. "I'm so sorry."

She shrugged. "It was a long, long time ago." She faced the television, but I knew she wasn't seeing Captain Picard.

"It was a lot for my mom," she said. "I didn't understand then, but I get it now. She became the sole earner for three young kids, two of them not yet old enough for school. She couldn't afford the mortgage and daycare too. Not without support. Mama was estranged from her parents ever since she got pregnant with me in high school."

When she paused, Quill.i.am started his nocturnal exercise on his squeaky wheel.

"They wanted bigger things for her, you know? I mean, she wanted them, too, but condoms fail. The U.S. might be the land of opportunity for many, but that doesn't include girls who get knocked up when they're seventeen."

Now I understood Jamila's high school girlfriends. I squeezed her shoulder.

"So we moved in with Daddy's mother, Nana. She was of a similar opinion. She thought they should've gotten an abortion and gone off to college like they'd planned and made something of themselves. She was probably right. It was what I'd have done. But then I wouldn't be here, so..." She shrugged.

"I'm glad they had you."

A smile flashed across her face. "My nana criticized Mama for not having a better job—she was a waitress—for not going back to school, and for having more kids than she could care for. I think she resented me a little, too, for ruining her dreams for her son."

I slid onto the floor beside her and slipped an arm around her shoulders. "It wasn't your fault."

She nestled her bony shoulder into my chest. "I know it wasn't, but Nana and I were oil and water. Always."

"What about your mother? Were you close with her?"

"Not so much. She was always working. She said it was for the money. I suspected she wanted to be out of the house and away from Nana's nagging and away from us kids, who reminded her of Daddy. Then she got an opportunity down in Houston in a restaurant manager trainee program. When she left, she said she'd be back when the program ended and get a job as a manager in Austin.

"But things didn't work out that way. I don't know if it was her choice or not. I was nine, and I thought grown-ups could do anything they wanted to. Of course, I thought she chose it. She stayed down there and said she couldn't take us with her since she worked all the time and didn't make enough to cover after-school care and whatnot. She sent money to Nana for us. Not a lot, but we always had new sneakers for the start of school and clothes for church on Sundays."

"Money isn't the only thing kids need." We had plenty, but there was still a hole in our family from our father's death. Charles filled some of it, especially for me as the youngest, but there was a part of my heart even he could never reach.

"Nana loved us, but she wasn't the warmest person. The last thing she wanted was for us to grow up living hand-to-mouth like our parents, so she pushed us hard.

"Looking back, I appreciate it. I wouldn't be where I am today without her hassling. But back then, I was mad. I was always shielding J.J. and Jevin from her, covering for them when they messed up. I learned how to forge her signature on their school notes." She chuckled. "They were always getting them. When Nana's network of church friends told her what they'd done, it was me who dried their tears and told them they were good enough."

I tried to picture Jamila as a stand-in mother. She was such a force at work, driving everyone to be their best. With Jackson and Cooper, she was intense, too, but I remembered moments when she encouraged them with a slap on their backs or when she comforted them with a hug. I could imagine her doing the same with her brothers. Maybe that was why she'd formed a trio with Jackson and his college roommate. Far from home, she needed a stand-in family and a pair of boys to keep out of trouble.

I let myself tug her closer to breathe in her floral scent. Her sharp shoulder poked me in the boob, but I didn't care. "You were right. They did great. So did you."

"We did all right."

"Better than all right." Then I asked her what I'd been curious about ever since I'd seen her home. "Is that why you bought this place? Because you sent all your money home to support your family?"

"That's part of it. I didn't grow up like you did. My nana lived frugally her entire life, and she'd paid off her home by the time we moved in. Her pension and what Mama sent covered food, clothes, and taxes, but there was never any extra. I saw how precarious life could be, so I chose a house I could pay cash for. It's comfortable, and it's all I need. It's plenty good enough." Her shoulders had crept up toward her ears.

I stroked a hand down her arm. "Of course it is. It's a beautiful home. Your neighborhood is nice too. Even your neighbor with the avocados."

"I got in trouble for that, you know. You didn't tell me Mrs. González needed help with her tree. I got an earful the next time I saw her."

"Oops." When I'd seen Jamila with her sweatshirt slipping off her shoulder, I'd forgotten everything else.

"She said something about a fancy Mercedes. Isn't that Audrey's car? What happened to yours?"

I winced. She'd told me her story. It was time to share my own.

"I still have a car, technically," I said. "You remember. My parents gave it to me for my eighteenth birthday. It's the cutest little red BMW coupe."

"I remember all right. I never believed people gave other people actual *cars* as gifts. Where do you even get a big pink bow like that?"

"I don't know. But every one of my high school friends got a car with a bow on it."

Jamila muttered something and shook her head. "So what happened? You crashed it?"

I sucked in a breath despite the shame that sat on my lungs like a lead crystal paperweight. "No. I met this woman on my first day of culinary school. Let's call her…Ruby. We started as study partners. We'd meet up at a café near school and go over our notes before exams. I went over to her place one time to make pies. I couldn't get the crust right, and she had a way with it. Her crusts were flaky and tender and…magical." I sighed, remembering.

"My nana always made a good pie crust," Jamila said. "I never got the knack of it."

"It's hard, right? Anyway, we hung out after to watch *The Great British Bake Off.* Everyone was talking about it, and I'd never seen it before. She teased me about it, then she started tickling me, and then all of a sudden, we were kissing." She tasted buttery like her pie crust.

Jamila stroked my knee.

I was glad she couldn't see my flaming cheeks in the dark. "The next week, I got to the café late, and she saw me drive up in my BMW. It's, you know, not very subtle in the neighborhood around the college. She asked me about it, so I told her how my parents gave it to me."

Jamila sat up. "You didn't."

I missed her warmth. "It was naive of me. I know that now. She asked me if she could drive it, and, of course, I said yes. We rode around for a couple of hours. She even took it on 101. Afterward, we ended up at this beachside restaurant. I paid, of course, and we walked on the sand holding hands and then made out against the pier." Her windblown auburn hair had been soft against my cheek.

"Oh, girl." Jamila shook her head.

"Look, I thought it meant something, okay? So that Friday, after class, she looked all sad, and I asked her why. She said she needed to go up to Sacramento to help her mother run some errands. Christmas shopping and whatnot. She said her mother had cancer. And that her car died. She couldn't afford to fix it right then. So I said, borrow my car. I mean, anyone would say that, right?"

"Nope."

I sighed. "Well, I did. I was happy all weekend that I'd helped her—and her mother. When she came back on Monday, she was so thankful and sweet. We made out again right there in the hallway at school. She'd forgotten to bring the keys, and I was so over-the-moon I didn't think about it."

"Girl..." This time, Jamila smiled indulgently.

"I know, I know. It sounds ridiculous now, but I didn't think anything of it. I was helping my girlfriend. It got to be exam week, and life was nuts. I knew hers was, too, and I let it slide. I figured we'd get together after exams, and I'd get the keys back from her then.

"But after exams, she ghosted me. By the time I figured it out, it was too late. I went to her place, and she'd left. The car wasn't in the parking lot. It was just...gone. And so was Ruby." My heart had crumbled like her pie crust when her landlord said she'd moved out. There was no room for sadness about the car.

"What did Audrey and Charles say?"

"You think I told them?"

"How could you not? That was five months ago."

I shrugged. "Every time they ask about it, I make an excuse. I don't feel like driving. I let my friend borrow my car. Both true. Since I'm always doing stuff like that, they just roll their eyes and drive. Sometimes I ask my brothers to drive me or call an Uber."

"Tell me you filed a police report."

I winced. "No. I guess I hoped she'd return my calls or texts. I figured when the registration came up for renewal, it'd be her problem, then she'd bring it back or contact me or something, but she never did."

I put a hand over my face. Jamila would never let anything like that happen to her. No one would ever try. Not with such a strong, confident woman. The kind of woman I could never be.

16

I FELT SO light after telling Jamila how I'd been duped, I was floating. I didn't feel the not-quite-plushness of her living room rug.

"Baby girl, your heart is too soft." Turning to face me, Jamila picked up a lock of my hair and twirled it around her finger. I savored the gentle tug.

"Ruby needed help. Well, I thought she did."

"You're always trying to help people—even me."

"Helping others makes me feel good."

She smiled, but it was a little sad. "Did she make you feel good?"

"Yeah. I believed her about her sick mother. I hope it was true and that I helped."

"No, baby. Did she make you *feel* good?" She gave a harder tug on my hair.

"Oh. *Oh.* You mean, did she get me off? No, we only made out."

Jamila's fingers stilled. "You can get off while making out. If you do it right."

I was still processing that when she asked, "What about with your no-expectations hookups after college? Did you get off with them?"

I shifted against the carpet. "Usually. Not always with the guys. It can be hard for me to…um, relax sometimes."

"You were pretty relaxed when you kissed me in Austin."

I buried my face in my hands. "Ugh, I wish I had one of those neuralyzers from *Men in Black.* I'd make you forget that night."

"Why would I forget that night?" She peeled my fingers away from my face.

"I'm super-embarrassed, okay? And I'm sorry. I didn't even ask before I kissed you."

"True. Though that doesn't mean I'm mad about it."

"But you just sat there! You didn't move!"

"I was surprised, that's all. I didn't know Jackson's little sister was bi, and I didn't know you liked me."

Lightness bubbled in my chest and held at the base of my throat. When I spoke, my voice was breathy. "How do you feel about it now?"

"Intrigued." She traced a finger down my throat and paused it at the hollow between my collarbones, right where the bubbles had lodged. "Though there are some reasons I should keep it a purely intellectual interest."

No! My heart thudded against my ribs. "Reasons?"

She pulled back and counted them on her fingers. "First, you're my employee."

"I'm helping you with PR," I argued. "I walked into your office and demanded you let me help you."

"Second, you're ten years younger than me. We have vastly different life experiences."

"Opposites attract. Isn't that what Paula Abdul says?"

Jamila rolled her eyes. "You weren't even born when that song came out. Besides, she made a video with a fucking cartoon cat. What the hell does she know?"

"I think she had a point." I crossed my arms.

Jamila traced a finger down my arm, but her words belied the sensual touch. "Third, and this is the real dealbreaker, you're my friend's little sister."

"A dealbreaker? Jackson doesn't own me. He gets no say in my love life."

Jamila tunneled her hand into my hair and scratched my scalp with her short fingernails. "Is that so?"

"Mm-hmm." Jamila's hand on me was heaven. I dared to reach a finger to her jaw and trail it down the long column of her neck the way I'd wanted to do all afternoon.

She shivered, then leaned into my touch. "Keeping in mind all the reasons I gave that this can be nothing but a casual, friends-with-limited-benefits thing, how would you feel about a do-over?"

My brain stalled out. "Friends with limited benefits?"

"I told you I don't do long-term. I especially don't do it with my friends' siblings. But we can scratch that itch you have for me. I'd be willing to add the occasional make-out sesh to our friendship."

A chill shuddered through my body, all the way to my teeth. I shook off her hand and twisted mine in my lap. "You're making fun of me, right?"

"No, baby." She laid her hand on the sofa cushion behind me. "Look, you've really helped me out over the past couple of weeks. You're all grown up now. And I'm a little curious about what it'd be like."

"You're curious," I said flatly. "You'd kiss me to satisfy your curiosity."

"If that's what you want to take from what I said, fine." She shrugged, but her gaze burned into me, anything but careless.

I narrowed my eyes at her. "You're into me too."

"Not what I said."

I pursed my lips. She was offering a kiss, maybe a little over-the-clothes action, as an experiment. No strings.

Was it enough? No.

But I couldn't walk away from it either.

"Why do you have to be such a flipping jerk?" I asked before I leaned in and kissed her, hard.

She froze like she'd done in the car on Tuesday night. But then her lips softened. I pressed into her, licking her plush lower lip.

She opened for me, and I swept in, seeking, searching, hungry.

She pulled away, leaving me gasping.

"Take it easy, baby girl. I got you."

She leaned toward me and slanted her lips over mine, teasing, advancing, retreating. Each time I chased her, she pulled back. Then she started again softly, slowly giving me more. Finally, I learned that if I relaxed, she'd give me all I wanted. All I needed.

Her chest pressed into mine. I ached to feel her skin against me.

I trailed my hand from her neck over her shoulder to her breast. I rubbed my palm over the small swell and felt her pebbled nipple through her thin tank top. God, she wasn't wearing a bra. If I'd known that, I wouldn't have had a coherent thought all night.

Was I imagining it, or did she press into my palm, as turned on as I was? She hadn't touched me anywhere my clothes normally covered, but every part of me was lit up like the Christmas tree at Union Square. I rubbed my thighs together, working the seam of my jeans against my swollen clit. My breaths came faster.

She still had her hand in my hair, and she tugged at the roots. A trail of sparks shot from my scalp down my spine, coiling in my belly. Would I come from this? I didn't want to. I didn't want to come until she touched my skin.

I tore my lips from hers and kissed across her cheek to her ear, where her floral perfume collided with the coconut of her hair product, and I was in a tropical garden with my heart's desire. "Jamila, I want you," I whispered.

She groaned into my ear. "No, baby girl. Not tonight."

"What?" I licked her earlobe. "You sure?"

"We're taking this slow. Don't you want to save some benefits for later?" Her fingers trailed across the back of my neck, sending tingles down my spine.

"No." The word came out sulky.

"Well, I do." She pulled away, and her hand left my skin.

"Why?" I whined.

"Don't want to blow it all at once. I want to keep you coming back for more."

"Sounds like you're a big tease." I stuck out my lower lip.

She leaned in and centered a light kiss on it. "We can end it right now."

"No!"

"You seem like someone who's not used to hearing the word no."

She was right. It was one of the many privileges of being a Jones. "Not often, I guess."

"You'll hear it a lot from me. We'll do things my way. Today, my way is that you go home. In fact, I'm calling you a rideshare right now." She grabbed her phone from the end table and tapped it.

"When will I see you again?"

"Monday at work." When she looked up from the screen, her expression was innocent, but her eyes held a wicked sparkle.

"But you won't kiss me at work."

"That's for damn sure. I'll take you out for drinks after, though."

"You will?" Hope flared in my heart.

"Promise." She leaned in for one more soft kiss, sealing the agreement. "Now, let's go. Your rideshare will be here in five minutes." She stood and hauled me up from the floor.

"In five minutes, I can help you clean all this up." I gestured at the takeout containers.

"Fine." She scooped up a few, and I snagged the rest and followed her to the kitchen.

When her phone pinged, she walked me to her front door and

swept her thumb over my kiss-swollen lips. "Night, baby girl. See you Monday."

17

THE NEXT FRIDAY while I was scheduling social media posts, Hannah let out a squeal.

"Check your email," she said. "Right now."

"Was that a good squeal or an oh-crap squeal?" I asked, switching windows on my laptop.

"Look, look, look!" She scurried around my desk and leaned over my shoulder pointing at an unread email. "It's the *Buzz Bizz* article and the photos. Open, open, open!"

I clicked the email and opened the attachments. I scanned through the article. The words *composed, self-assured, rational,* and *forthright* popped from the page. All good signs. I'd have to go back and read it later.

"Look at the pics." Hannah snatched my mouse and clicked to open them.

Jamila filled my screen looking sophisticated and graceful but also down-to-earth. Or as down-to-earth as someone wearing a thousand-dollar dress could appear. "She looks great, doesn't she?"

"Fabulous." Hannah's grin showed her perfect teeth.

"And the article? You read it?"

"It makes her out to be a goddess on earth. Totally the opposite of how she looked in that clip on TikTok. You did good, boss."

Excitement bubbled in my belly. "I'll ask if we can get the video from the interview so we can put some clips on TikTok. We'll drown out the bad stuff."

"Already asked. It'll be a total win."

I stood and held out my arms for a hug. "We did good. Thank you."

She crushed me, crinkling my starched shirt. "I think you've got a future in PR."

I'd never felt like this in any of my other careers. Not even when I'd made a pie crust that didn't completely suck. "Maybe you're right."

A throat cleared at the doorway. Felicia stood there with an envelope in her hand.

Releasing Hannah, I stepped around my desk. Felicia handed me the envelope.

"What's this?" I asked, slipping a finger under the flap.

"Paycheck." She turned to leave.

"What about Hannah?" How had I gotten a paycheck and she hadn't?

"I set up direct deposit," Hannah said. When I looked at her blankly, she continued, "My paycheck goes directly into my bank account. Have you never done that before?"

I scrunched up my face. "I've never had a paying job before. Just volunteer stuff and unpaid internships. My stepfather took care of the flower shop's finances."

She chuckled. "Must be nice."

Felicia let her disdain show in her curled lip. "Must be."

My face heated. "I-I..." I couldn't take Jamila's money. All I'd wanted to do was help her. I also couldn't be the entitled rich girl in front of these two hardworking women. "I need to see her."

Pinching the envelope between my fingers, I marched to Jamila's office, rapped on the door, and shoved it open.

Winslow sat in the chair facing Jamila. His posture was

relaxed, one ankle set over his other knee. The berry-pink pants revealed the eye-wateringly bright pastel polka dots on his socks, a total mismatch to his two-tone brogues. He drawled, "What PR emergency has arisen now?"

Jamila raised her hands, palms out. "I swear, I did nothing. I did that interview just like you told me. And I've been working like a dog all week."

Monday night, Jamila had taken me out for a drink like she'd promised, but she'd kept looking at her phone as it blew up with messages. QA had found another issue in the code, and the development team was scrambling to debug it. It was a game of whack-a-mole: as soon as they fixed one problem, another one erupted. It still seemed like someone was working against them—but not Rhiannon. I knew that now.

After one drink, I'd taken pity on her and told her to go back to the office. All I'd gotten was a fleeting kiss on the cheek. Jamila had leaped to help the coders, and there had been no follow-up kisses. I'd had to recycle the ones from Friday at her house to fuel my spank bank.

Not that I was complaining. Those kisses at her place had been incendiary.

"It's not a PR thing." I crossed my arms. "It's an HR thing."

"Uh-oh." Winslow chuckled. "I'll let you two work that out."

"HR falls under operations." Jamila raised an eyebrow.

"Not when it involves special cases." He raised a finger. "I had nothing to do with hiring her. That was all you."

"I seem to remember your being in favor of hiring a PR specialist," she said.

He pretended to think. "Nope. No recollection of that." He sauntered past me and shut the door behind him.

"What is it, Natalie?" Jamila propped her chin on her hand. Shadows gathered underneath her eyes.

Something pricked in my chest. I almost turned around and followed Winslow out to give Jamila a few moments of peace, but this was important. It affected us and the weird friends-with-benefits situation she'd established.

I lifted the envelope. "I told you I didn't want to get paid."

She rolled her eyes. "I told *you* you're doing work for me. People who do work get paid. I'm paying Hannah even though, technically, no one hired her."

"I hired her. You need her."

"Then, ipso facto, you are my employee. I don't allow non-employees to hire people to work at Jamilow."

Crap. That made sense.

"But...but what does that mean?"

A smile curled her lips though her eyes remained dull with exhaustion. "Well, baby girl, being an employee means you get a check every two weeks, the government taxes it, and we provide benefits, so if you're sick, you can go to the hospital."

"I don't need benefits or a paycheck. Not if that means you and I..."

"Can't have the other kind of benefits?"

"Have you ever had benefits with an employee?"

"Sure."

I waved the check, and the little plastic window rattled. "With *your* employee?"

"Fuck no."

"Then I'm going to—" I pinched the top of the envelope to rip it.

"No!"

I froze.

"Nat, I need you. To work here. Things are a lot quieter now." She glanced out the window. "No more news vans. Because of you. I don't want you to quit."

"But I want this." I waved between us, still not sure what *this* was but determined to hold on to it with both hands.

"Then we'll try it out. I can't promise anything but casual. If either of us decides it's not working, we can call it off. No harm, no foul. Still friends. Okay?"

Her teeth glanced off her kissable lip. Her gaze was cool as if she didn't care, but that one tell gave me hope that she might care about this as much as I did.

"And we're exclusive?" I asked.

She huffed. "Damn, girl, you think I have time to play the field?"

It wasn't a great offer, but it was the best I'd get. "Okay."

A grin dawned across her face. "Okay."

"Now what?" I folded the check and put it into my pocket. "Do we shake hands? Kiss?"

"We're not kissing in my office. There are boundaries to this. That's one of them."

"Got it. Drinks tonight?"

"The team is pushing to meet a deadline. I can't walk out of here while they're still working."

"Right." Her work was more important than whatever casual thing we were doing. "I guess—"

"Tomorrow," she rushed to say. "I'll take you out. Plus, I have a gift for you."

"A gift?" I grinned. "I love gifts."

"Come here." She grabbed something from her desk, then strode to the window that overlooked a slice of the parking lot. She handed me the black plastic object.

"A key fob?"

"It's a pain in the ass to get down here from San Francisco every day with no car. Click it."

I clicked the unlock button, and there was a faint chirp. I did it again and focused this time. A candy-apple red Porsche convertible flashed its headlights.

I stared at Jamila, mouth open. The BMW from my parents had been one thing. I didn't know anyone who gave a friend a car. Not even friends with benefits did that.

"They don't come in pink," she said. "I asked. And I told them they could skip the giant bow."

"You can't give me a car. That's not what g—" I had to choke back the word *girlfriends.* "That's not what friends do."

"Employers do it all the time. It's a lease. Call it a company car."

"But..." I didn't know what Jamilow's policy on company cars was, but I suspected PR specialists who hired themselves didn't get them after less than a month of work.

"Drive it to my place tomorrow. We'll go on a date."

A date. A genuine date. In an over-the-top gift.

"Okay." I closed my fist around the fob. "This is normally where I'd kiss you."

Her brown eyes burned into me, and her voice came out husky. "Save it for tomorrow."

I didn't know how I made it out of Jamila's office, but I floated back down the hallway to Hannah's and mine.

"All straightened out?" Hannah asked.

"What?" What I'd done was anything but straight.

"Your paycheck."

"Oh, right." Bemused, I pulled it from my pocket.

What the heck did one do with a check, anyway?

18

I WAS bold enough to pack a small overnight bag for my date with Jamila but less bold as I slung it over my shoulder and tiptoed down the stairs. I hoped Mother and Charles would sleep in after their arrival from Paris last night, but as I slunk past the dining room, Mother called out, "Natalie, darling. We're in here."

Sighing, I set down my bag in the hall and stepped into the dining room. Mother sat at the head, Charles to her right and Sam to her left. My sister slipped a slice of banana under the table to her tiny purse-destroying monster.

"Good trip?" I asked, bending to kiss Mother's cheek.

"Wonderful," she said with a soft sigh at Charles. "So romantic. Sit down, and we'll tell you all about it."

"Ew, no thanks." The bratty baby of the family was an easy persona to slip into. I grabbed a strawberry from the fruit bowl. "I'm on my way out."

"Where are you going?" Mother set her coffee cup into the saucer with a clink.

"Jamila's. And I might stay overnight at her place."

"Overnight?" Mother's eyebrows rose. "Is Jamila driving you too hard?"

I was hoping she'd drive me hard tonight, right into her headboard. I popped the berry into my mouth to keep from having to answer.

Sam looked up from her phone. "Nat's been working a lot lately. I hardly saw her while you two were gone."

I flared my eyes at her. Traitor.

"Jamila's an excellent influence," Charles said. "She can give you the direction you need."

"I bet she gives direction," Sam muttered. She was snacking in the kitchen last Saturday night when I'd returned from Jamila's, my hair wild and lipstick kissed onto my chin.

"When is your apartment going to be ready again?" I demanded

"Don't fight, girls," our mother said wearily. She'd said that phrase so often over the years it must have worn a groove in her throat. "Natalie, we were talking about Jamila's influence on you."

My cheeks burned. They must have been as red as the strawberries on the table. "She's happy with my work so far. I got her an amazing spread in *Buzz Bizz*."

"Honey, no one doubts your drive for success. You just need focus." Charles gave me a gentle smile. "Jamila has that in spades. We're hoping she'll rub off on you."

I held in a squeak. I hoped we'd mutually rub off on each other, in bed.

Snickering, Sam turned away to feed a blueberry to Bilbo Baggins.

"Okay, I'm out," I said. "I'll text you if I'm staying over. I might miss brunch tomorrow."

"Before you go," Mother said, "we need to talk about the picnic next weekend."

"Picnic?" I froze in the doorway.

"Representative Crawford's annual Memorial Day picnic. We'll go and use the opportunity to talk to him about our literacy agenda."

"Nope," Sam said.

I wished I could blow off Mother like that, but I'd never been that strong.

"Natalie, dear, whom are you bringing?" Mother asked.

I blinked. Last year, I'd gone with Daniel van der Poel. We often went to events as friends, but people were starting to link our names in a more serious way. Normally, I wouldn't have given a second thought to showing up to the picnic with him, but I didn't want to upset the delicate balance of whatever this thing with Jamila was, especially after the debacle of Billie Woods's Christmas party.

"I...I don't know. I'd forgotten."

"Forgotten? That's not like you. Take Daniel. I'll call his mother."

"No!" I winced as soon as I said it. These things needed nuance, and I'd been completely uncool.

"What? You two aren't on the outs, are you?"

"No. We just...haven't seen that much of each other lately."

"Is he dating someone?"

"I don't know."

"He just broke up with Bella Waddingworth," Charles said.

We both turned wide eyes to him.

"What? I hear things. Bob Waddingworth and I played golf last Saturday."

"Then it's a perfect time for you to go out with him," Mother said. "You need to settle down. Daniel is a good choice."

"Settle down? I'm only twenty-six!"

"I was only a year older than that when I had Jackson."

"Ugh. That was a different time, Mother. I'm not ready to settle down with anyone." Certainly not Daniel van der Poel, who cared more about his investment portfolio than about anyone I'd ever known him to date.

"A steady boyfriend would give you the focus you need."

I let Mother's words sit on the table like the plate of bacon, grease congealing on its cold surface.

After a beat, I said, "You let Jackson, Andrew, and Sam have careers before you pushed them to date anyone."

"Natalie." Mother's eyes softened. "You might have more success as a helpmate than as a career person. Like me."

Sure, I liked helping people. But that didn't mean I'd given up on finding a career. But my mother had given up on me and that stung. "Bye, Mother. I've got to meet Jamila."

"Think about what I said," she called after me. "I'll phone Daniel's mother."

"No, thanks," I called from the hallway, picking up my bag.

After that magical kiss with Jamila, the thought of going anywhere with someone like Daniel repulsed me. Even if I could never bring Jamila to a political picnic, I'd rather become a hermit like my sister than put on my socialite act again.

WE ONLY STAYED at Jamila's long enough for her to pack a picnic basket into the back of the red convertible and strap Quill.i.am snugly across her body in a soft carrying pouch. When he snuggled between her breasts and closed his eyes, I envied him a little. Then we were on the road, Jamila driving.

On the hour-long drive south, we talked about her week at work. I wished I'd paid attention to my computer-programmer siblings' code-speak so I could have understood the problem Jamila described. It had taken up her evenings all week, but they'd found a solution late Friday afternoon that had her giddily optimistic about the release date, a scant three weeks away. She tapped the steering wheel to the beat of a Lizzo song playing on the radio.

"We're going to Santa Cruz?" I finally asked as we took the exit.

"Yep." She grinned. At a stoplight, she pressed a button, and the roof retracted into a compartment in the back of the car.

I took a deep breath of salty air. "To the beach?"

"Yep."

"You should've told me. I'd have brought a swimsuit."

"More like a wetsuit." She shivered. "The water's ice cold. Besides," she said with a wolfish grin, "I like that dress on you."

"This one?" I fluttered my eyelashes and looked down at it like I didn't know exactly what I was wearing, a deep pink minidress so short I could barely sit without exposing myself. It had a tease of a cutout just below my breasts that, I hoped, would tempt Jamila's fingers to trace it.

"You know I do." She turned back to the road.

"It's not like I'd go swimming today. The swimsuit would be for the sunshine." Like a flower, I tilted my face up to the sun.

"Hmm. Maybe I should've told you to bring a suit," she purred.

Yes, please. "I could borrow one of yours."

"That could be arranged." She kept her eyes on the road and her hands on the wheel as we navigated through the city.

We pulled up in front of a two-story house that was enormous compared to her place in Menlo Park. In the narrow space between it and its neighbor, I glimpsed a sandy beach and blue water beyond. This was the kind of house I'd expected her to own. But now that I knew her better, I understood her need never to owe anyone anything. I respected her modest home in Menlo Park. And I marveled at this beach house. Jamila must have dropped multiple millions—in cash.

Grinning, Jamila let me admire it for a moment, preening at my awestruck expression, before she unlocked the door. She grabbed the picnic basket in one hand and my fingers in the other and tugged me inside.

The opulent home, one of several clustered around a stretch of sandy beach, had an open floor plan scattered with low-slung furniture and showcased a magnificent view of the ocean. Sunlight sparkled on the blue water, and the golden sand was dotted with the umbrellas and beach towels of the families who'd come to play in the sand and surf.

"Eat first or beach first?" she asked, setting the basket on the kitchen island.

"Can we do both? If you've got a beach blanket, we can take our lunch outside."

"Sure." She went to a cabinet and pulled one out. From another cabinet, she pulled a scrap of lilac-colored fabric. She nodded at a door. "You can change in there."

Taking the swimsuit into the powder room, I stripped off my sundress and shimmied into the bikini. I wished I had less cellulite on my thighs and that I'd thought to get a spray tan. At least I'd waxed everything in the hope that I'd get some naked time with Jamila. I met my own gaze in the mirror. Wearing Jamila's suit, I tried to channel a little of her confidence. *You're going to walk out of here—no,* march *out of here—and act like you deserve her.* Nodding at my reflection, I strode out.

Jamila was in the kitchen already wearing a white two-piece that was much more modest than the bikini she'd given me. Her smooth expanse of skin made my mouth dry as the sand outside. I wanted to touch her everywhere and see if her skin felt as silky as it looked.

She cleared her throat, and I snapped my gaze to her face. Did friends with maybe-benefits ogle each other? I needed a rulebook for this.

But she was staring at me too. Specifically, at my boobs.

"You should keep that suit," she said, her voice rough. "It doesn't fit me like that."

The lilac bikini had triangle-shaped cups, and some of my skin spilled out around where the spandex covered. Boldly, I looked at her top. Her breasts were roughly a cup size smaller than mine, but they nestled perfectly into the halter top. Her nipples were pebbled, and I wanted to rub my palms over them.

She cleared her throat again.

"Shall we?"

"Where's Quill? Is he coming with us?"

"Nah, I put him into his habitat for a nap. He's got sensitive skin. Speaking of which…" She grabbed a bottle of sunscreen and handed it to me. "Slather up, Empress Daywalker. You look like one of those Twilight vampires."

I shot her a flat expression. "Funny."

Still, I did as she said and rubbed the sunscreen from my neck to my toes.

"What about your face?" she asked.

"My makeup has SPF."

"Turn around. I'll get your back."

I turned, squeezing my glutes to try to make them look as firm as hers. The second her fingers hit the back of my neck, I shivered.

"Cold?"

"Yes," I lied. Clearly, our skin-to-skin contact wasn't affecting her the same way it affected me. My skin buzzed as she continued from my neck down my spine to the back tie of the bikini, then over each shoulder blade. Then—holy cheezits!—she poked her fingers under the string tie and smoothed her hands down my back, all the way to the ticklish spot at the base of my spine.

"A little bit under the waistband," she said, slipping two fingers inside. It was only her fingertips gliding over the very top part of my butt, but I couldn't help it. Every hair on my body stood erect. "Wouldn't want you to get burned." I shivered again and had to hold in a groan.

Suddenly, her lips were at my ear. "Later. First, you get your beach time. And lunch."

I pressed back against her, feeling the warmth of her skin against my back. "What if I want something else first?"

"We spent five minutes on sunscreen. Let's get some rays."

"What about you?" I turned around and held out my hand for the bottle. "Everyone needs UV protection."

"I'm covered." She snatched a garment from the counter and slipped it over her head. The swim cover-up was a gauzy white with long sleeves that hid her tempting curves and ended at the middle of her thighs. "Literally. Let's go."

She picked up the picnic basket, and I grabbed the blanket. On the way out, she tossed a giant sun hat onto her head, then smashed another onto mine. "Now we're both covered."

We stepped out onto the wood deck and descended a set of stairs onto the sand. We found a spot several yards away from the families with an unobstructed view of the beach.

I shook out the blanket, and Jamila unpacked the basket. She set out a bottle of sparkling water, cheeses, crackers, grapes, and strawberries. Carefully selecting a sample of everything, she set it on a melamine plate that she handed me before repeating with her own plate. She poured water into two clear acrylic cups.

"So fancy," I teased her.

"What'd you expect? Lunchables? I asked you out."

I widened my eyes. "So this is date food? Not friend food?"

"Date food." I wished I could see her eyes behind her mirrored aviators. "If it weren't for the no-booze policy on the beach, I'd have brought sparkling wine for you, princess."

I nibbled a cracker, savoring it for the romantic gesture it was.

"You like it?"

"Yeah. I do." I set a hand on her knee, which was splayed out toward me on the blanket. It was as silky as it looked.

She lifted my hand from her leg and held it briefly before setting it on the blanket. "I'd rather not do that here." She softened the words with a smile, but prickles formed in my chest.

"Why not? Those kids over there are making out." I tipped my chin at a teenage boy and girl. They'd tossed a towel over themselves, but anyone could see he had his hand under her bikini top. "I thought you were out."

"My bisexuality isn't a secret, but I try not to make it anyone's business but mine. Besides, as I recall, you're not out. Not to your family."

I grimaced, thinking of the nuclear war that would ensue if I brought a woman to the Memorial Day political picnic. "Not exactly."

"It's best to keep a low profile. Remember, I'm a Black woman in tech. All eyes are on me. Isn't that what my PR consultant would tell me?" She winked.

I groaned. "I guess. Though I was hoping not to be your PR person today and to just be"—I took a deep breath—"your person."

She held my gaze and her lips turned up playfully. I'd wanted this for so long, to be the object of Jamila Jallow's focus. Despite the day's warmth, the hairs rose over my exposed skin. I rubbed a hand over the goosebumps on my arm.

Breaking our stare, Jamila reached into the basket. "Try these. They're caprese salad skewers."

I pulled out a short skewer of mozzarella balls, cherry tomatoes, and basil leaves, drizzled with balsamic glaze. I worked off a bite with my teeth. "Mmm," I said.

"They're good, right? It's the first thing I learned to make for parties after I figured out Rotel dip and Texas caviar wouldn't cut it in Northern California. Even the way my nana used to make it, with a bit of spicy chorizo tossed in."

"Rotel dip?"

"Jesus Christ, you don't even know."

"That's sad you had to give up your favorite foods when you moved here."

She shrugged. "I had to give up a lot of things. It was worth it. I have my own company, and not even Pavel Thakor can stop me. We're going to kick Moo-Lah's ass with this new app. I'm about to shove it in his condescending face. Unless we haven't stopped the leak, and he's about to shove it in mine." She frowned and set down her plate.

"You think they might beat you to market?"

"We're so close, but these bugs keep setting us back. I wish I knew how close they were to launch."

"You don't think there's room for both of you in the market?"

"I don't know. If they beat us by a few days, it's probably no big deal, though I'd hate for him to scoop up all the press coverage and make us look like a copycat. If it's weeks…" She held up her hands. "They might get entrenched. It'd be tough to win back market share."

"Why did you decide to launch an app in life coaching?"

She shrugged. "It was my dream."

I snorted. "You dreamed about building an app for people to figure out what percentage of their salary to put into a 401(k)?"

"No." She traced a pattern on the beach blanket. "Growing up, all I wanted was a home where I felt welcome."

My body went cold. "You didn't feel welcome at home?"

"Nana didn't want us. She made that clear. I mean, she loved us, but I was always in the way. And my brothers?" She chuckled darkly. "They were always in trouble, you know?"

"Yeah." Jackson had been a troublemaker. I could only imagine the catastrophes a pair of him would have gotten into.

"So I dreamed up ways to get out on my own. Nana was always talking about college, and I knew that was the way. But things were a lot different from how they'd been when she went. My junior high teachers weren't much better. They'd gone to local colleges. Me? I wanted something bigger."

"Of course you did." I wanted to touch her and take away the bitterness that curled her lip.

"I worked my ass off to get good grades and took the hardest classes I could. My guidance counselor noticed. He told me about Stanford, but no one from my school had ever gone. He said I had a better chance of getting in if I went to the private high school downtown. They offered advanced placement classes, and some of the kids had even been accepted into Ivy League schools.

"But Nana couldn't afford private tuition. So I made an appointment with the deacon at my church. He was a friend of Nana's and, I thought, a friend of mine. The church was always collecting for communities in Africa. I figured they would help a kid in their own community. I went to his office and asked if he could get me a scholarship." She gazed out over the water like the deacon was standing there in the surf.

I waited for her to continue, but she didn't. She simply stared out at the ocean. Lightly, I touched her foot. "What did the deacon say?"

She startled like she'd forgotten I was there. "You don't want to hear me yammer on about what happened when I was fifteen."

"Yes, I do. I care about you, and I want to know what brought you here to this beach all the way from Texas."

She set her jaw. "He said, sure he could help. Then he asked what I'd give him in return. I started telling him about how I'd pay the church back when I got a job, but that wasn't what he wanted. When he touched me, I didn't know what to do. It wasn't until he slipped his hand inside my shirt that I slapped it away and ran out of his office." She shook herself and rolled her shoulders. "You do realize how much therapy it's taken for me to tell this story, right?"

I swallowed around the lump in my throat. "Oh my god, Jamila. I'm so sorry. What did your nana say?"

"She…she didn't believe me. She said the deacon would never do that, and I must have been mistaken."

I gasped. "No!"

"Yeah. She and I didn't talk much after that. And I never told anyone else. Not my brothers or my guidance counselor. No one at church. I thought I could trust the deacon, or at least Nana, but I couldn't. The only person I ever told was my therapist. And now you."

I sat for a moment with the gift of her confidence. I'd never tell a soul, not even Jackson, who'd probably go beat up that deacon, or at least ensure his personal data leaked onto the dark web.

"Did you find a way to go to the private high school?"

"No. I stayed where I was, working my ass off at school, and when I was old enough, at an after-school job at one of those tech places, you know, where they fix your phone when you break the screen? I loved being the badass in the back room who could solve the hard problems."

"But that's hardware. How'd you get into software?"

"Remember, I'm a bit older than you, and apps weren't even a thing, really, back when I was in high school. I got my hands on an early smart phone in the repair shop and saw the possibilities. I programmed a game for it to amuse my brothers, and they liked it, so I uploaded it to the app store. It took off, and when I put that on my Stanford application, I got noticed."

All it had taken for me to get into college was my family's name and decent grades. And then I'd discarded the opportunity. Along with so many others I'd been given. I set down my plate. My voice wobbled when I asked, "Was Stanford everything you'd hoped for?"

"Well, yeah. It was a lot harder than my high school, but I loved the challenge. I developed a network. It was where I met Winslow and through him, Billie, and I made friends with Jackson and Cooper. Your family welcomed me in a way I'd never felt back in Austin."

"And you never looked back?"

"More or less." She tilted her head from side to side, her enormous hat flopping.

"Wait, what did you do?"

She bit her lip like she wanted to hold back, but then she leaned forward. "I wished there had been a way for Mama to find housing she could afford so she wouldn't have had to beg Nana for a place to stay. That was my original idea, you know? To make a place to bring together people who were struggling. Someone who couldn't pay the mortgage but had a room, and someone who needed a room but couldn't afford a whole apartment."

"Why did you change it?"

"I knew how to program, but I didn't understand business all that well, not when I was twenty. That's when I partnered up with Winslow. He was a freshman with a head for business. He showed me market research and convinced me to nudge the app toward short-term rentals. We considered accepting advertising from apartment complexes and national hotel chains, but we ended up selling the app. A year later, it became that rent-out-your-house app everyone uses. We used the cash to develop In the Know, which was our first app as Jamilow."

I dared to interlace my fingers with hers on the blanket, and she didn't stop me. "I think your original vision was beautiful. Do you think you'd ever do something with it?"

"Oh, it's there. I created a new version people can use for free. We call it KnowHome. You just have to know where to look. Enough people use it for renting rooms and such that I'm satisfied."

"Really? I had no idea."

"We don't market it. It's got enough word of mouth in the right communities, so the people who need it can usually find it."

"That's amazing." Jamila put so much effort into looking tough on the outside that I felt honored she'd given me a glimpse of her soft center.

"The other stuff keeps us afloat. Winslow's projections on this financial advising app are through the roof. Though if Moo-Lah beats us, they'll take a lot of that income. KnowHome will be in danger. As a nonrevenue-generating service, it's the first thing the board will want to cut."

"Moo-Lah won't beat you. We won't let them."

She squeezed my fingers, then let go. "No, I won't."

I scrunched my nose at how she'd changed my *we* to *I*, but I forgot it as soon as she said the words that made my heart go pitter-patter.

"I think it's time to go inside and wash that sunscreen off of you."

19

AS SOON AS we were inside, I tossed the sun hat on the floor and pushed up against Jamila. She let me crowd her back against the door and kiss her, a soft slide of lips before I slipped my tongue inside her mouth to taste her fire.

A moment later, she whirled and pressed me against the door. She cradled my face in both hands and battled back, exploring my mouth. I moaned at the sweet invasion.

"Remember who's in charge here, baby girl," she muttered into my ear.

I gasped as she trailed a hand down my side to my butt and ran a finger along the waistband of my bikini bottom.

"You're a little sensitive here."

I full-body shuddered.

She chuckled. "Maybe a lot sensitive. We'll get there in a minute. First, let's shower off that sunscreen."

Leaving the picnic remains and the sandy blanket at the back door, she led me down the hall to a large bedroom. Under a lazily twirling ceiling fan, a huge metal-framed bed was made up in white linens.

Without pausing, Jamila tugged me into the en suite bathroom. It was a nice size, about the same as mine in my parents' house, all white tile with gray accents. There was an enormous soaking tub in one corner and a walk-in shower in the other. She turned on the overhead spray and stepped back out.

"Face the mirror."

I obeyed, turning my back to her and trembling with anticipation.

"You okay with this?" she asked, watching my face in the mirror.

"Yes." My pupils were huge. Her eyes were so dark I couldn't tell in the mirror whether hers were too, but the way her gaze roamed over my body told me she was very, very interested in what was under my bikini.

She untied the strings at the back, then the ones at my neck, and the top dropped to the floor.

"Ooh, baby girl. You missed a spot."

She was right. I hadn't gone under the swimsuit like she had in the back, and the sides of my breasts each had a strip of pink where the bikini top had shifted.

"I'll get you some aloe for that after you shower."

"After I shower?" I tried to meet her gaze in the mirror, but hers was fixed on my body. I hoped she could ignore my sunburn and concentrate on the parts of me she wanted to touch. "I thought we'd shower together."

Her gaze zeroed in on mine. "What would Jackson say if we did that?"

"I told you Jackson doesn't get a say in my love life. Neither does my mother," I added, more for my sake than hers. "Besides, I don't talk to him about it. It wouldn't come up."

"You mean what he doesn't know won't hurt him?"

"Exactly."

She bit her lip, the way I wanted to. No, the way I would. I turned, stretched up on my toes, and kissed her with all the hunger that had built up on the beach, exploring the sweet taste of the balsamic reduction on her tongue. Then I nipped her plush lower lip.

She groaned. "Strip. I'll meet you in the shower."

"I'll wait." I shimmied off the bikini bottoms and stepped out of them.

She scanned me all the way to my toes, then licked her lips. She grasped the hem of her cover-up and tugged it over her head. I took a mental picture of her in the white bikini, memorizing each curve, including the way her hips flared slightly over the high-waisted bottoms.

"Turn around," I said, my voice husky. "I'll get the fasteners."

I released the top hook, then the one in the middle of her back and tossed it to the floor. I set my hands on her hips. "Can I?"

"Yeah."

I hooked my thumbs into the bottom half of her suit and shimmied it down her legs. Taking a deep breath, I circled back in front of her. I took in the brown nipples that topped her small breasts, the flawless line of her taut stomach, and the trimmed triangle of hair above her sex. I wanted to explore every inch of her bare skin.

"Come on," she said. "Let's shower all that sunscreen off."

"And sand. Don't forget the sand." Why the heck was I talking about sand when I had a naked Jamila beckoning me into her huge, steamy shower?

"Don't worry, baby. I'll get every grain from between your toes. Hey, do you have a clip or something for your hair?"

"In my bag…" It seemed very far away at the front of the house.

"It's okay. I've got you." She pulled a shower cap from a hook on the wall, then she grasped my hair into a ponytail and coiled it on my head. It tugged a little, and I winced.

"Sorry, your hair got tangled in the wind. I'll brush it out later." She set the cap over my hair and tucked it behind my ears.

Grasping my hand, she led me into the shower. I turned my back to the main shower head so I could face her. She made an adjustment, and the body sprays kicked in, cold at first but quickly warming. She slid a sea sponge and a bottle of bodywash from a shelf.

"Wait. I, uh…" I dropped my gaze to the sponge.

"Is this another lobster situation? Seriously, these things are harvested sustainably. They're more like plants than SpongeBob SquarePants."

I wrinkled my nose.

"No problem." She set the sponge back on the shelf. "I'll use my hands."

She squirted the unscented liquid into her hand and rubbed it into a lather. She started with long strokes down my neck. I shivered at the slight pressure.

"You into that?" she asked.

"I don't know. I never have been before." Once or twice, a guy had put his hand on my throat, but I'd batted it away, sure I wasn't a fan of sexual asphyxiation. But Jamila's hands were different, softer, trustworthy. "Maybe I could be. Are you?"

"Not really. But we could try it later."

I liked the sound of *later*. It held a promise that casual with Jamila wouldn't be limited to once or twice like all my other hookups had been.

She slicked her hands over my right shoulder and down my arm, all the way to my fingertips. Then she repeated the movement on my left shoulder and arm. Her gentle touch felt like sunshine, like rain, like the lap of warm ocean waves. It was not enough, yet it was too much, all at the same time.

I held my breath as her soapy hands hovered over my chest.

"Turn," she said.

Shuffling around until the water hit my chest, I let the spray wash the lather from my arms. Again, she started at my neck, not simply washing off the sunscreen but kneading the muscles until I felt boneless enough to wash down the drain alongside the soapy water. Next, she washed my upper back, again massaging my shoulders and shoulder blades. She continued down the column of my spine with delicious pressure.

When she reached my lower back, she rubbed a circle at the base of my spine. I shivered.

"That's the spot," she said. "You're like a cat."

"A cat?"

"They like being scratched right above their tails. Growing up, we'd sneak food out to the stray cats on our back porch. That was their favorite spot."

I wiggled my butt to make the most of the sensation. "I can see why."

She slicked both hands down my glutes, and I gasped.

"Aha. You're an ass girl. Wouldn't have thought. Maybe you like a little spanking with your breath play."

"Spanking?" That sounded pretty demeaning. "I don't think—"

Smack. She didn't whack me hard, but the sound reverberated off the tile and glass. Tiny shockwaves echoed up my spine. I gasped.

"Oh, you don't?" she asked casually.

It wasn't just water slicking between my legs now. I squeezed the muscles of my pelvic floor. "Maybe."

She chuckled. "Turn."

I spun so fast I slipped, but Jamila caught my elbow. "Careful, baby girl."

She refilled her palm with the soap then smoothed it over my collarbones, onto my chest, and then, skipping my breasts, over my stomach. I sucked it in, wishing it were as toned as hers.

"None of that," she said. "I like how soft you are. Relax."

I did, enjoying the beat of the water on the back muscles Jamila had massaged.

She ran a fingertip around my breast. "Does it sting?"

"What?"

"Your sunburn." She glided a finger over the side of my breast. "No. Feels nice."

She traced around my breast with two fingers. Then finally, finally, she brushed her thumbs over my nipples. I groaned.

She repeated the move, more firmly. Sensation rocketed down

to my core, putting it on full alert. My muscles clenched. She thumbed my nipples again.

I reached for her, grasping her lower back and pulling her into me. Desperately, I strained my neck to kiss her, but all I could reach was her jawline. If I went up on my toes, I'd slip again and take us both down. A trip to the emergency room would be anything but sexy.

At last, she bent her head and kissed me, sweeping her tongue into my mouth as she continued to tweak my nipples. The pressure built between my legs. As if she could sense it, she pulled away.

"Not yet, baby girl. This is my orgasm."

"But I haven't touched you yet." Could she come from touching me, watching me?

"Your orgasm is mine. I'm in charge of it. You come when I'm ready."

Oh. Ohh. "Oh."

She returned to my nipples, swirling, tweaking, until I squeezed my eyes shut to savor the bliss. Suddenly, her hands were gone.

I opened my eyes.

She sank to her knees. Grinning wickedly, she said, "Forgot to do your legs."

She made a show of pouring more body wash into her hand, then slicked it over my right hip, then my thigh, front and back. She brushed over my knee, my calf, my shin, my ankle. My legs trembled.

"Can't forget these sandy toes," she said. "Hold on to my shoulder."

I gripped her shoulder as she lifted my foot to swipe between my toes. She set it down then picked up my other foot. She rubbed between my toes, then the bottom of my foot, then the top. Tingles rose up my leg and hovered at the nexus between my thighs.

Setting my foot back on the tile, she began a slow, sensuous ascent up my ankle, my lower leg, my knee. She found the ticklish spot behind my knee and chuckled when I twitched. "I'm coming back to that, later."

Another *later*. The tingles intensified.

But when she swept up my thigh, trailing her fingers up the inside, I forgot all about later. It was all about now, now, now, with my attention focused on where her fingers met my skin. Long and nimble, her fingers pressed into my skin, dancing up, tapping again. My breaths came short and shallow.

At last she found the sensitive spot on my thigh just below my pussy. Her touch was featherlight, not nearly enough.

"Yes?" she asked.

"Yes. Yes! More. *Please.*"

Chuckling, she grazed my lower lips. Fire blazed through my pelvis. More. I needed more.

"Shift a little to the right," she said. When I did, the spray hit my lower back, lighting it up and making me groan.

"That's my girl." Then, at last, she gave it to me. When she flicked her fingers up to my clit, my knees quaked.

"Hold on," she commanded.

I gripped her shoulders. She increased the pressure on my clit, circling the swollen tip. My orgasm barreled closer.

"Can I...can I come?"

"Good girl," she said. Her words of praise made me feel like I'd swallowed the sun. Light and heat blazed through every pore. "Yes. Come."

As she rubbed faster, I let go. I let myself feel it all: the water pounding into my back and dribbling down my legs, her hot breath on my sex, and her fingers, those magical fingers, wringing the orgasm from me. I shouted, then I groaned as she kept up the motion, prolonging my orgasm until I felt like a buoy at the mercy of the ocean waves.

At last, I whimpered. "Enough."

"For now," she said. But her fingers stilled and lifted from my body. "Can you stand on your own?"

I was still gripping her shoulders. "Sorry." I released her and stood. My knees held. Barely.

"It's all good, baby girl." Her tone soothed me.

She stood and poured more bodywash into her hand. She washed herself efficiently.

"Wait," I said when she brushed a hand over her chest. "Can I do that?"

"Not this time. I'm getting pruny. I need some lotion, then we'll move this to the bed."

"I'll do your lotion," I said, my mouth watering at the thought of slicking it over her skin.

"No, baby girl." She turned off the water. "I want mine in bed."

———

JAMILA FOLDED BACK the covers of the enormous bed, revealing crisp, white sheets. She lay down on the far side and patted the space next to her.

I kneeled on the bed, less because I was unsure what to do next than because it was a better position to admire her. Her skin held a sheen from the lotion she'd applied. It smelled so incredible that I'd taken some, too, and rubbed it over my arms and legs.

Now she was naked, toes stretched to the foot of the bed, arms spread in a T shape. Her curves were subtle on her slender body, her breasts flattening a little when she lay on her back. Under the floral scent, an earthy scent of arousal lingered, mine and hers. I closed my eyes and inhaled it.

"Second thoughts?" she asked.

My eyelids flew open. "No, just…savoring."

"You're sure? There's still time to go back to friends without benefits."

"No, I'm ready. Spread your legs."

Her only movement was her eyebrows lifting.

"Aren't I in charge now?" I asked. "Like you were in charge of my orgasm?"

She chuckled. "I may be the one receiving pleasure this time, but I'm always in charge, baby girl. Don't forget it."

I swallowed and waited for her instruction.

"Good girl."

There it was again. That sensation of pleasure, lighting me up.

"You can touch me. Start with my breasts."

She didn't have to tell me twice. I traced a line from her collarbone down her breastbone, then I drew a circle around her right breast.

"Not so tickly. Use more force," she said.

"Got it, boss." I prepared to squeeze.

"I don't like a brat. Use your sassy mouth on me."

I didn't dare respond, not even with a "yes, please." Squeezing the base of her breast, I lapped the tip with my tongue. I thumbed her nipple and then repeated the action with her left breast before returning to her right breast to circle it with my tongue. I sucked it, watching her reaction. When she arched her back, I knew I'd pleased her. Satisfaction warmed me all the way to my toes.

I didn't stop. I kept my mouth and hands full of her, high on her floral taste.

Her breaths shortened until her chest heaved under me.

"Okay, good girl," she said at last. "Put that mouth between my legs. First my pussy, then my clit."

I obeyed, kissing down her stomach to where her scent bloomed. I positioned myself between her spread legs and took a second to stare at her dark lips surrounding her glistening pink center.

I bent to taste her, starting at the center and spiraling out along her lips, staying away from her clit as she'd instructed.

"Harder," she demanded.

I used more force to stroke her with my tongue like I'd do with extra-cold ice cream. But Jamila was anything but cold. She was heat, and silk, and sweetness on my tongue. I never wanted to leave.

"That's it, baby girl. Just like that."

As I knelt between her legs, cool air hit my wet pussy. I was as turned on as she was. Her quiet grunts told me she loved what I was doing. I delved the tip of my tongue inside her, then trailed it up almost to her clit, then back down.

When she gasped, I buried my face in her, wanting to draw out her pleasure and the moment as long as I could.

"Shift," she said, her voice strained. "Knees by my chest. Ass up here."

I did as she commanded. We were parallel, not quite sixty-nine, and she had a full view of my ass. Wetness dribbled down my inner thigh.

"Back to work. On my clit now."

Resting one elbow on the bed next to her hip, I slung my other arm across her. Using my thumbs, I spread her wide, revealing her swollen clit. I started out gentle, recalling how sensitive my own clit became, but she gritted out, "Harder," with a smack to my butt cheek.

"You sure you want to do that with my mouth on your clit? There's, like, a bazillion nerves down here."

"You're a good girl," she said, tracing a line from my stinging cheek to within an inch of my center. "You won't hurt me."

I peered around my shoulder. She watched me from the pillow, her eyes half-shut in pleasure.

"Never." I got back to work, circling her clit once with my tongue before closing my lips around it and sucking for all I was worth. She put her hand where I needed it, not rubbing this time, but pressing, a reminder that she was in charge, but also an assurance that she'd take care of me. I hollowed my cheeks.

Her hips bowed up. "God*damn*, girl. Yes!"

As I sucked, she rubbed my pussy and then slipped a finger between my legs to tap my clit. Sparks raced up my spine. Holy cow. I was as close as she was.

I kept going.

I alternated sucking and licking until she cried out, her legs going stiff. Her hand stilled on me. I eased her down from the orgasm with softer laps and kisses until she relaxed. Looking forward to a cuddle—if she'd let me—I put a hand on the bed to press up.

"Stop," she croaked. "We're not done."

"But—" My protest died when she started rubbing me fast, and my orgasm roared closer. I rested my cheek on her thigh and gazed at the wet wreck I'd made of her pretty pussy while she stroked, pinched, and tapped until my legs shook and everything clenched. I moaned in relief.

"That's a good girl," she said as my knees gave out, and I flopped to the bed on my hip.

I looked up at her lazy smile. "Why was that such a turn-on? What's wrong with me?"

"Nothing's wrong with you, baby girl. You're hardwired to please people. That's why you like it so much."

"That tracks, I guess. And you're hardwired to be in charge?"

"Abso-fucking-lutely."

"Must be nice." What would it be like to get off on ordering people around and to have them listen to you?

She snorted. "Except when it gets me in trouble."

"You mean with that reporter?"

She stroked my hip like she stroked Quill. "Yeah, that…and one time in bed."

I really didn't want to think about Jamila in bed with anyone else, not with my core still buzzing from her touch, but Jamila never opened up about anything personal. I'd take everything she wanted to give me. "Really? What happened?"

She looked up at the ceiling, and I held my breath. She was so guarded.

"It was another friends-with-benefits situation but with a guy. He's just as bossy as I am."

"Hard to imagine," I joked.

"I know, right?" She traced a long line down my thigh. "We were fucking—it was one of those bored fucks, you know? We'd been hanging out, watching some ridiculous old movie. *Singin' in the Rain,* I think."

All the warmth drained out of me and was replaced with ice. She had to be talking about Cooper Fallon. That was his favorite movie.

"Anyway, he said, 'We're good together, Mila.' And I said, 'Yeah, we're good friends.' Then he said, 'What if we were more,' and that's when I started to flip out.

"He started talking about combining our companies, synergies and whatnot—he was an entrepreneur too. I didn't like that. Jamilow was mine. And Winslow's, of course. Then while I was still sitting there with my mouth hanging open, he said, 'We should get married. Then it's all fifty-fifty, and you're protected.'"

I blinked my eyes wide. "Protected?"

She pointed at me. "Exactly! So I said, 'Protected from what, exactly?' and he started on this bullshit about how we'd share risk and blah blah blah. Looking back on it, I'm sure he had my best interests at heart, but all I heard was that I couldn't make it on my own. That I needed his protection from failure. That I'd want some kind of old-fashioned marriage of convenience. That I didn't know what real love was, or want it." She stared into the distance.

She believed in love. She might present a thick shell, but underneath, she was vulnerable and romantic like I was. Tingles danced across my skin.

"What happened then?" I asked.

She focused back on me. "I kicked him out of my apartment, didn't speak to him for weeks."

I remembered that weird time right after they graduated from college when things had been icy with Cooper. Jackson couldn't invite them both over at the same time. He'd tried to pull the story out of each of them, but they were silent. He tried to force them together, but neither one of them budged.

"He left me about a thousand apology voice mails and texts.

Sent me a roomful of flowers. It was before either of us had made any money, so I had no idea where he got the cash." She paused, remembering.

"And then?" Were they still friends with benefits? No, they couldn't be. Cooper was engaged now. Still, I held my breath.

"I finally realized how hard it was for him to apologize and how much I missed his friendship. We talked and worked it out, but we never fucked again. And he never said another word about a merger, including the matrimonial kind."

My chest loosened. At least I didn't have to compete for her affections with Cooper Fallon, who was smart and confident and everything Jamila had to want in a partner. I'd never measure up to him. I felt magnanimous enough to say, "I'm glad you made up."

"Me too. I never want anything to fuck up our friendship again." She chuckled. "Now come on up here and take a nap. That sunshine wore me out."

Thank god Jamila was a cuddler. I needed her arms around me after the story about a friends-with-benefits-gone-bad.

20

"WHAT ARE YOU DOING?" Jamila scuffed into the kitchen in a pair of wool-lined slippers and a silky dragon-printed robe that covered all the secret places I'd worshiped last night.

"Making you breakfast," I said, tossing the perfectly diced onions and peppers into the pan. Jamila's beach home kitchen was fully stocked, which I'd found out as I'd wandered in shortly after sunrise.

"I don't eat breakfast." She didn't eat breakfast? I slumped. She shuffled to the coffeemaker and grunted when she found the carafe full of hot coffee. After selecting a mug from the rack, she filled it and sipped without blowing on it first.

I stirred the vegetables in the pan. She'd miss out on my perfect knife skills—I'd gotten an A on that, at least—and the gorgeous omelet I was making her. They hadn't shown us how to make them at culinary school, but I'd watched Telma enough times to know how to do it.

Suddenly, she leaned over my shoulder, breathing bitter coffee on my cheek. "I'll watch you eat. I enjoyed that last night—a lot."

My face went as hot as the pan. I hadn't even thought about what I looked like last night. Most guys didn't care. Quite the opposite: they seemed to think the messier, the better. My experience with women was that we were always checking each other out, comparing, judging. Jamila was the most talented, put-together person I knew. "Did you really like it?"

"Yeah." She slid a hand under my T-shirt and stroked across my stomach. "It felt amazing. And your ass is adorable." She squeezed it over my shorts.

I hummed and pressed into her hand. *Adorable.* From a beauty like Jamila, that meant something.

She sniffed. "Watch those. They're getting a little charred." I looked down into the pan. The edges of the onions had started to blacken.

"Oops." I whipped it off the heat and scraped them onto a plate. Most of them were salvageable. I poured in the eggs I'd previously whisked and began scooting them around the pan as they cooked. "You sure you don't want one?"

"Nah, I think better on an empty stomach."

"Okay." The joy had left my cooking. I'd imagined sliding a perfectly fluffy omelet onto a plate in front of her and those brown eyes of hers lighting up at the feast I'd prepared. Now she was going to watch me eat. That was definitely less appealing.

As was the omelet. Why was it so lumpy looking? Telma's never looked like this. Hoping for a culinary miracle, I sprinkled the onions and peppers down the center, picking out the scorched ones. I let it settle a minute as the edges peeled up, signaling they were overdone.

When I slid it onto the plate, it didn't fold in the middle like Telma's always did. It flopped. Then it cracked. I'd made not a perfect semicircle of fluffy deliciousness but a half-overdone, half-undercooked disaster.

"That's what they taught you in culinary school?"

Jamila had observed the whole debacle. Of course.

"Maybe they would've covered omelets next semester. If I hadn't dropped out." I stared at the unappealing scramble on my plate for a moment, then I slid it into the trash. "I'll eat fruit instead."

Jamila dropped an arm around my shoulder. "It's okay. I can't even cut up an onion without slicing my thumb open. My chef drops off ready-to-heat meals at the start of every week. At least you tried."

"I never cooked at home either. Maybe that's why I couldn't cut it at culinary school."

"Hey. Hey." She waited until I looked at her. "You left culinary school because of your soft, animal-loving heart."

"I guess." I stared into the cold, milky surface of my coffee. "Want to take our coffee to the patio?"

"Eh. Let's stay inside. Going out on the beach yesterday was a risk. Wouldn't want to tempt fate."

"A risk? I only got a little sunburned."

"No, baby. I mean, it's a public beach. Someone might see us. Together."

"But we are together. Right?"

"Baby." Her mouth turned down. "I don't do serious. Besides, what would my PR consultant say if my face got splashed all over Instagram alongside yours? You're not exactly low-profile. We'd be right back where we started with the focus on my private life and not on the company, where it belongs."

"You're right. Of course you're right." Saying it, even twice, didn't make me feel any better. I'd woken at her side unable to believe that I'd gotten exactly what I wanted and full of hope I could keep it. But that wasn't how Jamila saw it. I was a fling, not worth the PR risk.

Jamila reached around me to pluck a couple of blueberries from the bowl of fruit. She popped one into her mouth. "Come on. You can give Quill one of these. It's super-cute to watch him gnaw on them."

Grasping my hand, she towed me to the bedroom where Quill.i.am's habitat was set up.

He was awfully cute to watch. And when Jamila kissed me while I laughed, it seemed that everything might turn out all right.

———

"BAD NEWS," Hannah said as I floated into the office on Monday.

"What's that?" I set down my laptop bag, my attention sharpening. Saturday and Sunday morning with Jamila were fantastic, but I had a job to do. Only a couple more weeks remained until the launch, and I had to hold everything together until then.

"Photos." She tapped on her phone, and my phone buzzed in my purse. She'd texted me a link. I ignored my many social media notifications and clicked on the link.

"Photos of Jamila?" My stomach went ice cold. The first image showed her kneeling on our picnic blanket at the beach. The next one showed me sitting beside her, but the floppy hat hid my face. Yikes, I hadn't realized how that bikini displayed the rolls around my middle. Jamila hadn't said a word.

Horrified, I flipped through the rest of the images. Thankfully, whoever snapped the pictures hadn't cared about getting my face. In each one, either my hat or Jamila's obscured it. But in the last photo, they'd captured my hand on her knee. There was no mistaking the sexuality of the pose. Hannah pursed her lips and gave me a pointed stare. I admitted nothing. "No big deal. Jamila's bisexuality is no secret. And look, there's a ton of likes."

"Likes give it more visibility, not social proof." Before I could even dig into them, Hannah said, "The comments are a mix. Some people love that Jamila is living her best bisexual life, others condemn it at a family beach—"

"We weren't doing anything!" I snapped. Then I cringed.

"Don't do that with your face," Hannah said. "You're proud of your bisexuality just like she is. Maybe in the future, don't let Jamila get snapped in a flirty pose with her employee, 'kay?"

Proud of my bisexuality was a little more than I was comfortable with. What would Mother say if she saw these? She'd recognize me even without my face showing. She'd definitely recognize the ruby ring that glinted on my finger as it rested on Jamila's knee. I twisted the band.

"Of course I won't," I said. "I'm sorry."

"It'll be fine, as long as…shit."

"What?" I looked down at my phone and saw that Pavel Thakor, CEO of Moo-Lah, whom I'd started to follow, had commented. I clicked to read it.

So glad to see Miss Jallow enjoying herself. Meanwhile, at @moo-lah_corp, we're working hard on a groundbreaking app. #workingforyou #betterfasterstronger

My phone buzzed with a notification. Another link from Hannah. I clicked it.

The video played silently with captions. It was Jamila, earlier today if I judged the light right, her gorgeous lips turned down in a sneer. The caption read, *Flick off. My weekends are my Gotham business.*

"Wait, what?"

"The captions are G-rated. Jamila cursed out another journalist who asked about the pictures."

I dropped my head back and stared at the acoustic-tile ceiling of our office. "Why?" I groaned.

"They didn't show the question. It must've pissed her off."

I watched the video again. This time, my heart prickled. *My weekends are my goddamn business.* Like I was her weekend entertainment, not worth mentioning by name. Certainly not with the word *girlfriend*.

But she'd said we were casual. She'd reminded me we needed to stay hidden. Right as the photo had been snapped. She wasn't protecting me. She was protecting herself *from* me.

"I guess we need to go talk to her." I swiped the video away and checked the time. "We can get in right before the developers' stand-up."

"I'm going to sit this one out," Hannah said. "She'll be in a mood."

"Coward," I said mildly.

"Plus she's in with Winslow now."

"Why? She meets with him on Wednesdays."

"They're planning for a dinner tomorrow night with that guy from the financial partner. And then Winslow's off the rest of the week."

"They're meeting with Kenneth Royal from First Arbiter?" Jamila hadn't said a word yesterday.

"Yes, at La Colombe Bleue."

"You said Winslow's taking off? The app releases in two weeks. Aren't we all hands on deck until then?"

"It's Memorial Day weekend." Hannah shrugged. "Guess he has plans."

"It still seems like a crap time to go on vacation. I bet Moo-Lah's not..." I glanced down at my screen, where I'd pulled up Pavel Thakor's profile. His most recent post was a photo of him seated outdoors talking to a group of men. The photo was so closely cropped that I couldn't discern anything in the background. They could have been at a country club or a restaurant patio or even outside his building. He looked relaxed, throwing his head back in a laugh. I squinted at the picture, then zoomed in. Behind Thakor was the lower part of a pair of slim-fit raspberry slacks. I zoomed in further, but the image pixelated. Were those two-tone navy-and-brown brogues?

I had a sneaking suspicion I knew who they belonged to.

"Are you okay?" Hannah asked. "I've never seen you that still."

"I'm fine." I snapped a screenshot. "I'll be right back."

Gripping my phone, I strode down the hall to Jamila's office. I paused at Felicia's desk.

"Is Winslow in there with her?" I asked.

"Yes. He'll be out in a minute, though." She nodded at Rhiannon, who marched toward Jamila's office trailed by her team. In her blue shirt, she looked like an angry bluebird leading her flock.

"Why do I feel like I'm the only one doing my damn job?" She looked me up and down. Her gaze lingered on my hand. "And not making things worse?"

Fire rose from my cheeks to my forehead. "I'm handling it."

"Yeah, you are." She lifted her nose in a cutting gesture worthy of my mother.

Heat blazed down to my chest, but I was saved from an ill-thought-out response when Jamila's door opened, and Winslow stepped out in his two-tone brogues. Today, his pants were powder blue with tiny American flags embroidered on them. I glanced at the photo on my screen again. I wished I could tell if the shoes in the photo were navy and brown or black and brown or brown with a weird shadow.

I didn't trust myself to say anything to Jamila, especially with an audience.

"Winslow, a word?" I tipped my head toward the small conference room a few doors down from Jamila's office.

He smirked. "Sure."

Stewing over his smirk, I waited until I'd shut the conference room door to speak.

I flipped my phone around so he could see the photo. "What were you doing, talking to the competition?"

He squinted at the screen. "I'm not in that photo."

I zoomed in on the slacks and the tops of the shoes and showed him. "You're sure?"

"Everyone wears pants and shoes like those. Why would you think that was me?"

"It's not a good look to be talking to a competitor when everyone knows there's a leak."

"I've been with Jamila since day one. Since before she started the company. What exactly are you saying?" He folded his arms.

A tickle of doubt started at the back of my brain. He was right that he wasn't the only tech bro who wore ridiculous slacks and expensive shoes. There were a lot of prep-school trust funders in the Bay Area. (I should know; I'd dated my fair share.) But I couldn't afford another slip-up like the one I'd made when I'd accused Rhiannon. Jamila would go off on me like she'd done with that journalist.

"Speaking of incriminating photos, I see you've been doing a stellar job of PR." He raised his eyebrows. "This is a pretty weak attempt to deflect attention from being caught with your hand in the cookie jar."

"I don't know what you're talking about." I swiped away the screenshot.

"Look, you're a nice girl, so I'll give you some friendly advice," he said. "I've known Jamila a long time. She gets stressed, and she blows off steam if you know what I mean. Seems like you're her latest vent."

I plucked a bit of lint from my jacket sleeve. "I don't know why you're telling me this."

"You seem like the kind of girl who takes things to heart. Jamila doesn't. Her little dalliances mean nothing. Ask Cooper Fallon."

I couldn't help it. I stared at him, open-mouthed.

He chuckled. "Yeah, I've been around that long. I saw the fall-out. Jamila's all about casual. She'll never trust anyone enough to let it get any more serious than that."

How many times had she reminded me she didn't do serious? More than I cared to recall.

He brushed past me and set his hand on the doorknob. But before he turned it, he glanced back at me. "I'll give you this advice: keep your focus on your own responsibilities. And don't bother thinking Jamila will ever be anything but a hookup. She's not that kind of woman."

He opened the door and left, leaving me standing in the conference room, deflated.

He was right. She'd warned me herself. Why had I let myself hope that she'd fall for me? I was just Jackson's cute but annoying little sister. I'd never be the one for her.

Not the way she was for me.

21

"YOU LEAVING SOON?" Hannah asked as she slung her laptop bag over her shoulder Tuesday evening.

Blinking, I turned my gaze from the open door of our office to her face. "Yeah. I just want five minutes with Jamila first."

It was the evening of the dinner with Kenneth Royal, the CEO of First Arbiter, and I was nervous for her. We hadn't spoken since the photos hit the media yesterday. Hannah and I had done all we could to flood the socials with photos of Jamila's camp, video snips from Nita's interview, and anything we could find to distract, but the story kept spiraling.

Everyone wanted to know the identity of Jamila's mystery girlfriend. I'd stalked Jamila on social media long enough to know that these things followed a pattern: once they identified her, they'd dig up her background, follow her for a few days, post a few unflattering photos of her eating or sweating after a workout, then drop her as quickly as Jamila did. Outing myself as Jamila's girlfriend wouldn't help her a bit. Not to mention what Mother would say.

No, thanks.

I'd spent more time on social media than I should have, even as a PR consultant, scanning the comments for a hint that Jamila's beach babe was me. So far, nothing. But every ping, every red number ticking up, twisted my stomach tighter.

"Good luck," Hannah said. "See you tomorrow."

"Have a good night." I pretended to look at my screen.

A minute after Hannah walked out the door, I caught a flash of lavender. Jamila was on the move, striding down the hall. I scurried to the office door and caught her as she passed.

"Hey, Jamila." I jogged to keep up with her long strides.

"Natalie." There was no softness in the way she said it.

"Development going okay?"

"Actually, no. We hit another snag. I need to stay to help, but we've got this goddamn meeting tonight." She shoved through the security door into the main hallway.

I sped up to catch her. "With the…partner?" I said it low since we were outside the secure space.

"Yeah, and it's going to be a shitshow. I can't tell if he's more pissed about the photos or about the potential schedule delay." She muttered the last two words as she shoved through the restroom door. She went to the mirror to check her lipstick.

"Can I help?"

"Not unless you've got a magic wand that makes the bugs in my code go away."

"Sorry, I can't help with that. But I can help with the PR angle. I can tell him about the *Buzz Bizz* article and our other PR efforts."

She frowned at me in the mirror. "You're free tonight?" Glancing back at the stalls, she added, "To meet with him?"

"Yes, yes, of course. Anything you need." My stomach fizzed like champagne. Maybe she'd let me stay over too. We'd reconnect. I wouldn't feel so abandoned and needy.

"Okay, then." She recapped the lipstick tube. "Let's go."

———

ON THE DRIVE to the city, Winslow sat in the front seat of her SUV and briefed her on who would cover his various activities while he visited his hospitalized grandmother. When I found out about her heart attack, I felt a little bad about criticizing him for leaving.

Meanwhile, I sat silently in the back. They talked about important-sounding things like supply chains and marketing campaigns. My job with its social media posts, likes, and photo shoots sounded frivolous in comparison.

When she pulled up at the valet stand in front of La Colombe Bleue, I finally felt in my element. I'd been to the elegant restaurant dozens of times with my parents and a few times with dates. The valet opened the door, and I stepped out and brushed the wrinkles from my pencil skirt. I stood straight and tall and led the way to the door, not bothering to pause because I trusted the doorman to open it in time.

At the host's stand, Frankie greeted me. "Miss Natalie. I wasn't expecting you tonight. Will Mr. and Mrs. Hayes be joining you?"

"No, I'm dining with Ms. Jallow tonight. You'll find us a good table, right? Something private? We have an important meeting that requires discretion."

"Of course, of course." Frankie noted something on the seating diagram.

Jamila rolled her eyes. "Really?"

"You wouldn't want to entertain our guest next to the kitchen," I said. "Plus, I don't think your partnership is public knowledge. We wouldn't want to sit in the front window and give people a cause to speculate."

"That's actually a good idea," Winslow said.

"Actually?" I said. "I have tons of good ideas."

Now he rolled his eyes.

Frankie led us to a table in a private alcove where we wouldn't be observed.

"This is perfect," I said as Frankie laid my napkin across my lap and handed me a menu. "Thank you, Frankie."

Jamila didn't wait for Frankie. She spread her napkin in her lap and held out her hand for the wine list. "What I wouldn't give for a whiskey."

Frankie asked, "Can I bring you something from the bar?"

"No, thanks. I have to go back to the office tonight."

There went my hope of a repeat of last weekend. Now I wished I'd driven the convertible, so I wouldn't have to Uber back to the office in the morning.

"Your server will be with you in a moment." Frankie bowed and left.

"What do you think, Winslow, cabernet or pinot noir?" Jamila asked.

I sat, incredulous. Why hadn't she asked me about wine? I'd practically grown up in this restaurant. I could've told her the cabernets were uninspired, and she'd do better with a malbec. But she hadn't asked me. I twisted my napkin in my lap.

While they debated the wine choice, I spotted a man I recognized. Kenneth Royal's silver temples, gray suit, blue tie, and black loafers telegraphed to the world that he was a banking executive. Here was a way I could make myself useful.

I stood. "Mr. Royal, welcome. I don't know if you remember me. I'm Natalie Jones, and you know Jamila Jallow and Winslow Keating-Ashworth."

Jamila looked irritated, but she'd been irritated all night. I couldn't tell if she was still thinking about the bug or if this was a new annoyance. "Evening, Kenneth. Thanks for meeting us." Her "thanks" sounded like ground glass in her throat.

"We need to talk about the health of our partnership." He sat across from Jamila but turned his head to assess me. "You're Charles Hayes's stepdaughter."

"That's right. We've met at my parents' parties."

"Charles is a smart man." He looked me up and down. "You're not the one who owns a software company. You're the socialite."

Gritting my teeth, I sat up straighter. "I'm in charge of Jamila's public relations."

"I see. Social media posts and whatnot?" He said it like he had a mouthful of overcooked broccoli.

"Yes, and—"

Jamila cut me off. "Kenneth, let's focus on your concerns."

I sat back in my chair. Why had she brought me here if she was going to ignore me?

"I'm not sure Jamilow is a good match for FA with all this kerfuffle," Royal said. "It's been one thing after another. First, there was Winslow's scandalous marriage and then his sordid divorce. You punched that journalist and let yourself get snapped on the beach with some bikini bimbo. Now you've had yet another altercation with a reporter. Jamilow looks more like a soap opera than a software company to which our august financial institution wants to tie its reputation."

He leaned back, letting the shrapnel fly from that grenade.

Bikini bimbo? Had Jamila brought me here to apologize?

Jamila's expression was stone. "Jamilow is an innovative company that generates more creative ideas in one morning than your stodgy bank does all year. That's why you're partnering with us. So what if there's a little drama? You get a group of artists together, there's going to be some theatrics. However, I can promise no more media hysterics before the release."

She stared right at me.

Now I understood why I was here. This was her way of showing me the stakes of her life. She had no room for a public relationship with me or the inevitable attention it would bring. My job was to smooth everything over for public consumption and make Jamilow look like a suitable partner to a beige financial services company.

Well, I knew all about smoothing things over. This was what I'd been raised to do. I lifted my eyebrows, and our server glided to our table.

"We'd like a bottle of the Nicolás Catena Zapata, please. And I'll have a vodka tonic."

"Really, Nat?" Jamila muttered. "This is my meeting."

Flashing her my most glittering smile, I said, "Make it a double."

Once the vodka hit my bloodstream, it was easy to slip back into what everyone, especially Kenneth Royal, expected of me. I ensured everyone's glass was full. When I spoke, I fluttered my hands to remind everyone I was there as window dressing and not to take me too seriously. I tittered at what they said when it was even remotely funny. I patted Mr. Royal's arm and gave him my most winning smiles. Slowly, he softened like butter left out on my culinary school worktable.

My behavior had the opposite effect on Jamila. I didn't need to refill her glass because she hardly touched the wine. She grew more brittle as the night progressed, like chocolate ganache in the cooler.

Finally, dinner was over. Mr. Royal and his august financial institution were won over. He shook hands with Winslow, promising to call him the next time he needed to round out a foursome. He invited Jamila for drinks at his social club. He gave me a lingering hug and offered to give me a ride home in his town car. I declined politely and ordered a rideshare.

Winslow walked out with Mr. Royal, and I expected Jamila to go with them, but she gripped my wrist like a manacle and dragged me behind a potted plant in the vestibule. My heart fluttered with hope. Would she give me a hug to eradicate the oily feeling of Mr. Royal's? Or at least call me a good girl for making everything go so smoothly?

But she didn't do any of those things. Instead, she hissed at me. "What the fuck was that?"

"What?"

"Don't give me those doe eyes and pretend you don't know what I'm talking about. Why'd you put on the airhead act?"

"Airhead act? I was trying to help."

"I needed you to be my capable PR consultant, not some Barbie."

Barbie? The vodka in my stomach roiled. "Then you should've introduced me as your consultant. You dismissed me, and I didn't know what you wanted. I acted the way I thought you needed."

"I didn't mean to dismiss you." The stiffness went out of her spine. "I just…I didn't know what to do with you once you were here. It's a delicate time in my business with this partnership on the line." She rubbed the space between her eyebrows. "I'm sorry I'm not better at this shit."

I wanted to reach out and pull her into a hug. We probably could have gotten away with a friendly embrace, but we couldn't afford to take that chance. Not after the photos. Not when Jamila's new product launch was on the line. So I tried to put all my affection into my gaze as I said, "It's okay. I'm sorry I disappointed you."

"You can be the real you around me, you know," she said. "Next time, call me out. You don't have to wear that mask. Though maybe not directly in front of Kenneth. Wait until after the release."

The first genuine smile of the evening broke across my face. "I'll do my best."

"I will too. To make up for this disaster of a dinner, I'd like you to come hiking with me this weekend."

"Hiking on Memorial Day weekend? Might a sleepover be involved?"

"Abso-fucking-lutely. Bring an overnight bag and a swimsuit, no pajamas necessary."

I held in a squeal. A long weekend with Jamila sounded like heaven. I'd buy some cute hiking boots and put my hair up in a bandana. I thrilled at the imagined snap as she whipped it off and pushed me against the rough bark of a tree.

"Yes, ma'am," I said.

Her eyes went molten. "I like the sound of that."

Insufficiently screened by a potted plant or not, I tipped toward her but froze when my phone buzzed in my hand.

Jamila licked her lips, teasing me. "Guess you'd better go," she whispered, her voice husky.

"See you at work tomorrow, boss." With a flip of my hair, I sauntered out of the restaurant and slid into a Toyota that smelled like Axe body spray and hope.

22

"WHERE ARE YOU GOING?"

If I'd been thirty seconds faster, Mother wouldn't have caught me with my hand on the front door latch Saturday morning.

Slowly, I turned. "Out?"

I tugged down the high-tech hiking shorts I'd bought on my lunch hour yesterday. I'd rolled them up, half-hoping when Jamila saw the exposed lengths of my thighs, we wouldn't have to go through the pretense of a hike, and the only exercise we'd get would be in her bed.

"In that?"

She should talk. She wore a burgundy cashmere robe over her silk pajamas.

I cursed the swishy fabric that must have alerted Mother I was sneaking out. I liked my shirt though. It clung to my curves in a way I hoped Jamila would appreciate before she tore it off. It even had snaps instead of buttons.

Mother cleared her throat.

"We're going hiking."

She raised an eyebrow. "What about Representative Crawford's picnic?"

"Oh. Uh." I forced a smile. "I don't think I'm going to make it to that."

"And with whom are you hiking?"

"With a…a friend."

"A 'friend?'" Mother crossed her arms. "After your sister went off traveling with a *friend,* she got kicked out of university. But you're not like Samantha. I wouldn't have thought you'd sneak around like this. You've always been my good girl."

She knew how to hit me right in my heart. It throbbed at the force of the accusation she'd tossed at me. "I still am, Mother. I do everything you ask. Just not today. It's a beautiful day to be outdoors." I waved at the sidelight, where the sun hovered a palm's width over the horizon, still coloring the early-morning clouds pink. "And I've never been hiking before."

"I asked you to attend the picnic and talk with Representative Crawford about our literacy agenda."

"I know, Mother. But I go to social events like that all the time. I want to do something different today."

She stared at me for a long moment, her blue eyes boring into mine. Then she glanced through the sidelight. "Speaking of different, whose car is that?"

I should've parked the Porsche down the street, but I was so tired coming home from work yesterday that I'd pulled it into the driveway.

"It's a company car. For the commute to Jamilow."

"Why do you need a company car when you have a perfectly good—"

"Mother," I interrupted her. "I'm going to be late."

She pursed her lips. "While I appreciate what you're doing for Jamila, I'll be glad when this PR nonsense is over, and you can get back to your family duties."

Nonsense? My empty stomach curled in on itself.

"I'll give your regards to Daniel. When you're done with Jamila, you two should consider making it official."

"Official?"

"Your engagement. Daniel will go far with you at his side."

The scent of her Chanel No. 5 overpowered me. "I have to go." I opened the door and stepped outside.

"You haven't thanked me yet. For the photos."

"The…photos?" A weight pressed into my belly.

"The ones taken at the beach with Jamila. I purchased the ones that showed your face."

Holy cow. "There were photos of my face?"

"Of course there were. You're a Jones."

My jaw dropped. "Why didn't you buy all of them?"

"I asked, but he wouldn't sell them all. Either the Jamila story is too big, or someone else paid him more to release them. So, if Jamila is the friend you're going hiking with, use discretion. I don't think she can afford another blow-up like that."

"Um…thank you." My face was hotter than the barrel of my curling iron. Did Mother understand my relationship with Jamila? Including the sexy parts? No wonder she was pushing me toward Daniel.

"I wish I could have gotten them all. I've always liked Jamila."

"You like her?" I held my breath. Maybe she wouldn't be furious with me for falling for Jamila.

Who was I kidding? It was one thing to like a woman; it was something else entirely to like the idea of your daughter being with her, especially in a weird friends-slash-boss-with-benefits situation.

"Of course I like her. She's practically another daughter to me. Jamila is driven the way I've always encouraged you girls to be. She reminds me of me."

There it was.

She wished brilliant, ambitious Jamila were her daughter and not aimless Natalie, drifting along on whatever breeze blew past.

"I've got to go, Mother." I shut the door and trudged down the stairs to the leased convertible.

———

WHEN WE REACHED the part where the rough trail—the one used by bobcats and, apparently, Jamila Jallow—crossed the smoother one, I bent with my hands on my knees to catch my breath.

As much as it pained me, I huffed, "Hold up!"

"What?" Jamila doubled back from where she'd already started to climb again. My new hiking boots had rubbed a blister on my heel that ruined my admiration for her shapely hamstrings and glutes in her hiking shorts.

She pulled her canteen out of her tiny hiking backpack and screwed off the lid. "Oh, yeah, great view."

Right. The view. The one I couldn't see because of the sweat dripping into my eyes. I straightened and pressed my hand into the stitch in my side. Hiking, at least with Jamila, was harder than it looked and not nearly as fashionable as I'd envisioned when I chose the cutest pair of boots at the sporting-goods store.

She'd refused to follow the flattish path that wound gradually up the mountain, the one everyone else used. No. She forged ahead, following markers, which she'd told me were the "blazes" of "trailblazing," on paths that I'd have thought only the most surefooted deer could follow. Her long legs easily scaled the rocks and exposed tree roots we used to ascend the slope. My hamstrings begged me to turn back. But Jamila would never quit until she'd scaled the mountain and beaten it into submission.

"Drink some water," she said. "We're almost there. Only another half hour or so to go."

"Half an hour?" I wheezed. Half an hour was no big deal on the treadmill. But this was more like the elliptical. An elliptical with rusty nails hammered into the pedals to prick my heels with each step.

"Hey." She put a hand on my sweaty shoulder. "You okay?"

Before today, I hadn't known my shoulders could sweat. I unclipped my fancy new canteen from my belt and took a gulp. "I'm fine."

"The view up top is amazing. It's totally worth it." Her fingertips danced over my breast to the belt of my hiking shorts.

I shivered at her touch. "I deserve more than a panoramic view if I make it to the top. What's my reward for surviving this death march?"

"Death march? It's only graded moderately strenuous."

I snorted. "For a mountain goat."

"There aren't any mountain goats in California. Only bighorn sheep."

"Fine. This path is better suited to bighorn sheep than to humans."

"Bighorns don't hang out down here. If you want to see them, you've got to climb that one." She pointed to a taller mountain in the distance.

"Maybe next time." That was a lie. If I wanted to see a sheep, I'd go to the zoo. Where the paths were flat and more conducive to handholding.

"I guess hiking's not your thing. Thanks for being a good sport, baby girl." When she tugged me tighter, I didn't care about my blisters or how red my face might be. I focused on her lips, soft and kissable.

"Maybe I need some motivation to keep going," I murmured.

"I've got some gorp in my pack." She nuzzled my temple.

"Unless that's what you call your vibrator, it's not the kind of treat I had in mind."

"On your left!" A voice called from a few yards away.

We'd heard that call from faster hikers and bikers all morning, but this voice sounded terrifyingly familiar.

Instead of burying my face in Jamila's chest like I should have done, I sprang away from her and faced the threat. My heart stopped beating when I saw my brother, Jackson, standing on the pedals of his mountain bike, trailed by his adopted son, Noah, on a similar bike.

Ho-ly crap.

"Nat?" He held up a hand to signal a stop.

"Jackson? What are you doing here?" I could hardly squeeze out the words with my heart ping-ponging in my chest. Of all the places he could be on a Saturday in May, he had to be here, on the same mountain, on the same trail as Jamila and me.

"Just riding my favorite trail," he said. "I think you're the one who should explain what *you're* doing here. Don't you normally spend Memorial Day weekend helping Mother schmooze with politicos?"

"It's my favorite trail too," Jamila said. Her voice was buttery smooth. "I invited her."

I gaped at her. With all her talk about casual and secrecy, was she really going to tell Jackson about us? My heart accelerated, and my fingertips buzzed.

"Hey, Jamila." He chuckled. "First, she comes to work for you, and now you're out together on the weekend? The PR stuff must be going well."

"Yeah," she said. "Natalie's really saved my bacon. I asked her to come with me as a thank you."

My heart thudded once as all my hopes and dreams fell—*splat* —on the dirt.

"That's fantastic. You might've liked a reward that was less strenuous, huh, Nutter Butter? Like a trip to the spa." He guffawed.

"Rude," I sniffed. "I was having a delightful time until you came along."

Turning my back to both my brother and Jamila, I limped to Noah and hugged him. Like me, he was hot and sweaty, and his helmet clanked against my head.

"Having a good time?" I asked.

"Yeah." His thirteen-year-old voice came out grumbly and gruff. He cleared his throat. "Are you?"

I glanced over my shoulder. Jamila and Jackson weren't paying attention, too focused on their own breezy conversation. "Eh."

"You should come riding with Jay and me next time. The ride up is kinda hard, but on the way down, we fly. It's so cool."

"Does Alicia know about the flying?" My sister-in-law was one of the most cautious people I knew. She and my brother epitomized opposites attract.

He squinted one eye. "We keep it on the down-low. Besides"—he rapped his helmet—"we play it safe."

Safe wasn't a word I associated with my brother. However, he'd surrounded himself with careful people like Alicia and Cooper. Jamila, though, was anything but safe. Was she telling my brother the truth? That we'd been about to lock lips when they'd come up behind us? From the way Jackson was laughing, I doubted it.

"What's so funny?" I asked testily.

"Nothing, Nutter Butter." He sauntered toward me and reached out with one of his long arms to ruffle my hair.

I leaped away. "Cut it out!" I tugged my hair elastic out and finger-combed the tangles he'd made. Then I scraped it back into a fresh ponytail and snugged it tight. When I looked up, Jamila watched me with hunger in her eyes.

Maybe we could still salvage our hike—and my reward.

"Noah says he can't wait to reach the summit," I said. "Guess you guys should get going."

"Yeah, let's go, little man." Jackson picked up his bike and straddled it. "Nat, we'll miss brunch tomorrow. I'll see you next weekend. Later, Mila." He kicked off and stood on the pedals to climb the incline. Noah did the same, and soon they disappeared around the bend.

Jamila shook her head. "That was close."

Suddenly, the energy drained out of me, and it wasn't only exhaustion from our hike. "I don't suppose you told him about us?"

She blinked her eyes wide. "About *us?*" She lowered her voice. "You mean, did I tell him I'm casually fucking his little sister?"

Her words shredded my heart like dull steak knives. I wasn't a hundred percent sure my crush had escalated into love, but my feelings toward her were anything but casual. "Well, when you put it like that—"

"Look." She stepped closer, not as close as we'd been before Jackson interrupted us, but into my personal space. With a knuckle under my chin, she lifted my head until I looked her in the eye. "This is very new. I think it's reasonable to see how things go before we go telling the world about us."

Her reasoning was…reasonable, but my feelings were not. "Jackson is one of your closest friends. Wouldn't you tell him about someone you were seeing?"

"Normally, yes. But this isn't a normal situation." She whirled around, flipped off her cap, and ran her fingers through her short hair. "You're his kid sister."

She grumbled her next words, but I understood every word.

"We shouldn't be doing this."

The knives in my heart twisted. Maybe she was right. If she didn't care enough about me to talk to my brother, we *shouldn't* be doing it.

"Come on." But instead of leading me up the mountain, she turned back down.

"We're not going to the summit?" I asked.

"Nah. You're tired. I've already pushed you too far."

She trudged down the mountain, never turning back.

23

WHEN WE STEPPED inside Jamila's house, she bent to untie her hiking boots and spoke for the first time in almost an hour. "Want to jump in the shower?"

I didn't relish the thought of sweating all over the leased Porsche on my drive back to San Francisco. Plus, we'd come back early enough that Mother might still be home when I returned, and she was the last person I wanted to see in my stormy mood.

"Sure." I toed off my boots, grabbed my overnight bag, and headed toward the guest bathroom.

She grabbed my wrist. "With me?"

"But I...I thought..." I sucked in a deep breath. "You didn't say a word on the drive back from the trail."

"I had to think. And now I'm done thinking. I want to do something else." She tugged me closer and dipped her nose toward my neck.

I pulled away. "What are we doing, Jamila? I can't be your dirty secret. I don't need a car or a paycheck from your company. What I need is someone who isn't ashamed of being with me in public or in front of my family."

"I know." She twirled the end of my ponytail around her

finger. "I'm sorry about earlier with your brother. I wasn't prepared, and I didn't know what to say."

My shoulders lowered an inch or two. "What would you say if you saw him now?"

She paused for a moment. "I'd tell him you're not a little girl in pigtails anymore." She tugged my ponytail, making my scalp tingle. "You're a grown woman. A sexy grown woman. And I'm very, very interested in you."

"Very interested? What does that mean?" My heart pounded.

"It means I want to fuck you. And keep doing it for a while."

As on board as I was with the sex, fucking for "a while" didn't satisfy my romantic heart. "A while?"

"A while. With my past partners, that didn't interest me. Look, I need some time to figure my shit out. I suck at talking about feelings. This is the best I can do right now."

Was that a plea in her eyes? They were soft and warm as melted chocolate.

I wanted to drown in them.

"I'll take it." I kissed her softly on the lips. "For now."

Her arms wrapped around me, and the kiss turned dirty. Dirty because I smelled my gross sweat.

I pulled away. "Let's get in your sexy shower. Half of that hiking trail is stuck to my face."

"I like you dirty," she said, dropping a kiss on my lips. "I also like cleaning you up. Let's go."

We left our dusty boots and socks in her laundry room, then she led me by the hand to her bathroom. It wasn't as spacious as the one in her beach house, but the shower was big enough for two. She flipped on the rainfall showerhead and turned to me. "Strip."

It was just like the dirty daydream I'd had this morning when I got dressed. I set my fingers on the neck opening of my hiking shirt and pulled apart the sides with a pop. Her lips parted. Letting a smile tease my lips, I repeated the deliberate action with each snap on my hiking shirt. Jamila's irises grew more molten with each ping of the fasteners. I shrugged out of it and let it flutter to the floor.

I'd worn my sexiest sports bra—if any sports bra can be called sexy—the one with cups that didn't hide my figure. The fasteners in the back meant I didn't have to struggle out of damp spandex. I flicked open the hooks and tossed the bra on top of my shirt. She stared at my breasts as steam rolled out of the shower around her. I unfastened the buckle of my shorts and slowly drew the zipper down.

I'd forgotten about my canteen, and its weight sank the shorts to the tile floor with a clank.

"Oops," I said, smiling mischievously.

"Oops," she echoed. "Leave it."

Finally, I shimmied out of my cotton panties. Biting my lip, I rotated so that my backside was to her and bent to pick up my clothes. "Where should I put these?"

"In the hamper." Her voice sounded strained.

I tiptoed to it across the warmed tile, then returned to stand, naked, in front of her. She reached into my hair to pull out the elastic holding my ponytail. I shook my hair out over my shoulders.

She picked up a lock to twirl it between her fingers. "I like your hair."

"I like yours too." I reached up to stroke her short, springy curls. "Can I wash it for you?"

"We'll see. I might not have the patience."

I pouted. "Will you wash mine then?"

"My curly-girl stuff might not work on your hair."

"It's okay. I can wash it again in the morning. I want your hands in my hair."

"You got it, baby girl. Now, go on in and wash yourself."

"You're not coming?"

"I want to watch you."

If she wanted to watch, I'd put on a show. Slowly, I turned and opened the shower door. I took an exaggerated step inside, which stretched my overworked quads, hamstrings, and glutes. I moved under the rainfall showerhead, turning my face up to it and running my fingers through my hair, slicking the wet strands toward the back of my head.

When I turned to peek at her, she smiled wolfishly. "Wash up, baby girl. I want you all clean when I get in there."

Grabbing her body wash, I poured some into my hand and lathered it up. I stroked it down my neck, over my shoulders, and down my arms. I rubbed down my belly and my legs while she watched. "Come do my back?" I asked.

"In a minute. You haven't done your breasts yet. Or between your legs."

"I was hoping you'd take care of that." I flashed her my most seductive smile.

"I want to watch you do it."

I tingled with anticipation. I cupped my breasts and squeezed, thumbing over the nipples.

"Slow down," she said. "We've got all afternoon. Don't forget the handheld."

"The handheld?" I spotted it on the wall. Lifting it from its cradle, I switched it on. "Cold!" I squealed as icy droplets hit my skin.

She chuckled. "It'll warm up."

After a few seconds, it did. I thumbed my nipple with one hand while I directed the shower wand between my legs. It was nice, but—"Does this have a massage setting?"

When her hand closed over mine, my eyes flew open. Water glistened on her naked skin.

"Want something done right, gotta do it myself," she muttered. But she didn't bother repressing her smile.

She flicked the button on the shower wand and it pulsed the way I needed it, a pattern of pressure that felt like a hand between my thighs. She directed it onto my lips, which plumped and opened while my core tightened. My breaths sawed in my chest the same way they'd done on the mountain. Now that I had both hands free, I worked my nipples, gasping at the sensation.

Keeping the spray pointed at my pussy, she explored me with her hand, tapping my clit until I moaned.

"That's it, baby girl. Give it to me." She tapped faster, rocketing the sensation to my core.

And I did.

I couldn't refuse anything she asked of me. My orgasm gripped me like a fist, wringing the pleasure out of me in waves. As I came down, my knees weakened, but Jamila caught me with an arm around my waist.

"I've got you, baby," she crooned in my ear.

Groaning something even I couldn't understand, I slipped my arms around her waist and rested my cheek against her shoulder. I felt safe in her embrace as the warm water rained down over us. The shower was my cocoon, and I never wanted to leave it.

"Can you stand?" she asked at last.

"Yeah."

She eased her arm from around my waist, and my legs supported me. "Turn around. I'll wash your hair."

Her fingertips against my scalp made me feel both boneless and weightless. It was exactly the care I needed after that hike up the mountain and the crushing encounter with my brother. She wrung out my hair and reached for the conditioner. She rubbed a dollop into her own hair, raking her fingers through her tight curls.

With her arms raised, her breasts were too tempting to resist. I palmed them both and licked one nipple. Her hand landed on the back of my head and held me there.

"Yeah, baby. Like that."

I tunneled my other hand between her legs, gently caressing, then tapping her swollen clit like she'd done to me. Her breath hitched.

I sucked her nipple into my mouth, latching on and flicking it with my tongue. She shuddered and held me tighter.

"Don't stop."

I didn't. I tapped harder, then softer, testing out the pressure until she bucked her hips against my hand, grinding against my palm. After a few more seconds, she stilled, groaning.

With one last lick, I released her breast and kissed up to her neck. I never wanted my mouth to leave her skin. How long could we stay here in the heaven of her shower?

She bent to capture my lips, a satisfying mess of a kiss with the water pouring over us. With both hands pressed to my back, she held me close. When she released my lips, she muttered, "God-damn," and shook her head.

"What?"

"Just…that was good. Who knew the little princess would be such a firecracker in bed?"

"You mean, in the shower."

"I mean, wherever I want you, baby girl."

I shivered even under the warm spray.

"Let's get out before we get pruny." She turned off the shower and wrapped me in one of her fluffy towels.

We dried off and then used her jasmine-scented lotion to moisturize. She clucked her tongue at the blisters on my heels and found a couple of bandages for them, which she insisted on applying while kneeling behind me.

When we tumbled into her enormous bed together, clean and exhausted, I was completely satisfied. And cautiously happy.

I traced a circle around her belly button. "So you'll talk to my brother about us?"

"Is that what you want? To tell him right now?"

"Well, not *now* now." I dipped my tongue into the divot. "There are other things I'd rather do now." I kissed a line down her stomach and paused at her pubic bone. "I don't want to keep us a secret. I don't want to sneak around."

"Sure, with Jackson, but I'm not going to tell Audrey. That woman is terrifying."

"I'll take care of Mother. After you've told Jackson and he agrees to back me up."

"Admit it. She terrifies you too."

"She's my mother. I'm not scared of her. Though I hate it when she's angry with me."

"We'll still need to keep it on the down-low at work. I don't need another scandal."

Wincing, I rested my chin on her hipbone. "News flash: everyone at work knows."

"Shit! Really?"

"Yeah. Winslow and Hannah for sure. I suspect Felicia and Rhiannon too."

"Fuck me." She rolled her eyes up to the ceiling. "I was hoping to maintain a little professionalism."

"We'll stay professional at work. We'll keep up boundaries there. As long as I can cross them at home." I brushed across her nipple with my thumb, and she shivered.

"That works for me," she said, her voice husky.

"But you'll talk to Jackson?"

"Yeah, I'll text him right now." She reached for her phone.

"Not now." I batted away her phone. "Can't you see I'm trying to sex you up?"

"Then get on with it, princess. Less talking, more eating me out." She slid down to give me better access.

"My pleasure."

24

THE NEXT MORNING, I woke to the scent of coffee. When I opened my eyes, Jamila sat on the edge of the bed holding a mug in front of my face.

"Get up. I'm taking you to breakfast."

I sat up and took the mug from her. She'd made it how I liked it: sweet and lightened with oat milk. I savored the first heavenly sip. Then I remembered what day it was.

"It's Sunday. My mother's expecting me at brunch today."

She winced. "I forgot. Do you have to go?"

"You could go with me," I said, my heart in my throat.

She traced my collarbone with her fingertip. "I don't think I'm ready for brunch with Audrey. Not while we're still figuring this out. And not until I've talked to Jackson."

"You heard him yesterday. He won't be there."

"Right, but I don't think I could sit there at your mother's table and eat brunch like I don't want to hoist my girl into my lap."

"So I'm your girl now?" My heart thudded like I was in spin class after drinking a double espresso.

She pretended to look around the bedroom. "I don't see anyone else here."

Gently, I shoved her shoulder. "You know what I mean."

"I'm new at this, okay? I'm not sure what it's supposed to feel like. But when I woke up this morning with you sleeping beside me, my first thought wasn't, 'How do I get this bitch out of my house so I can get some work done?' So I guess that means you're my girl."

I fluttered my eyelashes. "You know just what to say to make a woman happy."

"*Now* I'm wondering how to get you out of my house."

"You are not." I leaned forward. "You like me." I kissed her, a soft brush of our lips.

"Maybe I do." She spun a wayward lock of my hair around her finger.

"Okay. I'll text my mother that I've changed my plans." Spending more time with Jamila like this, in our happy bubble, was worth risking my mother's disappointment.

"You will?" She leaned forward and laid a lingering kiss on my lips.

"Yeah. Since it's a holiday weekend, we can come back here after and hang out?"

"You got it. We'll chill with Quill."

"Or..." I snuggled into the warm sheets. "We could skip breakfast and stay in bed."

"Nope. Get up. My girl likes to eat breakfast. The place we're going gets crowded if you get there too late."

"Fine. I'll need a minute to do my hair though."

"Only a minute. You know I don't care about all that."

That was a lie. I knew Jamila cared about appearances. I was glad I packed a dress. When I walked into the kitchen half an hour later, she whistled.

"You like it?" I twirled, letting the skirt flare out around my thighs.

"I do. Though I might be tempted to ruck it up at the restaurant."

"At breakfast? You wouldn't!" Though the thought of her

touching me in public—heck, the thought of being Jamila Jallow's girlfriend in public—made my heart race.

"Nah. I wouldn't. But all bets are off on the drive home." She tugged on my braid. I'd made a long one down my back as an ironic callback to what she'd said about pigtails yesterday. "I also can't guarantee I won't pull on this while I finger you."

"Yes, please," I said, my voice breathy.

"Let's get going, then."

The drive was longer than I expected, almost all the way to San Francisco. Jamila parked near a standalone building in the parking lot of a strip mall in the south suburbs.

"Must be a five-star breakfast to be worth this drive," I said.

"Cooper recommended it. Nothing but the best for my girl." She leaned over and kissed my temple. At the mention of Cooper's name, the coffee from earlier burned in my empty belly. My friendship with Jamila wasn't as strong as hers with Cooper. Would we survive an awkward breakup?

"What's the matter?" Jamila asked, tipping up my chin.

I gazed into her eyes, soft with concern. Why was I worried? Except for one tiny mistake, I'd turned around her public image. She couldn't stop calling me her girl, and that was half a step away from calling me her girlfriend. We had fabulous sex on two consecutive weekends. And now she was taking me out in public like I'd asked. Like a girlfriend.

"Nothing. All good." I pecked her lips. "I'm going to order the biggest stack of blueberry pancakes they'll give me." A glance in the window showed tables nestled close together, the waitstaff bustling between them with pots of coffee and trays of food.

She chuckled. I followed her inside the restaurant where I inhaled the scents of butter, coffee, and syrup. My stomach growled.

She'd been right about the crowd. People sat on benches lining the small lobby, and the hostess had two or three grease pencils sticking out of her bun. Smiling at the curly-haired man in front of her, she pulled out one of her pencils and made a note on the seating chart.

Focused on the chalkboard listing the daily specials, I bumped into Jamila's back when she stopped short.

"What's wr—" But I saw what was wrong. As if we'd conjured him by saying his name, Cooper Fallon stood beside the man at the hostess's stand. The dark-haired man was his boyfriend, Ben. And standing next to them were my brother and his wife.

"Crap," I muttered.

But it was too late to turn back. They'd spotted us, thanks to Jamila's unmistakable height.

"Mila!" Cooper called. My stomach burned again at the nickname. She hadn't asked me to call her that. I hadn't been brave enough to try it, not yet. It was another proof of where I stood in the hierarchy of Jamila's affections.

Dropping my hand, she shuffled around the other patrons toward them. I followed in her wake.

"Can we squeeze in another chair?" Cooper asked the hostess, who held a fistful of menus.

"Two, babe," Ben said.

"What?" At last, Cooper spotted me. "Natalie! What a surprise. Of course." To the hostess, he said, "Can you make it six?"

As the hostess grabbed more menus, Jackson hugged me. "What are you doing here?"

I glanced at Jamila. From the shock on her face, I could tell she wasn't prepared to talk to my brother about us. Still, she was the most confident woman I knew, so I hoped she'd follow through on her promise and find a way to tell him we were together. She'd make him think it was the best idea he'd ever heard. Then when I told Mother I was dating a woman and would never, ever marry Daniel van der Poel, he'd stand beside me and support me.

I gave her my most encouraging smile and brushed her hand with my fingertips. *We can do this.*

She flinched at my touch and crossed her arms. "We're having a working breakfast."

My skin went cold like someone had turned on the fire sprinklers.

"Working on a holiday weekend? You are a taskmaster," Jackson said. "Or maybe the taskmaster is Nat." He knuckled my head, messing up my French braid.

I slapped his hand away. "Stop it."

"Just showing you some brotherly affection."

"Well, stop. I don't like it."

His eyes went wide. "You don't?"

"I'm not twelve anymore."

"Right. Sorry." He held up his hands.

I tried to tuck my hair back into the plait, but it was hopeless without a mirror. Giving up, I hugged Alicia. "Good morning. Feeling okay?"

"Yeah." She rubbed her slight baby bump. "We'll feel better once I've consumed some carbs."

Jackson slid an arm around her waist. "We'll get you some saltines in a minute."

She smiled, love pouring out of her blue eyes. "Thanks."

I glanced at Jamila, but she'd set her jaw just like yesterday after we'd met Jackson and Noah on the trail. Her eyes held a hard glint like smoky quartz. Cooper tugged Jamila away, and with a hand on her back, followed the hostess into the restaurant. I trailed behind my brother and his wife.

The round table would've been perfect for four but was tight with six. I squeezed between Cooper and Jamila. My brother sat across the table from me.

"So. What are you guys doing way out here?" I patted my sweaty temple with my napkin. They all belonged in north San Francisco, not the south suburbs.

Ben leaned forward. "We found this place on a weekend trip down to the beach. Their pancakes are to die for. And this guy likes their egg white omelet even though egg whites suck all the joy from breakfast." He elbowed his fiancé. "So now, whenever we have time, we come down here. Plus Cooper and Jackson had some best man stuff to talk about."

"Best man stuff?" My brother asked. "Does this mean you're asking *me* to be your best man? What about Mateo?"

Cooper shot his fiancé a narrow-eyed stare. Ben rolled his eyes.

"Yes." Cooper cleared his throat aggressively. "Will you be my best man? Mateo is in the wedding party, but I-I want my best friend standing next to me."

"Coop!" Jackson's voice cracked, and his eyes glittered. "I'd be honored."

"Aw." Ben clasped his hands under his chin. "You guys are too cute. Now that that's settled"—he picked up his menu—"I'm stuffing my face with carbs."

I glanced at Jamila. How did she feel being left out of this bromance? From the way she stared down at her menu, not great.

"Mila, I"—Cooper cleared his throat again—"I was going to take you out, too, but since you're here, would you also stand up for me?"

She grinned at him, all traces of her earlier stoniness gone. "Of course. Y'all are still planning it on the island in the fall?"

"Oh my god, it's going to be gorgeous," Ben said. "There'll be a chuppah on the beach, and Cooper found us a rabbi on the island. And then dinner and dancing in the restaurant. We've got the whole resort to ourselves."

"I don't remember agreeing to dancing," Cooper grumbled.

While they argued about whether or not Cooper would be required to dance in public, I stole a glance at Jamila. She watched them argue, a bemused look on her face.

"Hey." I touched her thigh under the table, and she startled. "Are you okay?"

"Of course," she muttered. "I'm just surprised, is all. It's been a weird morning."

We hadn't expected to meet her besties. But I didn't love that she'd called the morning weird. Earlier, she'd called me her girl. She'd taken me out to breakfast. But now she felt far away, and despite the contact of our knees under the table, she'd erected a wall between us.

By the time the waiter came to take our order, I'd lost my appetite.

But Jamila hadn't. She flashed her biggest grin at the waiter, whose cleft chin reminded me of Hayden Christensen from *Star Wars*. It would've been a lot for anyone, but the full force of Jamila's flirting—because that's exactly what it looked like—was too much for him. He blushed, dropped his pencil, and skipped over me entirely when he took our order. Ben had to grab the waiter's sleeve to pull him back to hear my clipped request for a short blueberry stack.

As the others talked and sipped their coffee, I felt trapped in an invisible cage like a mime down on the Embarcadero. Jamila drove the conversation toward business. She asked Alicia about her company and her plans to hire another consultant to cover her maternity leave. She talked stock prices with Jackson and Cooper. Jamila even asked Ben about his work for a local foundation and whether he thought charitable giving would increase as the country emerged from the recession.

She said not one word to me.

But I laughed at her jokes. I picked at my pancakes, and I hid all the hurt behind a vacant smile. I knew my role. My family taught me well.

Jamila was here with her peers, her friends. I was the dorky little sister, too uninteresting to invite to the conversation. As long as I remained silent, they wouldn't notice I was there and send me off to play with my dolls.

Maybe that's what Jamila meant when she called me her girl. I was a plaything, something she'd pick up when she thought about it, then toss aside when she was no longer in the mood.

I'd been a fool to think we could be more.

While they lingered over coffee, I ordered a rideshare. This close to the city, it didn't take long.

As it arrived, I stood. "Thanks for breakfast." I didn't say it to anyone in particular, sure one of the billionaires would pick up the tab. "I'm heading home."

"What?" Jamila finally met my gaze, and I knew she saw my pain when her eyes crinkled at the corners. "You're leaving?"

"Yeah. I'll see you at work on Tuesday."

She scraped back her chair. Glancing around the table at her friends, she said, "I'll be right back."

Jamila followed me outside to where a sickly green Toyota Prius idled. She grabbed my arm. "What are you doing? I'll drive you back to my place. Or yours if that's what you want. I thought we were spending the weekend together."

I shielded my eyes against the sun behind her. "I thought so too. I guess I was wrong." *Wrong about how you feel about me,* I didn't add.

"I don't understand. We were having fun."

"You said you'd tell Jackson about us."

"You expect me to tell him in front of my mentee, my best friend, and his fiancé that I'm fucking his little sister? How the hell do you think that'd go?"

"I don't know since you didn't even try!" I cursed the waver in my voice.

"Look, I can't. Not right now. I need his support and Cooper's. I need my family. Once this media mess dies down and we launch the new app—"

"Then you'll have another excuse." I took a deep breath. "I need a minute to think. Okay?"

She opened her mouth to say something, then closed it. She pressed her lips together for a long moment, her gaze hopping between my eyes like she'd find the answer in one of them. Finally, she said, "You're coming back to the office on Tuesday?"

"Yeah."

She squeezed my shoulder. "Thanks. I need you, you know."

My rational brain knew how much effort it took for her to say that. Yet it wasn't enough.

"Okay," I said.

I got into the Prius. This one smelled like patchouli. I blamed my tears on that.

25

I ARRIVED home a few minutes after eleven, which was when Mother served Sunday brunch. I wasn't hungry, and I wasn't dressed for brunch. Even so, they'd expect me to make an appearance.

Throwing back my shoulders, I strode toward the dining room but stopped when I heard a laugh from the den. I turned toward the sound and found Sam and Charles sitting on the floor, sorting through puzzle pieces on the coffee table. Bilbo Baggins snored under the table.

"Hi," I said, checking the time on my phone. "What's going on?"

Charles looked up, smiling. "Since it was just the three of us, we decided not to do a big brunch. There's still coffee if you'd like some."

"Where's Mother?"

"I brought her coffee and toast in bed. The representative's picnic yesterday took a lot out of her. I thought she could use the rest. Did you want to see her?"

"No, thanks." I dropped my purse on the floor and approached them to peer at the puzzle. They were still finding the edge pieces. "I'll wait until she's up."

"Then join us." He patted the Aubusson next to him, and I settled in. It reminded me of rainy days when I was a preteen, when Charles and I used to do puzzles together. Sam rarely joined us, always working on a computer program or homework.

I pulled some light-blue pieces toward me. It might be a landscape with a blue sky. I'd always done the boring parts of the puzzle, leaving the more interesting sections—flowers, signs, collections of toys, or antiques—for Charles. I didn't want him to get bored and wander off like my siblings did. He never had.

Sam slid a blue piece to me, a question in her eyes.

Charles voiced it. "We weren't expecting you back so soon. You said you'd be gone for the long weekend."

"Yeah. Those plans didn't work out." I tried two pieces together, but they didn't fit.

"I'm sorry." He rubbed my back, and I leaned into him the way I used to do when I was younger.

My older siblings had more memories of our biological father than I did. I had flashes of Jasper Jones: the scent of his aftershave as he brushed out my hair or the monitor lighting his face in blue when I tiptoed into his office late at night after I'd had a nightmare. He was always up working, one of those sweet energy drinks I wasn't allowed to have on his desk. He'd get me a glass of water and let me sit on his lap, his arms bracketing me as he typed.

Charles had been more of a father to me. He was on time for dinner every night, in the front row at the choir concert, holding my hand at Mother's parties until I was old enough to follow her example and flit around on my own. He'd been a rock-solid presence in my life since I was ten. But before he was my stepfather, he'd been a single guy. Maybe he'd know something about my predicament.

"Did you ever date anyone in secret?" I twirled a piece in my fingers.

"Me?" Sam asked. "No. My college dating experience was such a disaster I gave up on it entirely."

I winced. I hadn't meant to bring up her sextortion scandal. Mother hadn't been kind about it.

"But you're with Niall now," I said.

"True, but I fell for him while we were still on that awful tour together. We didn't date until we were already committed to each other."

"What about you, Charles? Any secret dates?" Surely, I wasn't alone in this.

"Nah. Sneaking around isn't for me. Your mother wanted to keep our relationship quiet because it started less than a year after your father passed, but I couldn't be in the same room as her and not want to stake my claim. So I proposed instead."

I leaned away from him so I could get a good look at his smiling face. "Wait, when?"

"About three months after I met her. I was leading the team working out your father's estate, and I fell in love the first time I saw her."

"You did not! How did I not know about this?"

He shrugged. "You were working through your grief. You didn't notice much else."

"I guess not." I didn't remember a lot from that time. It was probably for the best. "But would you have dated her in secret if she'd insisted?"

"I suppose. I'd have done anything for her." He shrugged. "Still would."

That was exactly how I felt about Jamila. I walked away this morning, but I'd go back. She had her own suite of rooms in my heart. I couldn't imagine ever being strong enough to evict her.

"Is that what Jamila's asking you to do?" Sam asked, sliding another blue piece toward me.

My heart stopped in my chest, and I shot a look at Charles. "What happened to sister code?"

"What's sister code?" she asked.

Charles looked not at all shocked. "A secret relationship is a big thing for Jamila to ask of you. Though I understand, especially after those photos."

Of course he knew about the photos. Mother would have told him. Did she also know about our relationship?

She couldn't. If she did, she'd have set me up on dates with a slate of eligible bachelors.

"Please don't tell Mother?"

He pressed his lips together. "You should tell her yourself."

"It might not last long enough to be worth disappointing her. What should I do? I should refuse, right?" Bilbo stood under the coffee table and stretched, then scratched at my ankle.

"Can you?" Charles asked.

Slumping, I allowed Bilbo to crawl into my lap. He curled up in the hammock of my skirt. "I don't think so."

"Then you'll have to figure out a way to get to a place where you aren't dating in secret. What are the barriers to dating publicly?"

I set aside the obvious one, Mother. "She doesn't want anything to disrupt this deal with First Arbiter. No more scandals."

"And you're helping her with that," Charles said, logical as ever. "You're keeping the other disruptions out of the media for her."

"I guess. It doesn't seem like enough." I stroked Bilbo's silky fur and didn't care that his black hairs stuck to my skirt.

"It's not like you can make the development go faster," he said. "Those things take time."

"Especially with the problems they've been having," I said.

"Problems with the development?" Sam set down the piece she'd been examining. "Jamila has the best team in Silicon Valley."

"Well, they're struggling on this," I said. "Bugs in their code."

She frowned. "That doesn't sound right."

My sister was the smartest person in computer science I knew, even smarter than Jackson. "Remember how she thought someone was selling company secrets to the competition? I, uh, I tried to dig into that but failed." Rhiannon haunted my nightmares, her face lit up in Mateo's headlights. "I still suspect someone is working against her."

"If you could figure that out and remove the saboteur," Charles said, "she could get her product to market faster. Then you wouldn't have to be a secret. What are the clues?"

I tried another two pieces together, but they didn't fit, either. "I wish I were as smart as the detectives in your police procedurals. I haven't found any clues, at least nothing substantial." Just that photo of Pavel Thakor and what might or might not have been Winslow's garish pants.

"You're plenty smart. Sometimes the detectives have to do a little digging to turn up those clues."

He was right. It was like poking a cake with a toothpick to see if it was cooked in the center. Bribing Rhiannon hadn't been the best move, but I knew something wasn't right with Moo-Lah. I wouldn't try to bribe Pavel Thakor. A billionaire like him wouldn't be tempted by cash. However, I could talk to him. Surely, there'd be no harm in that.

"Thanks, Charles. I'll give it a try."

Sam slid another blue piece across the table, and I clicked it into the piece I'd been trying to match.

They fit together perfectly.

26

I HADN'T ANSWERED her texts on Memorial Day. Instead, I'd succumbed to my guilt from blowing off the congressman's picnic and Mother's Sunday brunch by asking Telma to teach me how to make an omelet. When we'd finished, mine weren't as gorgeous as hers, but they didn't crack down the middle and the filling stayed (mostly) inside.

I sent Telma home early, promising to have the kitchen spotless by the time she returned to work on Tuesday morning. Then I served a holiday brunch to my parents and Sam.

Sam didn't attach a lot of emotion or attention to food, but she dutifully ate her omelet and shared some egg and vegetables, but no cheese, with Bilbo. Charles pronounced his omelet delicious and praised my work. Mother pursed her lips but said nothing about culinary school or my future.

After cleaning the kitchen, I scanned social media and found something that pushed my heart up into my throat.

I'd followed Pavel Thakor's entire leadership team on social media. On Sunday afternoon, one of the fools posted a photo and tagged the location as a golf course in Cabo San Lucas. The caption read, *Best #leadershipretreat ever,* and a foursome huddled together, longnecks in hand, in front of a towering palm tree. Standing next to Moo-Lah's CEO, his nose pink from the sun, was Winslow Keating-Ashworth.

My mother had drilled into me that ladies didn't swear, but I let a few choice words fly when I saw it. Then I made a plan.

———

TUESDAY MORNING while I dressed for work, I responded to Jamila's text.

> I'll be in a little late, but I'm on my way

Instead of taking an Uber to Jamilow, I asked the driver to drop me off at Moo-Lah's building, which was just down the road. But as our dot approached the destination on the map, I started to second-guess myself. My last plan, the one where I'd tried to entrap Rhiannon, hadn't worked out so well.

I looked down at my lavender jacket and purple plaid Prada skirt. It had looked stylish and authoritative this morning, almost like something Jamila would wear to one of her power meetings. Now it looked like what a socialite would wear to a garden party. No one would take me seriously.

"A hundred bucks for your sunglasses," I said to the driver. They looked more unrelenting than my oversized, pink-tinted ones.

"A hundred bucks?" He snorted. "They're Maui Jims."

"Five hundred, and throw in that scarf." I pointed to the gray paisley fabric draped over the front seat.

After I'd Moo-Lahed him the cash, I got out of the car and shook out the scarf. I took a cautious sniff. It smelled like cardboard pine tree air freshener and leather seats. I set it over my hair and wound it around my neck Grace Kelly–style. Sliding on the dark-tinted aviators, I checked my reflection in the front window of the Moo-Lah building. All right, I could be any age.

I pushed through the revolving door and marched to the front desk. Roughening my voice, I said, "Audrey Jones to see Mr. Thakor."

The security guard raised her eyebrows doubtfully. "Do you have an appointment?"

"Of course I do. Do you think I'd waste my time coming all the way out here if I didn't?" I set my hands on my hips in a power pose. "Announce me, please."

She narrowed her eyes but picked up her handset and spoke to someone. I held my breath. Would my mother's name inspire enough fear to admit me to the executive floor?

"They say you're not on his calendar, but if I can verify your ID, I'm supposed to let you upstairs."

ID? Nuts! I thought about lying and saying I'd left it in the car, but maybe I could bluff my way over this hurdle. I slid my license out of my wallet and passed it over.

"This says Natalie Jones." She eyed it.

"I go by my middle name, Audrey. It's right there." I held my breath, hoping she didn't know my mother had taken Charles's name when they'd married and was actually a Hayes, not a Jones.

"All right, Ms. Jones."

It was all I could do not to dance as she inserted my license into a scanner, then handed it back to me along with a visitor badge.

"Elevators are that way." She pointed. "Fourth floor."

I slipped the lanyard around my neck. "Thank you." I lifted my chin and glided to the elevator, which I entered with a clump of casually dressed Moo-Lah employees.

As I rode up, I surreptitiously checked myself in the mirrored wall. Wow, I did look a little like my mother. I curled my upper lip in a superior expression. Perfect.

I got out on the fourth floor, where a receptionist's desk barred my way to the executive offices beyond. Moo-Lah's space felt more closed-in than Jamilow's. Its solid office fronts blocked the natural light, and LED lighting hummed.

I drew myself up again. "Audrey Jones to see Mr. Thakor."

When the receptionist stood, I noticed his hands trembled. "Of course, Mrs. Jones. Right this way."

How easy was this? If my PR career didn't work out, I could get a job as a corporate spy.

The receptionist handed me off to an administrative assistant, who immediately picked up her handset. "Mrs. Jones is here," she said. She listened for a moment, then waved at a forbidding-looking wooden door. "Go right in."

I set my hand on the cool handle and pushed inside. The office was your typical masculine seat of power with dark wood furniture, a thick hunting-design Kashmiri carpet, and an enormous window overlooking a stand of pine trees and the distant Santa Cruz Mountains.

Gray strands sparkled at the crown of Pavel Thakor's thick, black hair as he sat behind his massive desk. He looked up from his papers when I crossed the expanse of thick carpet.

"You're not Audrey Jones," he said, his lips turning down. He lifted the handset of his phone.

"I'm her daughter, Natalie." I stood tall, trying not to think of what Mother would say if Thakor called her and told her what I'd done. "I need to talk to you."

He set down the handset, but his stony jaw told me I had seconds to ask my questions.

I pulled out my phone and unlocked the screen. I turned it to face him. "Why were you golfing with Winslow Keating-Ashworth in Cabo San Lucas?"

His lips thinned. "Happenstance. We ran into each other at the resort and played a friendly round of golf."

I flipped to the next photo. "And this is you with Winslow too."

"That picture doesn't show Mr. Keating-Ashworth."

"Those are his shoes behind you. I'm sure of it."

"What are you implying, Miss Jones? Silicon Valley is a small place. Everyone knows everyone. We're friendly here." He spread his hands like he had nothing to hide.

Slipping my phone into my purse, I planted my hands on my hips. "I think you're a little too friendly with Winslow. I think you've been stealing secrets."

He rose from his chair, taller than I remembered from my mother's parties. "That's a serious allegation, Miss Jones."

I straightened. "Corporate espionage is serious business."

"Fortunately, it's not a business I engage in." He lifted the phone handset. "Get me security," he snapped. "I need Miss Jones escorted out. Now."

I planted my heels in the carpet. "Those photos are proof, and they're on social media."

"Those photos prove nothing. You have zero evidence. You've come to my office with baseless accusations. Say anything to the media, and my lawyers will come down on you with shock and awe."

"I'm not afraid." I tried to sell the lie with another imperial lift of my chin.

"You should be. I'm calling your mother."

I barely kept myself from wincing. "She'll back me up."

She wouldn't. I'd be in so much trouble when she found out. He was right about my lack of evidence. Why hadn't I learned from my mistake with Rhiannon?

Winslow was the leak. I'd find proof somehow. He had to have left a trail.

There was a knock, and a security guard opened the door. It wasn't the woman I'd spoken with downstairs, but a big, beefy guy with biceps bursting out of his black Moo-Lah golf shirt.

"I'll find that evidence," I said, "and then we'll see who's escorted out of this building."

Thakor only laughed. "Don't enter my property again."

Even though he was twice my size, the security guard kept a tight grip on my arm as he marched me out of the building. A taxi waited for me, and the guard stood at the curb, arms crossed, until it had driven me out of sight of the building.

I scrunched down in the back seat. In hindsight, going in without actual proof was a mistake. But I'd find some. Next time, I'd have a better plan.

————

I WAS GOING over the crisis communication binder with Hannah that afternoon when someone—okay, let's face it, it was probably me—lit a match to my career in PR.

Felicia knocked on the open door, her expression grim. "Jamila's office."

I shut my laptop and grabbed a notepad and pen. "Let's go, Hannah."

"Just you, Natalie. You won't need that." Felicia nodded at the notepad.

"Oh?" Maybe it was a personal meeting. Jamila's text had implied she wanted to see me, but we hadn't spoken since I'd walked out of brunch on Sunday. We should talk about that. I remembered Charles's advice. I needed to stand up for what I wanted. Unless Jamila wasn't ready to go public. She might insist we dial things back. Though two o'clock on a Monday was an odd time to discuss our personal relationship in her office.

I swallowed, but the lump in my throat remained. As I followed Felicia to Jamila's office, my heart went wild in my chest.

When I walked in, I knew Jamila hadn't called me in to talk about our relationship. Because she wasn't alone.

A ball of dread formed right behind my ribs. Winslow Keating-Ashworth, his nose and cheeks sunburned, sat across the desk from her. His scowl told me he knew what I'd done that morning.

I glanced at Jamila. Her face was stone. Her eyes glittered not with fun and affection the way they had on Saturday when we'd set out on that hike. They sparkled with fiery anger.

"What the fuck, Natalie?" Her voice was taut as a tripwire.

I remained silent. How much did they know?

Winslow filled the silence. "We know about your little field trip this morning. I received a copy of Moo-Lah's visitor log. You signed in as Audrey Jones, but that's a scan of your driver's license."

I stole another look at Jamila. I wished I'd come back with a shred of proof to show that I'd been justified in bluffing my way into Thakor's office.

"Do you have nothing to say for yourself?" Winslow stood. "How long have you been selling Jamilow's secrets to Moo-Lah? What did you give them today, the product specs?"

It took me a second to catch up. "Wait, what? You're accusing me of being the leak? I wasn't around when the leak started! I don't have the product specs."

"Who says it's a single mole?" He stepped closer. "You saw an opportunity to make some cash after you and Jamila broke up." I gasped and looked back at Jamila. Her hands were flat and tense on her desk like she was holding on for her life.

"But I…but…I went there to accuse you! You're the leak!"

"Me?" He put a hand to his chest. *"I'm* the leak? I've been Jamila's right hand for fifteen years. She trusts me implicitly. I have too much invested in this company to have any motivation to damage it."

Motivation! I hadn't thought of that. Not for Winslow. Why would he want to hurt Jamila or her company? A lot of his wealth had to be tied up in stock options and such. I'd leaped to another half-baked conclusion.

Still, there was the matter of the photos.

"Where were you last week, Winslow?"

"I went to visit my grandmother."

"Where?" I persisted.

"In Mexico. She was vacationing there when she fell ill. But we're talking about you now."

"Pavel Thakor was in Mexico! You guys golfed together!"

He crossed his arms. "We ran into each other one day on the golf course. And?"

"And…and you…" But I couldn't bring up the other photo. I knew those were Winslow's feet in the picture, but no one else could see it. My credibility was already hanging by a thread.

"Speaking of photos," he said, "how odd was it that none of the ones of the two of you on the beach showed *your* face? It's almost like someone deliberately avoided identifying you. Yet, it set up Jamila for another fall."

"Deliberately?" I sputtered. "I didn't even know where we were going that day!"

Jamila's face had gone still, like a mask. There was no smile, no sparkle. Nothing but pain reinforced by impenetrable steel.

Finally, she spoke. "I can't believe you'd try to hurt me by selling secrets to Moo-Lah."

"I'd never do that."

"Thakor says otherwise."

"What?"

Winslow stepped between me and the desk like he wanted to shield Jamila. "Thakor's email said you offered him details about our launch."

"But I—no. I didn't. I don't know why he said that. I accused—"

"That's sad, Natalie." He shook his head. "You should know better. Here's a tip: keep your personal life separate from work. Then your feelings won't impact your job."

"Leave your laptop in your—the office," Jamila said, her voice hollow. "Felicia has your final paycheck."

"What? You're firing me?" Anger blazed up. I hadn't done what they said. I'd made a mistake by breezing into Moo-Lah without proof, but people didn't get fired for mistakes like that. Did they?

Winslow snorted. "You're surprised?"

"You can't—" But I didn't finish my sentence. It appeared they could fire me even if I was a Jones. No need to quit this time.

Winslow drove it home. "We can and we have. If you try to approach another competitor, we'll get our lawyers involved. I don't think you'd enjoy the accommodations at the Dublin minimum-security federal prison."

Bees buzzed in my brain. Jamila knew I wouldn't do what Winslow accused me of. I stared at her, hard, like I could make her look up from her desk. But she didn't.

That's when Bruno, who'd beamed at me and said, "Good morning, Miss Natalie," a few hours ago, opened the door.

Bruno watched, arms folded, while I gave Hannah the password to my laptop. He didn't allow me time to answer her questions about why this was happening or what she should do next.

"You've got this," I said. "I have faith in you and the binder."

He trailed me to Felicia's desk. Frowning, she held out an envelope. I ignored it. Instead, I reached into my purse and pulled out my keyring. Sighing at the inevitable damage to my manicure, I worked the Porsche's fob from the loop, wincing when my thumbnail tore right against the quick.

I held out the key. "Can you give Jamila this?"

She took it from me. Grudgingly, she said, "Need a bandage?"

I glanced down at my thumb where a spot of blood welled.

"No, thanks." I wouldn't take another thing from Jamila, not even a bandage. Not when, after all we'd shared, she didn't trust me. I popped my thumb into my mouth to soothe the wound.

For the second time in a day, a security guard escorted me out of a Silicon Valley office building.

Today's Uber back to the city was the worst yet.

"Sorry about the smell," the driver yelled over the wind whipping through the car. "Last passenger had food poisoning."

27

HANNAH CALLED three times in a row before I finally picked up.

"You know I don't work there anymore, right?" I leaned against the outside wall of the boutique on Sacramento Street.

"I'm calling to check on you. As your friend, not your employee." I could almost see Hannah's eyes roll.

Guilt seized my stomach. "Sorry."

"I'm in front of your house, but you're not here."

"You didn't have to go all the way there." It was rush hour, and traffic crawled on the street in front of me. Someone laid on the horn.

"That's what friends do. Where are you?"

"Shopping on Sacramento Street." I looked down at my empty hand and flicked the bandage that still covered my raw thumbnail a week after I'd torn it on the key fob. I'd spent all afternoon browsing the shops, but nothing held my interest.

"Ah. Retail therapy."

"I guess." Maybe I should try some real therapy.

"How...how are things at the office?" I asked. "You're still there, right?" A pang zipped through my heart. I'd hired Hannah. Had they tossed her out along with my files?

"Yeah. They need me. Jamila's been at it again."

"At what?"

A silver Lexus pulled up at the curb. It wasn't a convertible, but the window lowered, and Hannah ducked her head. "Get in, loser. We're going for ice cream."

I crossed the sidewalk and leaned in to look inside. "Did you just *Mean Girls* me?"

She snickered. "I've always wanted to do that."

I buckled my seatbelt as she pulled away from the curb. "What did you mean, 'Jamila's been at it again'?"

"You weren't watching?"

I picked at my bandage. "No. I turned off my notifications."

"Oh, boy. There was another development disaster. Someone lost a bunch of code. They had to push out the launch."

"No! It was supposed to launch on Friday!"

"Yeah, not happening. First Arbiter got so frustrated they killed the deal, so Jamilow only has half a product."

"That's not fair!" Jamila must have been devastated at all that hard work down the drain.

Hannah turned onto a street with less traffic. "That's not even the worst of it. Turns out, they'd been playing both sides. FA had a deal with Moo-Lah on the side."

"They can't do that! Wasn't there a noncompete clause?"

She shrugged. "It'll take a while for the lawyers to work it out. Meanwhile, Jamilow is starting over from scratch. Everyone wanted an interview to see what Jamila thought. And she let them know," Hannah finished darkly.

"Uh-oh." I flicked my phone screen to life and searched. The recording of her comment was the first result.

"No, I'm not mad," she said, her glittering eyes belying her words even on my phone. "Pavel Thakor is so low he's got to look up to see hell. Now get out of my way."

"Yikes." The final frame caught the curl of her lip in a spectacularly unflattering way.

"Dozens of memes. I made one myself, trying to spin it as a girl-power kind of thing. But the haters are louder."

Effortlessly, she pulled into a prime parking spot in front of a small gelato shop.

With a hand on her arm, I stopped her from getting out. "How's she doing?"

"Not great." Leaning back, she scanned my face. "She's obsessed with finding a new partner and turning this around. She hardly talks to anyone but Rhiannon."

"What about Winslow?" I asked.

"He hasn't been around so much. Apparently, his divorce just got finalized. He's been scrambling to liquidate his assets. I heard he refused to let his ex have any of his Jamilow stock or options."

"That's…that's loyal of him." I choked on the word *loyal*. Five days ago, I'd accused him of disloyalty, and I still believed it to my core. But I was the only one.

"I guess. Now, let's go. You need some fat and sugar."

We exited the car and went into the shop. On a Tuesday afternoon in tourist season, it was crowded.

Hannah picked up our conversation from earlier. "I'm sure Jamila would've understood if Winslow had to give up some shares. Billie's a reasonable person. They're friends. She's already on the Jamilow board."

"Wait. Winslow's ex is Billie Woods?" My face went hot at the memory of my embarrassing behavior at her Christmas party.

"Isn't that weird? Apparently, there was a scandal when he married a board member, but Jamila stood by them both. Doesn't seem to have hurt Jamilow in the end." Hannah stepped up to the counter and ordered a banana avocado gelato.

I asked for extra-dark chocolate with cherries. "Calories didn't count while you're wallowing, right?" I half-joked.

"Think of all the calories you burn tossing and turning. I bet crying uses a bunch too. Especially ugly crying. You haven't been crying, have you?"

"No, not so much." Crying hadn't felt like the right reaction. I'd felt more empty than anything. When Jamila took back her trust, she scooped out the rest of me with it.

"I don't think Jamila has ever cried in her life." Hannah took her cup of gelato to a high-top table with metal stools. "She was one of those kids who, when she fell on the playground, really thought rubbing dirt on it made it feel better."

I hummed and shoved a bite of gelato into my mouth. I bet she'd cried when her dad died and when her mother left and after that terrible man she'd trusted tried to bargain her innocence for private-school money. Plus that day in my brother's office when that reporter's hateful words had reddened her eyes. But Jamila didn't want anyone to know about her past or her softer side. She must regret showing it to me now.

Suddenly, the gelato didn't taste right to me. Cold and sweet were wrong. I was fire and bitterness. I didn't want to be sitting here in this gelato shop, spooning creamy, chilled sweetness into my mouth and gossiping about people I used to work with. I wanted to fight for Jamila. Even if she didn't love me the way I loved her.

I had to talk with Billie Woods.

I stabbed my spoon into my gelato. "Can you take me home?"

"Sure." Hannah savored a spoonful of her dessert, rolling up her eyes.

I tapped the table, ready to move. "Now?"

"Now?" She swallowed.

"Right now. I can drive while you finish your ice cream. Please?"

Normally, I'd have finessed it. Being polite, staying out of the way, and helping from the sidelines was my comfort zone. But for Jamila, I'd burst through the barriers of acceptable behavior. I'd use every tool I had to make her hurt less.

"I guess it's important, huh?"

"Absolutely." I tossed my ice cream in the trash. "Let's go."

———

I FOUND my mother in her favorite place in the house, the conservatory. She wore a kerchief over her blond bob and gardening gloves to repot something with long, strappy leaves. I'd never cared much for her plants. She never let me help with them.

"Hi, Mother." I kissed her cheek.

"Back from shopping? Did you buy something nice for Charles's birthday?"

Crap. I'd forgotten. "Not yet. His birthday's not until next Sunday. I still have time."

"Of course." She patted the soil around the plant's roots, then peeled off her gardening gloves. Then she looked at me. Really looked, the way only a mother can.

She tilted her head. "You look a little better today."

"I, uh. Yeah. Yes. I feel better."

"Are you ready to tell me why you quit your job?"

I leaned against the potting bench. "I didn't quit. Jamila fired me."

Her blond eyebrows shot up. "Fired? Does this have anything to do with the call I received from Pavel Thakor?"

I winced. "I accused Winslow Keating-Ashworth, her COO, of corporate espionage. And I may have done it while impersonating you."

She pursed her lips. "Your job was public relations, not sniffing out spies. Jamila shouldn't have asked you to do that."

"She didn't. That's why she fired me."

"Why did you think Winslow was doing anything wrong?"

"I saw a photo of him somewhere he shouldn't have been, and I made a connection. But it was only circumstantial. He somehow turned it around so I looked like the traitor. Jamila's sensitive to things like that, you know. Betrayal of trust."

"That's why she and Jackson get along so well together. He's loyal to a fault."

Right. Which reminded me of how pissy I'd been the weekend

before I'd accused Winslow. If Jamila had been looking for an excuse to cut ties with me, I'd made it too easy.

"Do you think Jackson would be upset if—" I clamped my mouth shut. The words had spilled out like pearls from a broken necklace. I couldn't ask my mother about dating Jamila. I remembered the look on Jamila's face when Winslow had produced that visitor log and the copy of my identification. She would never forgive me. Why should I reveal my bisexuality now, when it didn't matter?

"If what, darling? Do I think he'll be upset when he finds out Jamila fired you? Probably more at her than at you. Though, really, I don't understand why it was your business at all."

"I…I made it my business."

She stroked my cheek. "That's my Natalie, always trying to help everyone."

That wasn't right. Not in this case. If it had been anyone else, I would've shown them the picture of Winslow on that golf course and let them deal with it, but I hadn't been satisfied with that. Not with Jamila. Because my feelings were too strong. Because I loved her. And love wasn't something you hid from your mother, not even if your mother held all kinds of heteronormative ideas about a woman's role in society.

"Mother, I"—I took a deep breath—"I need to tell you something."

"Yes?" She stroked a lock of my hair into place on my shoulder.

"I love Jamila."

She brushed a stray hair off my sweater. "Of course you do. We all love her."

"No. Mother." I clasped her hand to keep her from plucking every imperfection off me. "I love her romantically. She's my person."

"Your person? What kind of Gen-Z nonsense is that? Is that from an Olivia Rodrigo song?"

"Mother, listen to me." I waited until she met my gaze. "I'm bisexual, and I'm in love with Jamila Jallow."

"For goodness' sake. She's ten years older than you. She's practically an older sister to you."

"She is, and I love her."

She stared at me for a moment. "Does she love you? I mean, I know she's bisexual, too, but..."

That "too" broke me. She'd just accepted my sexuality and all the messiness it would introduce to her carefully ordered life.

I threw my arms around her. We weren't really a hugging family, but my feelings were too big to contain.

"Thanks." I sniffled.

"Don't do that." She pulled back and dabbed under my eyes with her thumbs. "You'll get all puffy. And what do you have to thank me for? I'm your mother, and I love you. But what about Jamila? Does she feel the same way?"

My chin trembled. "No. We"—I swallowed down the details I'd been about to give—"we dated for a little while, but it didn't work out."

"My poor little girl. Maybe you should go down to Mexico for a few days. Let the ocean breezes blow away your troubles."

Mexico, where horrible Winslow had gone to spill his secrets while pretending to have a sick grandma. It reminded me of what I needed to ask.

"Mother, I need a favor."

"Of course you can use my credit card. How else would you afford a trip?"

"No, not money, a connection. You know Billie Woods, right?"

"Certainly. From the library foundation. Remember, I told you to go to her party when Charles and I were out of town at Christmas."

As much as I'd prefer never to see Billie again, I had to do it for Jamila. "I need to talk to her."

"Why do you need Billie? This probably isn't a good time for her. She's recently divorced, you know. She's out of the country at Pangkor Laut. I suppose you could go there instead of Mexico."

"I don't have time for that. I need to talk to her about her divorce. I think it might have something to do with the leak at Jamila's company."

"You think she knows something about it?"

"No, but I'd bet my favorite Fendi bag that her ex had something to do with it."

"And you think this could win Jamila's affections?"

I slumped. Jamila's trust was like the boarding door on an airplane. Once it was closed, there was no opening it again. "No, but I still want to help her."

She gave me a rueful smile. "And you need Billie for that?"

"Yes."

"I'll call her. It's early in Malaysia, but she might pick up for me."

"Thanks, Mom."

"My phone is over there on the charger. Get it for me?"

I spotted it on the small table next to the door where my mother deposited her jewelry before digging in the dirt. I scurried over to grab it and carried it back to her.

She dialed.

"You're not going to text first?" I'd hate to get an unexpected call, especially before—I checked the time difference on my phone and winced—ten a.m. on her Malaysian beach vacation.

"Why would I do that?" She held the phone to her ear. "Hi, Billie, it's Audrey Hayes."

I rolled my eyes. Billie had to know who it was from the caller ID.

My mother listened for a moment and smiled. "That's wonderful. I hope I'm not disturbing you?" Her cheeks pinked. "Well, then. I won't keep you long. My daughter Natalie has some questions."

She paused, then nodded. "Here she is." Holding a thumb

over the microphone, she handed me the phone. "Be quick. She's entertaining a guest."

"A what?" My jaw dropped open. "You mean a guy? I don't want to—" But I did. The sooner Jamila got rid of that snake, Winslow, the better.

I took the phone. "Hi, Billie, it's Natalie."

"Natalie," Billie drawled. "I haven't seen you since you made a fool of yourself at my party."

I cringed. "I'm sorry about that. I was having a bad night."

"Of course you were. Everyone could tell you had it bad for Jamila Jallow. Except for Jamila herself." Her laugh was a merry tinkle, like seashell wind chimes.

"I still do. Which is why I have a question about your ex, Winslow." I grimaced. She knew who her ex was.

"I'd rather not talk about him right now."

"I know, and I'm sorry. I was wondering if, um…if there were certain provisions to your divorce settlement? Specifically ones having to do with Jamilow. I understand he kept his stock and options?"

"Yes. He was *very* insistent on that point. I wanted to split it down the middle, fair is fair and all. I wanted to continue to support Jamila myself. We've been good friends for years, since Stanford. I was her RA, you know, when she was a freshman. I was the first person she asked to be on the Jamilow board."

"Really? And then you married Winslow."

"Not my best decision as it turned out. He can be charming when he wants to be, you know. I let myself get swept away by the attentions of a younger man. Seems like it's a pattern for me." She chuckled.

I couldn't let her get sidetracked by her guest. "Tell me about the Jamilow shares."

"Right. He said he'd give me the equivalent in cash value, which turned out to be a bad deal for him. We set the value back in January, but the stock price has been dropping steadily since the PR flap, then precipitously this week when Moo-Lah launched their product. I guess it's been a good thing for me, not so good for Jamila and Winslow, eh?"

"Uh-huh." My mind spun. He'd held onto all of his stock and options and hadn't asked to renegotiate despite the dropping price? What was his angle?

"He got the stock. I got all the cash and property—except for his condominium in Los Altos." Her voice turned bitter. "It's where he used to keep his mistress, but she left him too."

"Why do you think—"

"She probably couldn't stand it either. All he did for the past two years was talk about Jamila. Jamila this, Jamila that."

Oh, no. I remembered all the time he spent in her office. Their easy banter. "You think…you think he's in love with Jamila?"

"In love?" She laughed, sharp and cold. "He resents her. He never stopped talking about how she was—pardon my French— fucking up the company they'd built together. How much better he'd run it if only he could get control."

My heart skipped a beat. "Get control? He said that?"

"Every goddamn day. Until I left him. Then I'm sure he said it to the mirror."

"If he somehow found the cash to exercise his stock options, how much of Jamilow do you think he could control?"

"Oh." She paused. "I hadn't thought he'd actually follow through. If he exercised them all, he'd hold not quite forty percent. That's the same amount Jamila kept for herself."

Not quite enough to wrest control from her then. But—

"What if he had a partner who was also buying up shares while the price was low? Or if he had another source of income?" Like a bribe from Moo-Lah.

"As long as he kept it on the down-low, he could surpass her holdings or be strong enough to challenge Jamila as an activist shareholder."

"He could vote her out," I said. "Or execute a hostile takeover by Moo-Lah."

My mother gasped.

Billie exclaimed, "The snake! Do you think that's what he did?"

"I think he's the source of the leak to Moo-Lah. I think he's been driving the stock price down so he can amass more shares. Do you think he would do that to Jamila?"

"Ten years ago? Never. Now? I'm afraid so. He might be kind to her face, but behind her back, he's...not a nice person."

"Holy shit." I winced. "Sorry, Mother."

"The COO plans to take over Jamila's company? Holy shit," Mother repeated.

"I need proof," I said.

"I have a document outlining his Jamilow holdings," Billie said.

"What about any cash he might have received from Moo-Lah?"

"I'll email my attorney. If it's there, she should be able to find it."

"Okay, that's good." It was the proof I needed.

A deep voice murmured on Billie's end of the line.

"Need anything else, sweetie?" she asked. "Because I've got a hot date with a Malaysian tycoon."

"No. Thank you. You've been very helpful."

"I'll shoot off that email right now," she said. "Good luck."

"Thanks." Energy buzzed in my fingers and toes. I had a lead on something that would prove Winslow was the leak, one that would stop him from hurting Jamila any more than he'd already done.

28

THE NEXT MORNING, Wednesday, I sailed into Jamilow's headquarters like I owned the place. I didn't, but I hoped that by the end of the day, Jamila still would.

Bruno stopped me. "Miss Jones, you don't work here anymore."

"I know, Bruno. And I know you're doing your job, but you have to let me upstairs."

"No, I don't. Jamila said—"

"It's okay, Bruno." Hannah stepped off the stairs and strode to us. "She'll log in as my visitor."

"I'm not sure I can let—"

"Bruno." I leaned over the curved desk. "I'm here to save Jamila. And the company."

He frowned. "Sounds like you're going to cause trouble."

He had a point. "I probably am. Want to come with us? Then you can walk me out if I cause the wrong kind of trouble."

"Fair." He lifted the handset and called someone. When the replacement guard arrived, I marched up the stairs, a neon-yellow visitor badge clipped to the neck of my boring navy sheath dress, the one I wore to funerals. On the second floor, heads turned as we made our way to Jamila's office. Felicia barred the door, arms crossed.

"You can't go in there. She doesn't want to see you." She shot an accusatory glare at Bruno, who shuffled his feet.

"I have something she needs to see. Something you all need to see. Let me in. All I need is five minutes."

"Five minutes." Her lips thinned. "Seems like you can do a lot of damage in five minutes."

"I promise, I don't mean any harm to Jamila. I want to help her. Please?"

The last voice I wanted to hear came from my left. "Absolutely not."

Slowly, I turned. Today, he wore the same raspberry-colored pants, his two-tone shoes, a white shirt with the collar open, and a navy blazer. "Winslow."

"Was our message not clear on your last day, Miss Jones? You're not welcome here."

"I need to see her." I raised my voice higher than was acceptable in an office where people were trying to work. "She needs to hear what I have to say."

"She does not," Winslow hissed, "need to hear any more from you. Bruno, escort her out. In fact, escort them both out. Hannah, you're fired too."

"You can't do that!" I didn't know my voice went that loud. "Hannah's done nothing wrong!"

"She let you in, didn't she?" He reached toward my neckline and snatched off the visitor badge. "Get them out of here, Bruno."

"What the absolute fuck is going on out here?" Jamila stood in her doorway with her hands on her hips looking like an avenging goddess. "Have y'all lost your damn minds?"

"Jamila, I need to talk to you. All I need is five minutes. Please?" I clutched the satchel that hung from my shoulder.

She glanced down at her smartwatch. "Five minutes. Starting now." Turning, she went back inside her office, and I followed. So did Winslow, Hannah, and Bruno.

Jamila eased into her chair like she carried the weight of the entire building on her shoulders. In that moment, I realized she did. Not only did Hannah and Bruno owe their jobs to her, but Felicia and everyone outside that door did too. She might have been trying to prove herself worthy to her nana, her mother, and everyone else who hadn't believed in her, but as a result, she'd built a business that employed hundreds of people and made money for thousands more. And I was about to make her life a whole lot more complicated.

I stood in front of her desk, feet planted as wide as my narrow skirt allowed. "Last time, I came in here with some pretty flimsy accusations. Today, I have proof."

I reached into the Saint Laurent satchel I'd borrowed from Mother and pulled out the papers I'd printed from Billie's attorney's email. "This is a statement showing Winslow's stock holdings and options."

"What the hell is that supposed to prove?" Winslow tried to snatch the papers from me but stopped when Jamila held out her hand for them.

She scanned them, nodding. "Nothing I didn't already know."

"Right, but here's where it gets interesting. In his recent divorce, Winslow kept only the Jamilow stock holdings. They represent approximately half the couple's wealth, and Billie kept the other assets." I handed over the next set of papers.

"Where did you get that?" Winslow snapped. "Those documents are private."

"A friend gave them to me." I leaned forward. "Winslow owns a significant amount of Jamilow stock outright. He also has unexercised stock options that would almost equal your own holdings, Jamila. He could exercise those options to buy up that stock for pennies on the dollar."

Jamila rolled her eyes. "I think we all know how stock options work. It's nothing nefarious. Winslow earned those options as part of his executive compensation and as one of my earliest employees."

"But," I said, "since his divorce, he doesn't have enough cash to exercise those options, much less buy additional shares at market price."

"Wait," Jamila said, a smile curling her lips. "I thought you were a fashion designer-florist-chef-PR consultant, not a financial expert."

"I'm a Jones." I shrugged. "This is what we talk about at dinner. Anyway, what's most interesting is this recent transaction in Winslow's bank account the day after his divorce was final." I dropped the last paper on her desk. "A deposit for twenty million dollars from an offshore account owned by Pavel Thakor."

"What?" Jamila wasn't smiling anymore. Her eyes went wide.

"Not only did Winslow accept a bribe from your competitor, but I suspect he's planning to use it to exercise his stock options and possibly buy additional shares. He plans to take on a majority interest in Jamilow. My guess is that he's planning to remove you as CEO and possibly attempt a hostile takeover by Moo-Lah. And I suspect he had something to do with the development issues too."

"That's ridiculous," Winslow sputtered. "Jamila, are you going to believe this child? She prances in here in her designer clothes with some papers she shouldn't have—who knows if they're legitimate—making claims she can't otherwise substantiate."

Jamila rose slowly. "Did you, Winslow? Did you accept money from Pavel Thakor? From Moo-Lah?"

"No, I—" He clamped his mouth shut. "I need to speak with my attorney."

"Why?" Her voice lost all its volume, all its brashness. That *why* was a young girl overburdened with the care of two rambunctious younger brothers asking her mother why she wasn't coming back, asking a church deacon for an easier way, asking her nana to believe in her.

My heart broke for her. For what I'd had to show her about a man she'd thought was her friend.

That man stood in her office, jaw set. "Jamilow could be so much more. You never wanted to succeed the way I knew we could. You had all these fairytale ideas about helping people in crisis and educating people out of poverty, but our business would best serve people who already had cash to drop on a paid app, those who bought things we could advertise and who had the net worth to take advantage of a partnership with FA. You could never see the vision of all we could be."

I regretted leaving my knives at culinary school. I arched a razor-sharp eyebrow. "You mean all that Jamilow could be if you were in charge?"

"Exactly." He had his hands on his hips, taking up space he didn't deserve.

I glanced at Jamila. She stared, unbelieving, at the papers that had upended her world. She needed time to process it all.

"Everybody out," I said. "Including you, Winslow. Better call that attorney." I made a shooing motion with my hands, herding the people out of her office. I paused at the door.

"I'm really sorry, Jamila," I said. "I wish it wasn't true."

She said nothing. Her shoulders slumped under the enormous weight of betrayal.

Softly, I closed the door behind me.

———

WHEN I GOT HOME an hour later, all I wanted to do was put on my sweats, eat a tub of ice cream in bed, and watch Darren Star shows until my eyes shriveled in their sockets. But my sister and her dog sat on the bed I wanted to crash onto.

"What are you doing here?" I asked. We'd never been the type of sisters to hang out in each other's rooms, sharing secrets, giving each other makeovers, or talking about boys, as much as I'd wished we had.

She stroked Bilbo's black fur. "I'm leaving today, remember? I didn't want to go back to Ohio without hearing how the big confrontation went. Mother told me what you found out."

"It...went." I flopped onto the bed, my hands over my eyes. Bilbo nudged my hand with his nose, and I lifted it to pat him. "It broke her heart to be betrayed by someone she trusted. Someone she thought was a friend."

"What happened to Winslow?"

"Security walked him out. Jamila has to have her lawyers file the papers before the feds can get involved."

"Do you think he'll leave the country? That bribe was enough to make anyone comfortable on some island."

"Maybe." I shrugged against the fluffy comforter. "But they'll probably seize his U.S. assets like his stock shares, so at least he won't trouble Jamila again."

"How did she take it?"

"Not well. I expected her to blow up, but she shut down. I'm worried about her."

"Of course you are." Sam wasn't the type of person who casually touched, but she squeezed my hand, the one that rested on Bilbo's side. "Do you think she's changed her mind about you?"

I remembered Jamila's blank expression. She hadn't even thanked me. I understood. I'd tossed a grenade into her company and walked away. Plus I hadn't done it for her gratitude. I'd done it because it was the right thing to do.

"I don't know. I'm not the most important thing going on in her life right now, am I?"

There was a knock at my door, and Charles poked his head in. "Natalie. And Sam! I thought you'd already left."

"Not yet. I needed to talk to Nat for a minute."

"Mind if I interrupt?"

"Come in," I said.

He stepped inside my room. "I got a call from Jamila today. I think I have you to thank. Frankly, I was a little hurt when she partnered with FA, but she came to me in the end. Thank you,

Natalie. My board is already salivating over a partnership with Jamilow."

He went on about synergy and revitalization for his stodgy bank, but I stopped listening. Jamila had gone to Charles?

My sister asked, "Did she say she'd done it because of Nat?"

He tipped his head to the side. "No, but I assumed…"

"Sorry, Charles," I said. "That was all Jamila. We're not working together anymore."

"Oh." His face fell. "And you're not, uh…doing other things together anymore?"

I winced. "No."

He walked to the bed and pulled me up so he could hug me. "I'm sorry. I know you care about her."

I relaxed into his hug. "It's all right. I helped her in the end, so at least I have that."

"And you have some valuable experience to put on your resume."

"My resume?"

He pulled away to look me in the eye. "I've never seen you as happy as you were while you were working at Jamilow. Part of that was because of Jamila, but you truly enjoyed the work. I think you should give PR another go. If Della Lippman doesn't have a position for you, I'm sure she knows someone who does."

"Huh. Maybe you're right." Jamila would never recommend me to anyone, but Hannah could give me a recommendation to her aunt. The thought of diving back into public relations work sparked excitement in my gut, the way culinary school, the florist shop, and the fashion program hadn't.

"I'm almost always right," he said, releasing me. "Now, Sammy, you've got to get to the airport. Come on, I'll drive you."

"You sure you'll be okay?" Sam asked, peering into my eyes.

"Eventually, yeah."

"My place will be done when I'm back in two weeks. Come see Bilbo Baggins and me then?"

"Yeah. Okay."

She patted my shoulder. Bilbo was more generous with his love. He jumped into my arms and licked my chin. I didn't even flinch. Maybe I'd get a dog once I got my life together and moved out of my parents' house.

For the first time, that felt possible.

29

AFTER ANDREW DROPPED me off in front of Jackson's townhouse on a Saturday evening in early July, I glanced up the street and felt like I'd been punched in the stomach. A red convertible Porsche like the one I used to drive when I was with Jamila was parked in front of his place.

I squinted at it. In the sunset glare, I couldn't be sure it was red. It might be brown or orange. And it might be a different year.

I shook my head. She wouldn't have kept the car after I'd given her back the key. She'd have ended the lease early because that was the smart financial move.

Both Charles and Jackson said she was fine, but I wished I could see for myself. I'd stare into her beautiful eyes and see if the pain of betrayal was still there, or if a glimmer of hope had replaced it. Before I got close enough to read the license plate or identify the driver, it pulled away.

I snorted at my ridiculousness. It was silly to get worked up over a car that reminded me of Jamila. It was also silly of me to stalk Hannah's carefully curated Jamilow social media account. I had to set a timer for ten minutes, or I'd get sucked into it forever. It was even sillier of me to masturbate to memories of the few nights we'd spent together.

Okay, maybe that wasn't so silly.

I'd probably treasure those memories forever because *hot*, but it was laughable to think it had ever meant anything. I was another fling to her and not special enough to deserve her love.

I rang Jackson's bell, and like he'd been waiting there for me, he opened the door.

"Ready for date night?" I asked, forcing a saucy grin onto my face.

"You bet. Thanks for babysitting—"

"I'm not a baby." Noah pushed his way to the door. "Tell Jay I'm *thirteen,* which is too old for a babysitter."

Remembering all the times my family treated me like a baby—heck, they still treated me like the baby—I flashed him a lopsided smile. "You don't need a babysitter. But Val does, and I need all the help I can get. You'll help me, right?"

"Yeah, I guess. I know where all her stuff is."

Valentine toddled up to us and raised her hands. "Up."

Noah bent and picked her up, parking the toddler on his hip the way I'd seen Alicia and Jackson do a hundred times. My heart gave an enormous thump.

"So it's me helping you," I said.

Valentine leaned forward, reaching her chubby fists toward me. "Tee-Tee Na."

I took her from Noah, inhaling the baby shampoo from her bath. "Auntie Nat's so happy to see you, Val."

She snuggled into my neck, and I couldn't contain my grin. It was real this time.

"Hey, Noah, can you give us a minute?" Jackson asked. "I need to talk with Auntie Nat."

"Queue up a videogame for us," I suggested. "Nothing too gory, okay?"

"We can play after Val's in bed," he said. "We'll watch one of her movies first."

"Mon-sah," she said, leaning back toward him.

"That's right," he said. "The one with the blue monster."

She squealed as he hefted her again and bounced her into the living room.

Jackson led me past the television through the kitchen into the laundry room and shut the door. Their cat, Tigger, was curled up on top of the dryer, napping in the ray of sunshine that spilled through the small window.

"Uh-oh. Must be serious if we need a closed-door conversation," I joked. "Wait. Is it serious? Is everything okay with Alicia?"

"She's fine. The baby's fine. She's taking a minute to get dressed. She's been working like a fiend trying to get everything ready for her maternity leave. This is about you."

"Me?"

"And Jamila."

"Holy crap. Was that her in front of your house? Was she just here?"

"You saw her?"

"Just her car."

"Yeah. She came over to talk. She told me something very interesting."

"Oh?" I took a deep breath, willing my racing heartbeat to slow.

When Jackson leaned against the dryer, Tigger lifted his head. He stood, stretched, and rubbed his cheek against Jackson's shoulder. He scratched behind the cat's ears, but his gaze didn't leave my face. "She told me she popped your bisexual cherry."

My face flamed hotter than the summer sunshine streaming through the small window. "Don't be gross."

"Don't play innocent. She told me you two were…intimate."

I rolled my eyes, remembering Jamila's *casual* label. "She hardly deflowered me. I'm twenty-six years old. I've had dozens of partners, of various genders."

He clapped his hands over his ears. "Didn't want to hear that."

"Then don't bring up anyone's sexuality, jerk," I said, testy over the memory of Jamila's constant reminders we were scratching an itch. "It meant nothing."

"Nothing?" he asked.

"She made that abundantly clear. And we're not intimate anymore. Not since she fired me."

"So that day on the mountain and the next day at brunch, you were together?"

"Yes."

"I see. Does Mother know?"

"I told her when I needed her help to get the truth about Winslow."

"She was okay with it?"

My blood boiled. I clenched my fists. "I'd have thought you of all people, best friend to two queer people, would support me!"

"I support you. I'm worried about you, though. I wish you'd come to me for help with Mother. Maybe with Jamila too."

"I don't need your help."

He held out his hands. "I know. You're not a little girl with pigtails anymore. You've got a grown-up job. But as your big brother and as her friend, I'd've felt better if I'd helped."

"Sometimes people don't want help, Jackson." The back of my neck prickled. I'd forced my help on Jamila. Maybe if I'd asked first, I wouldn't have ruined the friendship I cherished.

"I'm sorry. Forgive me?" He gave me the saddest puppy-dog eyes ever.

I rolled my eyes. "I guess."

"Really, you're okay? Especially with Mother?"

"We're fine. I think she'd be happier if I'd meet some rich guy, fall madly in love, and pop out half a dozen grandchildren, but she also wouldn't mind if I met a rich woman. Even though I'm working for Della now, she worries about my future."

Despite how busy she was on her product launch, Jamila had shocked me when she'd called Della Lippman to tell her she should hire me. I hadn't had a chance to leverage Hannah's connection before Della offered me a position. And then Jamila had sent me the most adorable flowering cactus. The note had simply said, *Good luck on your first day. I know you'll bloom in your new job.*

It had said nothing about love, as much as my squishy heart had wanted to interpret the gesture that way. The cactus wasn't a joke about her prickly personality or a reminder of Quill.i.am, no matter that the tag identified it as a hedgehog cactus, *Echinocereus fendleri*. She was so busy retooling her product that she'd probably gotten Felicia to do it, and it was purely coincidental. The job referral? Just another way to ensure I'd keep my distance.

He squinted. "So you're okay?"

"Yeah. I think I've finally figured out my life. I'm happy at work, and maybe someday, I can find love again."

"You loved her?"

"Yeah." I wouldn't admit that I was such a sad sack that I still loved her, a month after she'd dumped me and fired me in one go. "You were nice to her, right? When she told you about us? She was afraid of what you might think."

He straightened. "I hope you gave me more credit than that. You'll always be the baby of the family. I might tease you a little—"

"Or a lot!" I punched his arm.

He caught my fist and held it. "But you and Jamila are grown women, capable of making your own decisions. If two of my favorite people in the world end up together?" He shrugged. "Wouldn't be the worst thing."

I wished Jamila could've understood that. Maybe if she hadn't been looking for an excuse to end things, I wouldn't have lost her trust.

I hugged my brother tight. "Thanks."

"For what?"

"For believing in me. For thinking I'm, y'know, worth something."

"Nutter Butter."

And there it was, the noogie I'd been dreading. He'd probably still noogie me when I was sixty. Or eighty. But it didn't feel terrible. It felt like love.

"You are worth something," he said. "You're worth a lot. So what if it took you a minute to figure your shit out? I'm still figuring my shit out. We all are—even Jamila."

He released me, and I stepped back, finger-combing the tangled mess he'd made of my hair.

"Why don't you spend the night here and hang out with us tomorrow? We're going to a barbecue."

I blew out a breath. "Sure. Why not?" It'd be better than sitting in my room, staring at Jamila's nonexistent personal social media and regretting what I'd lost.

30

THE NEXT DAY, as we drove south down 101 in Alicia's SUV, the pit in my stomach deepened. I hadn't been this close to Silicon Valley in two months, and I wished I could distract myself from the too-familiar landmarks by putting on some headphones and playing a game on my phone like Noah was doing. Valentine was strapped into her car seat in the middle of the backseat and had worked off one of her tiny Nikes. I fished for it on the floor, then snugged it back on her foot.

"How much farther?" I asked as I saw the sign for the Marsh Road exit.

"Why?" Jackson glanced at me in the rearview mirror, his hands loose on the steering wheel. "Got somewhere better to be?"

"No, I just…" I didn't finish the sentence when Jackson pulled off at the too-familiar exit. I pulled the seatbelt away from my breastbone. "Where exactly is this barbecue?"

"At a friend's."

"Jackson." Alicia set a hand on his shoulder. "She should know."

"But I promised."

"What should I know?" I leaned forward into the gap between the front seats.

"No, no, no, no!" Val chortled.

"The barbecue is at Jamila's," my brother said. "It's a pre-celebration of her product launch."

"Dammit, Jackson!"

"Swear jar!" Noah said despite his headphones.

"Dammit, dammit, dammit!" Valentine kicked her sneakers in her car seat between us.

I pinched the bridge of my nose. "Sorry. But why didn't you tell me?"

"Are you not ready to see her?" My brother asked, stopping at a traffic light.

"I...I don't know." Especially not wearing a too-long pair of Alicia's pre-pregnancy jeans that I'd rolled up at the ankles and her T-shirt that read, "You may all go to hell and I will go to Texas."

"If you're not ready, we can drop you off somewhere and pick you up in a couple of hours," Alicia said.

It sounded tempting, to hide out in a boutique or café and not have to face Jamila again, not to see the stony expression on her face and remember a time when her eyes sparkled with passion as she looked at me when we were casual, but it felt like a whole lot more.

Yesterday, I'd told my big brother I was a grown woman, and it was time for me to act like one. I could face her. I could be friendly. I could chat with her about her upcoming launch and be happy for her and proud of myself.

"It's fine," I said, staring out the window at the other modest homes on her street.

Jackson pulled up in the first available spot on her street, practically back at the stop sign. Mrs. González must love that cars were parked along both sides of the street. After Jackson freed Valentine from her car seat and unloaded practically an entire discount store's worth of inflatable toys, we followed a set of pavers around the side of the house to the open gate in the wooden fence. We took the short path to the pool, and Val squirmed in my arms, pulling my hair until I looked at her. "Poo! Poo! Poo!"

"Yes," I said. "It's a nice pool. Want to go in?"

"Can you hold her for a second while we say hello?" Jackson asked. "I'll get her into her suit in a minute." When I nodded, he and Alicia made a beeline for Jamila, who stood at the far end of the pool with a familiar sun hat on her head and one of those insulated can holders in her hand.

When our eyes met across the backyard, her gaze scorched me to my bones.

I wasn't ready.

Not yet. I'd just wrapped my head around the fact that I'd be seeing her today. I hadn't prepared a plan or a script, especially not one to deal with her anger. How could I avoid humiliating myself when I remembered the last time she'd worn that hat and what had happened after? I could never forget and go back to who I was before. I'd promised myself I'd never fall back into the simpering persona I was at Billie's party.

Noah dumped an armful of pool toys near the steps into the shallow end. He'd save me.

"Need some help?" I asked.

"With what?"

"I don't know. Setting things up."

"Nah. I'm all done." He gestured at the haphazard pile of a swim vest, a unicorn floatie, a set of diving sticks, and a half-dozen pool noodles.

He reached for the waistband of his track pants, shooting them down his skinny legs and stepping out. He wore swim trunks underneath, and his shirt was a rash guard. Leaving his flip-flops poolside, he cannonballed into the pool. I stumbled back to avoid getting soaked.

Noah bobbed to the surface, wiping his long hair out of his eyes. "You coming in, Auntie Nat?" he shouted.

"No, I'm good. I'll wait for your dad to get Val." I was grateful for the excuse. I'd need to work up a lot more courage to bare my skin again in front of Jamila.

"Hey, Natalie." A tall, handsome blond guy stepped up to me with a longneck in his hand.

"Tyler! And Marlee." I greeted his wife and hugged them both. Marlee and Tyler were about my age, and we often found each other at parties. "Congratulations, you two. I don't think I've seen you since you got married."

When Marlee hugged Val and me, her oversized sunglasses tangled in my hair, and we laughed as we unwound ourselves.

"Tell me all about your wedding," I said.

"It was small." Marlee winced. "We couldn't invite everyone we wanted—"

I waved off her excuse. "Don't worry about it. I understand." Tyler and Marlee didn't come from money. They'd paid for the wedding themselves while supporting Marlee's father in a memory-care facility.

"It was magical." Marlee sighed in ecstasy. It did seem like a fairytale, especially when she showed me a photo of the guests lighting sparklers at sunset. Marlee had started telling me about their honeymoon when Ben, whom I hadn't seen since that disastrous brunch, bounded up and hugged her, followed by Tyler, then me. Cooper trailed behind him but didn't hug anyone.

"See, babe? I told you." Ben scanned me, head to toe. "She's wearing her clothes. And I-just-got-fu-uh-uh-screwed hair. Sorry," he whispered, eyeing the baby. "You owe me fifty bucks. I'll take the other part of our wager when we get home." He winked.

"Wager?" Combing my fingers through my hair, I worked out a knot Val had made with her sweaty hands.

"You and Jamila. I knew when we met you at brunch that day. Cooper didn't think so. And guess who was right?" He chuckled.

"No, we're not—" I kept myself from saying *anymore*. "Not together. These are Alicia's clothes. I babysat overnight last night."

"Oh." Ben's lips curled down. "But I hoped you'd—"

Cooper leaned forward to put his mouth at his fiancé's ear. "I'll take *my* winnings at home," he purred.

Ben full-body shivered. "Let's finish making the rounds. I feel an early departure coming on."

"Ha-ha." I forced a grin onto my face. "Engaged couples are the worst, right?"

But Tyler squinted at me. "You and Jamila, huh?"

"No, no, not a—" I had to stop the word again. "Not at all."

"She needs someone like you," Tyler said. "To help shoulder all her burdens. I thought Winslow was that person, but we all see how that turned out." He scowled.

"I think I need a drink." I was choking from all the words piling up in my throat like a multicar crash on I-80.

Tyler pointed me toward a table set up in the shade, and I made my way to it, avoiding the circle of people around Jamila.

The bar wasn't a self-serve cooler of beer. There was a bartender. And she was Rhiannon. I winced when I saw her, dreading whatever cutting remark she had for me.

"Hi, Natalie. What can I get you?" She eyed me warily.

"Oh. Um…do you have a sparkling wine?"

"We've got a Napa blanc de blancs."

"Perfect. Thanks." I watched her pour the wine. "It hardly seems fair that you work all week, and then you have to work at Jamila's party."

"Nah, this is my choice. Jamila made me come since, you know, I basically built the product. Despite that snake, Winslow." She scowled. "I like to hang out here. It gives me a way to talk to everybody, but I don't have to put myself out there. They come to me."

"Smart." I held up my glass in a toast and took a sip of the bitter wine. The bubbles made my nose itch.

"Hey, speaking of smart…" Rhiannon looked down. "You were a fool to think I was the leak, but you figured it out in the end. I never thought… Anyway, thanks for sticking to your Jessica Fletcher shit."

"Um. You're welcome? But I didn't do it for you."

"I know who you did it for." Her gaze met mine. "We both care about her in different ways. I appreciate what you did for all of us."

I nodded. "Maybe now we can be friends?"

She snorted. "Friends? I didn't spit in your *sparkling wine.* That's a start."

"Fair. Thanks for that. I guess I'll see you." Though I probably wouldn't. I wouldn't be going back to Jamilow, and the next time Jackson offered to hang out, I'd ask where we were going before I got into his SUV.

"Be sure you get some food. I'm not picking up your drunk ass later." She pointed at a giant grill, tended by two enormous men.

With a halfhearted smile, I scuffed toward the grill for my next awkward encounter. Not even my mother's stuffy parties were this torturous.

"Hey, J.J. Hey, Jevin."

"Nat-a-lie." Jevin drew out the syllables of my name with an appraising look. "Lookin' good."

"Cut that out." J.J. elbowed his twin in the ribs hard enough to make him grunt. "She's Mila's girl."

"Oh, no, I'm not—"

"I don't see a ring." Jevin winked. "She's fair game until then."

"That's just nasty, bro. Natalie." J.J. smiled at me, and it was heartbreakingly similar to Jamila's smile. "What can I get you? The best ribs you've ever tasted, or a so-so burger from my brother?"

"Get your head out of your ass, J." This time, it was Jevin's turn to elbow his twin. "She's a vegetarian. I got your veggie burger right here, sugar." He pulled a toasted bun from the grill and slid a patty onto it.

"Sorry. Forgot." J.J. lifted his Texas Longhorns hat and wiped the sweat from his brow with the back of his wrist. "Sides are over there." He pointed at another table that held serving bowls. "Stay away from the casserole with the potato chips. It's got chicken in it."

"Got it. You two doing okay? It was nice of you to come out here for Jamila's launch."

"Well, that's not all we—"

"Yo!" J.J. punched Jevin's arm. "There goes your mouth again, flapping like a rusted old screen door." He gave his twin a baleful glare.

"Sorry, man. She'll find out soon enough."

"Who'll find out what?" I looked for Jamila in the clump of people next to the pool. "You aren't planning a practical joke, are you?"

"There's an idea." Jevin rubbed his clean-shaven chin. "Maybe Mila ought to go for a swim."

I puffed myself up. "You try it and you're going for a swim. And I don't think your Air Jordans would like that very much." I looked pointedly at his spotless vintage sneakers.

"This one's not messing around." Jevin raised his spatula. "No funny business. Promise."

"Thanksgiving's gonna be fun," J.J. muttered.

"Go eat that veggie burger before it gets cold," Jevin said. "And be sure to try the potato salad. It's our nana's recipe."

I trudged toward the table of sides where I spotted the potato salad and dropped a dollop onto my paper plate. I scooped up some salad and a fudgy brownie—I certainly deserved the indulgence after being dragged to Jamila's against my will—and found a vacant table in the shade of a sycamore.

I spread my napkin in my lap. The potato salad looked good with chunks of potatoes clumped together by a creamy dressing. Something green, celery perhaps, added color. I reached for my fork, but I'd forgotten to pick one up. I scooted my chair back and set my napkin beside my plate.

"Looking for these?" Jamila handed me a clear plastic fork and knife. When I looked up at her, the sun blazed behind her head, its rays spilling out like a crown. She wore her white bikini top with a light, almost transparent shirt and a sarong printed in bright red, orange, and purple.

"Yeah. Thanks." I took the cutlery from her. Why had she come over? She could have ignored me for the entire party. No, as the hostess, she had to say hi to everyone, including the person who had the wrong kind of feelings for her, the person who'd blown up her world.

"Can I join you?" She pointed at the folding chair next to me.

I nodded. While she settled into the chair, I poked the potato salad with my fork. My appetite was gone along with any cool I had left.

"Thanks for coming." She twisted the tail of her shirt.

"Jackson brought me here under false pretenses. I didn't mean to crash your launch party."

She gazed into my eyes. "I wanted you here."

"Me?" I put a hand on my heart to slow its gallop. "You wanted *me* here?"

"Only you. I don't care about anyone else."

"Not even my brother? Or your brothers?"

"Well, okay, I care about the brothers."

Half a smile sneaked onto my face. "What about Rhiannon? And Alicia?"

"Fine." She threw up her hands impatiently. "I invited all of these people here because I care about them. Get your wrench out of my romantic gesture."

"Romantic gesture?"

"I know, I know. Not the words most people associate with me. But it's what you want, isn't it? Still?" Her eyes went soft like lava cake. "It's why I sent that hedgehog cactus. Am I too late?"

Despite the warmth of the sun, goosebumps rose on my skin. "Too late? What are you saying?"

"I'm saying you're the one for me. When we were together, my feelings scared me. I'd never felt that much for anyone else I'd dated. Never let myself feel, but with you, I couldn't help it.

When I thought you'd gone behind my back, it hurt." She winced and patted her breastbone. "Right here."

"Like when your mom left," I said.

She wrinkled her nose. "No, that was definitely worse. I never wanted to feel that way again, and I thought if I could control everything, I wouldn't have to. But you made me lose control. I was mad."

"I know." I set my hand on her knee, palm up, and she grasped it.

"When you stormed back in and told me Winslow was the one who'd betrayed me, I kind of went numb. Like, a blue screen in my brain. It took a minute to reboot. By then, you were gone."

"I thought you might need a minute. You and Winslow were close."

"Yeah." She shook her head. "He'd tried to talk to me about his ideas for running the company, but I shut him down. I thought it was a healthy disagreement. I was wrong."

"I'm sorry. I wish I could've been there for you."

"You were." The intensity was back. "You showed me what I'd missed. I still have the majority interest in Jamilow, thanks to you. You saved my company." She cleared her throat. "Thank you."

I glanced down at our joined hands. Her long, dark fingers spanned my paler skin. "That's kind of extreme. *You* saved the company. I only gave you information you needed."

"And pushed me until I accepted it." She shrugged. "But I didn't ask you to come here to talk about the company."

I snorted. "As I recall, you didn't ask me to come here at all."

"I did! I asked Jackson to bring you."

I gave her a dubious look.

"Okay, fine. Maybe I need to work on my interpersonal skills, but that's what I'm asking you. Can you give me grace to improve? While I spend too much time at work. While I keep putting my foot in my mouth in front of journalists and their cameras."

My sparkling wine had gone flat in its plastic cup, but bubbles rose inside me. "What are you asking me, Jamila? Because this doesn't sound like a great offer so far."

"I'm being honest with you. This is what you get." She waved a hand over herself. "I'm prickly and sweary and nothing like what a princess like you imagines for herself. But if you want to be with me, I promise to try my hardest to be what you need."

My heart stilled. "You want to be with me? You trust me again?"

"I trusted you all along. I couldn't help it. That's why it hurt so much when you…"

"When I went all Nancy Drew on you?"

"Yeah. I thought we were close enough that you'd have told me before you did something that extreme."

I swallowed. "I…I…was afraid I'd screw it up like I always do."

"Baby girl, I'd love you even if you did screw it up."

"Wait. You love me?"

"Goddammit! See, I can't get this right. I thought with the call to Della and the cactus, you'd understand."

"I hoped, but I didn't know." My heart fluttered.

"I'm sorry. I told you I suck at this. Yes. I love you."

My chest was almost too full to breathe. "We can be public? I can be your…your girlfriend?"

She gripped my hand almost painfully tight. "I want to be all in with you. I'll even let you be in charge sometimes. Whatever you need. Because I need you."

I leaned toward her and whispered, "Call me baby girl again?"

"I love you, baby girl." She kissed my lips, a gentle press.

"And I love you…Mila. Can I call you that?"

"Only when you're happy with me. Not when I make you mad."

"You'll never make me mad." I kissed the corner of her mouth.

"Oh, I promise, I'll make you mad. Not on purpose, but I will. And I'll be really"—she kissed my lips—"really"—she kissed my jawbone—"really sorry."

I shuddered. "Will there be makeup sex?"

"Absolutely."

With effort, I pulled back. "Then I'm all in too."

The hard angles melted from her face. Only her plush lips, her warm eyes, and her gorgeous cheekbones remained. And they were all mine.

"Are you out to everyone you care about?" she asked.

"I told my mother and Charles. My sister. My brothers. I think everyone else either knows or suspects. Or they love me enough not to care."

"Then let's tell everyone here."

"Everyone?" I surveyed the party guests, but that was old Natalie scanning the crowd. New Natalie didn't care what anyone thought. It wasn't my job to please them or make them happy. The only person I cared about pleasing was myself—and Jamila.

"Okay," I said.

Gripping my hand, she tugged me up. "Here's the plan. We tell them we're a couple, then we sneak off to my room."

"But everyone will know what we're doing!"

"And that's a problem because…?" She trailed a hand down my lower back, underneath the waistband of my borrowed jeans to the spot right at my tailbone where I was ticklish. Shivers spread from where her skin met mine, igniting a flame in my core.

"No problem," I squeaked.

"Thought so. Hey, everyone!" she shouted.

And while she told the crowd of our friends about our relationship, I crowed inside. The most fabulous woman in the world loved me. Only me.

And I loved only her too.

EPILOGUE

MY GIRLFRIEND, as it turned out, loved parties.

Her pre-launch backyard barbecue last weekend for family and friends was nothing compared to the actual launch party on the rooftop patio of the Jamilow building.

When I'd worked downstairs, I had no idea this was up here. The building was only two stories tall, but the rooftop overlooked the distant treetops and the sparkling lights of Mountain View. If you stood close to the west side, you could see the inky blot of the pond below. Reflections of the rooftop lights shimmered on its surface.

"What are you doing over here?" Jamila's whisper was hot in my ear, and I shivered.

I took the champagne flute she offered me. "Observing."

She made a show of feeling my forehead with the back of her hand. "Natalie Jones is *observing* a party? She's not at the center, networking? This might be serious."

I clasped her hand and lowered it to our sides. "Hannah did a great job."

"Yeah, I'm glad I hired her."

"Excuse me?" I dropped her hand to gesture at myself. "I hired her."

"No one works at my company without my approval. She was a great hire."

I sighed, letting it go. We were a team. We'd hired Hannah, who had thrown an amazing launch party. All Jamila's billionaire business associates were there, except for Winslow Keating-Ashworth who, along with Pavel Thakor, was currently the subject of a federal investigation. Reporters and tech bloggers packed the rooftop.

"What are you doing over here?" I asked. "You should be over there talking to a blogger or an investor. Not here with me. You're missing your party." I gave her shoulder a gentle push.

"I'm right where I want to be." She turned her back to the party and set her hands on my waist. "Did I mention I like this dress?" Her hands roved the short distance to the hem and curled under it.

I trailed my hands from her shoulders to the back of her neck and played with the short curls at the back of her head. "You did mention it when I got to your place. And again, in the back of the car on the ride over here."

"Ah, right," she breathed in my ear before kissing my neck. "I can't be responsible for remembering what I say when you wear a skirt that short. I'm shocked your mother let you leave the house in it."

I shoved her shoulder. "I might still live with my parents, but they don't have a say in what I wear."

She pressed me back against the wall. "Maybe someone should. That skirt is indecent. It makes me wonder what you're wearing underneath." When she caressed my bare butt cheek, her eyes went wide. "Nothing?"

"Jones women don't go commando in public." I lifted my chin. "It's a thong."

"A thong." She found the G-string and slipped her thumb under it, stroking the sensitive spot at my tailbone. "Maybe I should take you to my office for a more thorough assessment."

Shuddering, I grabbed her rogue hand, pulled it out from under my skirt, and gripped it.

"Later. In your bed, not your office." I nudged her to face the party. "Have you talked to any of the COO candidates?"

"I've got to say, it was brilliant of you to invite them here. I felt a couple of them out. They could be interested in the job. Though I'll have to order a full background check on any serious candidates. No more corporate spies," she grumbled.

"No more corporate spies," I agreed. "Or friends."

"Speaking of not-friends, what's *he* doing here?" She pointed at a tall man, his gray hair sparkling in the strands of Edison bulbs that crisscrossed the center of the rooftop. He looked vaguely familiar.

"Who is he?"

"That's Harris Weston. He used to be CEO of Synergy until he tried a hostile takeover."

That was why he looked familiar. He used to be on Mother's invitation list until he tried to drive a wedge between Cooper and Jackson. "I didn't invite him. Do you think Hannah did it by accident?"

"Doesn't matter," she growled. "He's not welcome here." Dropping my hand, she strode toward him. I followed as fast as I could in my heels.

A glass of something brown was in his hand as he talked with a group of well-dressed people near the bar. He wore a Dolce & Gabbana suit that should have looked out of place on the casual rooftop but somehow made everyone else look underdressed. His pale blue tie brought out his blue eyes, which were truly lovely. In fact, he was handsome in a way I might have fallen for, if I were into silver foxes and if I weren't so gone for Jamila. His white teeth flashed when he smiled.

His smile dimmed when he saw Jamila.

She looped her arm through his. "A word, Weston?"

He nodded his goodbye to the group. "Of course, Jamila."

They walked to the dark side of the rooftop behind the bar,

and I followed to make sure she didn't throw a drink in his face or try to push him over the edge. She was seething, so either option seemed possible.

She yanked him to a stop and hissed, "How dare you show your ugly mug at my party?"

He held up his palms in an "easy there" gesture. "I came here with—"

"I don't care if you came here with Barbara Jordan and Ruth Bader Ginsburg and their attendant angels. You. Are. Not. Welcome. Not at my party." She punctuated each word with a stab of her long finger to his chest.

"Fine." This time when he smiled, it wasn't friendly. It was cool and calculating. "I accomplished what I needed to." Brushing off the divot Jamila had left in his tie, he strode away to the exit.

Jamila pulled out her phone and hit a button. "Bruno. Make sure Harris Weston leaves the building. He's the asshole leaving the rooftop." She pocketed her phone.

I stepped closer. "What do you think he accomplished?"

"Getting his ass escorted out of my building. Getting his photo put up at the security desk like a check bouncer at Buc-ees."

"No, Mila, we're not doing that. You don't need to be tough with me."

"Right." She slipped an arm around me but stared at the door closing behind Weston. "I don't know. Could be, he just wanted to show his face at a tech party again. Claw his way back into everyone's good graces so he can sweet-talk his way into another CEO job or a board position. Or it could be something more nefarious."

I shivered. "Say *nefarious* again."

She tucked her nose under my ear. "Should we do some role-play around the word *nefarious?*"

"It's hot when you say it with your twang."

She straightened. "I do not have a twang."

"You do when you want to. When you want to throw someone off your trail. You're not considering hiring that PI again to check out Weston, are you?"

"No…"

"That didn't sound like a real *no*. No more PIs. We talked about this. Everything on the up-and-up."

"Fine. Though I wish I knew what he was up to."

"I'll ask around. See what I can find out through unofficial channels."

"Good girl." She wrapped an arm around me and tugged me closer. "Maybe you missed your calling as a private investigator. You did so well figuring out what Winslow was up to."

"No." I leaned my head on her shoulder. "I'm happy where I am. Della Lippman is the best mentor I could ask for."

Her hand slipped to my hip. "You sure you wouldn't rather come back and work for me? I'm not sure I can afford to pay you what Della does, but the benefits…" She slipped her fingers under my skirt and skated them to my butt cheek, which she rubbed in a circle. "The benefits are amazing."

I tried not to think about the wetness seeping into the tiny triangle of my thong. "The benefits of being your girlfriend are pretty spectacular. I will not be screwing my boss again, thank you."

"Mmm. Have you given any more thought to a visit to my office?"

"Absolutely not. You're the star of this party Hannah worked very hard to put together for you. You're staying here on this rooftop to shake the hand of the last person who leaves."

She squeezed my butt, then pulled her hand out from under my skirt. "Fine."

We both wore heels, so I had to go up on my tiptoes to whisper in her ear. "I promise, good girls get a reward at home."

She raised her eyebrows. "I'm the good girl in this scenario?"

"We'll take turns?" I bit my lip.

"I like it." Her dark eyes sparkled. "Let's see how many outrageous things I have to do to make people leave early."

"I think you're unclear on the good-girl concept."

"Show me, then? You know I love to watch you work."

"Do you?" I took a step toward the party, glanced back at her over my shoulder, and batted my eyelashes. "Then follow me."

She did.

————

Thank you so much for reading *Tempt Me*. Please consider posting a review on your favorite retailer, BookBub, or Goodreads. Reviews help other readers find new authors like me.

Want to see Natalie and Jamila in their happily-ever-after at Ben and Cooper's wedding? Sexytimes ensue in a beach cabana…with only one key! Join my newsletter at michellemccraw.com/Jamila or use your phone's camera to take a picture of the QR code below to download a bonus epilogue!

If you like age-gap rom-coms that feature strong, independent women, you might also enjoy my 40 and Fabulous series. It's set in the Synergy universe, so you might see some familiar faces in its pages. The series starts with *Frenemies and Lovers,* a fake-dating, age-gap vacation romance featuring Natalie's brother Andrew and his 13-years-more-mature crush. It's available from your favorite retailer. Read on for a sneak peek!

FRENEMIES AND LOVERS

A FAKE-DATING AGE-GAP STANDALONE
ROMANTIC COMEDY

1 FLIPPING ANGELS

CARLY

> To-do list—October 22
> ✓ Request limit increase for credit card
> ✓ Pick up client's gowns at boutique
> ~~Take gowns to client~~ Give Audrey Hayes a piece of my mind

EVERYTHING about the Jones-Hayes mansion in Presidio Heights was exquisite, from the graceful curve of the staircase leading to the front door to the delicate amber spider mums spilling over a planter on the doorstep. The first time I'd come here, I'd stood on the doorstep like a slack-jawed noob, listening to the doorbell's lovely, melodious chime. To a girl who'd grown up in low-rent apartments, it sounded like angels singing.

I banged the side of my fist on the heavy wooden door. Audrey's flipping angels could shove their tiny harps where the sun didn't shine.

The door swung open, making me wobble back on my two-seasons-ago Jimmy Choos. The pretty, smiling young woman who answered wasn't my frenemy.

She was her daughter, Natalie, a stunning blonde in her midtwenties, about the age I'd been when I'd entered her mother's social sphere. But Natalie hadn't bumbled her way in like I had. No, Natalie had been born into San Francisco's tech royalty.

No one would kick her out the way they'd done to me.

"Mrs. Winner. Would you like to come in?" As Natalie pulled the door wider and stepped aside, her high-waisted beige trousers swished. Her periwinkle-blue silk blouse was Brunello Cucinelli, if I wasn't mistaken. Natalie was the youngest of Audrey's children, but she had the best sense of style, vastly superior to her brother's. I would *not* think about him today. Not while I stood on his mother's doorstep.

"It's Ms. Rose now." I stood as tall as I could on the doorstep. "Or just Carly. Is your mother here?"

"She's in the conservatory. Shall I show you to her?" Her phone buzzed in her hand, and she glanced at it.

My phone hadn't rung in weeks. Except for today's call to cancel my job. I sucked in a deep, calming breath through my nose. "No, thank you. I know where it is."

"Great. See you later." She bounded up the grand staircase, leaving me in the foyer.

I'd been to Audrey's home often enough to be able to find my way around. I used to come with Brad for formal events and dinner parties. One time, when we were on the friend side of our frenemyship, she'd brought me to the conservatory to show off an orchid she'd coaxed into a pink bloom so ethereal I thought it might crumble like sugar if I touched it.

I rounded the pedestal table in the center of the foyer with its enormous arrangement of alstroemeria and stalked through an arched doorway into the hall that led to the back of the house.

My heels echoed off the Spanish tiles as I passed the doorway to the dining room. Audrey usually held committee meetings there and presided over them like a queen in her armchair at the head of the table. I strode past her private wing, the black and white powder room, and her husband's office.

Finally, when I smelled green things, I flung open the French double doors that led to the glass-enclosed room. I slowed my steps, watching for wet places on the tile. Avenging furies didn't fall on their asses.

Everywhere I looked was verdant. Trees grew from pots that two people could fit inside. Leaves the size of an elephant's ear nodded in the gentle breeze from a fan. Graceful pink and white flowers cascaded from hanging baskets and planters. Although it was autumn outside, here, it was spring.

"Audrey?" I called.

"Over here."

I followed her voice toward the trickling fountain in the center of the room. She sat in a rocking chair facing the garden outside. She wore yoga pants, a simple white T-shirt, and a man's plaid flannel shirt—in her signature color, red—thrown over like a jacket. She'd tied a matching kerchief over her blond bob.

I'd never seen her dressed casually before, not even when we'd gone to the rainy, muddy groundbreaking for the library their family foundation had funded. Without her Dior 999 lipstick and couture armor, she looked as small and fragile as one of her orchids. But I knew the truth.

As one of the most powerful women in the city, she could bar anyone's entry into the upper echelons of San Francisco society.

And today, she had put up her metaphorical keep-out sign in front of me.

I balled my fists at my sides.

She wore no makeup, and her unmasked wrinkles made her look almost as old as she was. With four grown children, I knew she had to be in her sixties and not forty-five as she'd claimed for the past ten years.

I was forty-five. And I was not going to think about her children right now. Especially not her second son.

There was a small bench beside her, but fury kept me on my

feet. I stomped up and towered over her, planting my hands on my hips.

Her pale lips opened in surprise. "Carly, what are you doing here?"

The nerve! As if she didn't know exactly why I'd come here madder than a wet hen.

I took a deep breath. When I was this angry, my Texas twang tended to pop out, but I wanted to inspire the fear of god, not laughter.

"What you did was low, Audrey. We used to be friends." Sort of. "Before..." I swallowed down the words *my divorce* and, even worse, *my downfall.* "We worked together on more committees and galas than I can count. You know I'm a hard worker, professional and talented. I'd have done a good job for Bianca and started to build my business. There was no reason for you to go behind my back."

"Behind your back?" Audrey shook her head slowly, her diamond earrings glinting in the afternoon sunlight. "Whatever are you talking about?"

"Bianca Waddingworth." I parked my fists on my hips. Feigning ignorance was beneath her. "I was supposed to be styling her for her birthday party tonight. She texted me to cancel because *you* told her to."

"Me?" She planted a perfectly manicured hand on her chest. "Why would I do that?"

"You're trying to kick me to the curb." A fresh wave of anger tightened my throat. "News flash: you're too late. Brad already took care of it."

"It seems like something you could have predicted," she said in that cultured voice of hers. "Since he left Eleanor for you."

Why did she have to be right? Brad hadn't told me he was married when we met. And I was positive his new fiancée hadn't known we were still living together when she knocked on my door eighteen months ago. But if I let Audrey distract me with that disaster, I'd never get my point across.

"All I want—"

"Hey, Carly, a question for you while you're here." Natalie's voice at the door to the conservatory startled me. She was bare-foot, and I hadn't heard her approach. "If someone is sixty-something and in decent shape, what type of gown would you recommend for a formal party? She's a yoga nut, if that helps."

I paused. That could have described a dozen women in her mother's social circle. "Good arms, then," I mused.

"That's right. And she's a blonde."

That narrowed it only slightly. But I had a sneaking suspicion she was asking for styling advice for the woman who'd backed out of paying me to do it. Still, Natalie was a nice girl. I only wanted to jerk a knot in her mother's tail. "An A-line. Sleeveless, of course. In red."

Natalie approached me, looking down at her phone. "Here's a red sequined gown. But which shoes?" She showed me a photo of a pair of glittery gold pumps. "These?" She swiped to show a pair of strappy black sandals. "Or these?"

"Does she have a neutral dress shoe? Something beige?" I asked.

"Good idea." Natalie tapped on her phone. "She should've asked you to style her."

"Who?" I gritted my teeth.

"Bianca Waddingworth."

She did. And then she canceled. But that wasn't Natalie's fault. It was her mother's. "Maybe next time," I said with a sweet-tea smile, hoping my tone didn't sound as strangled to her as it did to me.

"Will these work?" She flipped her phone around to show me a photo of a pair of rose-gold rhinestone-spangled sandals.

"Perfect."

"Thanks. I'll let her know."

Damn it, I'd just styled Bianca Waddingworth. For free. *And* let Natalie take all the credit. I sucked in a breath, but the conservatory's moist air weighed heavily in my lungs.

Natalie looked between her mother and me, her gaze lingering on my fists jammed onto my hips. "You two okay?"

"Fine, thanks." I broadened my smile.

"We were talking about Carly's styling business," her mother said smoothly.

"Nice. I'm sure you can refer lots of clients her way, Mother."

"Perhaps Carly's style would be better suited to a different type of clientele." Audrey's smile was brittle. She muttered low enough that only I could hear, "The kind down on Capp Street."

I sucked in an outraged breath.

The doorbell chimed, and Natalie glanced down at her phone. "I lost track of time. I'll get the door, but then I've got to go." She pecked her mother's cheek. "See you at the party. Will we see you there, Carly?"

Pain speared behind my right eye. "No, I'm not on the guest list tonight."

Her cheeks went red. "Oh. What about the gala at the Merchants Exchange?"

"A gala?" I repeated. The event would be chock-full of potential styling clients.

"On November first. You should come. Is there room at our table, Mother?"

Audrey looked like she'd sucked on a lemon. "I don't think so, darling. I'm sure Carly would prefer to sit with the new wives."

Because after nineteen years of marriage, I was still a new wife. An interloper. I balled my fists.

"Still, you should come, Carly. You haven't been to anything since…" Natalie grimaced.

The doorbell rang again.

"Saved by the bell!" Natalie said, trotting toward the exit. "Really, you should come."

Across the room, a buzzing erupted from a phone resting on a wireless charger. Audrey ignored it, so I did too.

"I don't care about being invited to parties anymore." Staying home was preferable to facing down my asshole of an ex and his fiancée. "But I do care about making a living for myself."

Audrey pursed her lips. "I heard your divorce settlement was less than ideal."

Heat licked across my forehead. I wished I could go back and shake my twenty-five-year-old self, the one who'd blithely signed away any future interest in Brad's business ventures. The ones I'd supported through dinner parties and networking for almost twenty years. But even if I didn't have his money, I still had my pride, and my dirty laundry was none of her business.

"I came to talk about my clients. I need women like Bianca to hire me."

She rose from her chair. She was shorter than me, but fire ants are small too. "Why do you think I had anything to do with Bianca canceling?" Her pale-blue eyes glinted.

"Of course you did. You've always had it out for me. You and the other first wives." I'd never said it out loud, not to Audrey or any of her cronies. But it had been true since the day I walked into that first party on Brad's arm, so much younger than his friends. Back then, she terrified me. Now, I was old enough not to give a damn about what she thought of me. I only feared what she could do to my business. "You're kicking me when you think I'm down."

I straightened my spine. I'd show her, and all the other first wives, that even without Brad, I was a force to be reckoned with. Someday, Audrey's circle would beg me to style them for their parties. "I'm not down. Far from it. I'm going to show you, and everyone—"

"Mother?" A familiar voice echoed down the hall, sending lightning up my spine.

I couldn't keep the images from my mind. His sexy saunter as he approached me that night in Monterey. His outrageous suggestion that I meet him in his hotel room. The way his face lit up when he opened his door to find me standing there.

His handsome face, slack with pleasure, as he groaned my name.

"In here, Andrew," Audrey called. She raised an eyebrow. Her son could move his eyebrows independently too. "You were saying?"

Shit. I couldn't face him. Not in front of his mother. Not after I'd left him asleep in his hotel room six weeks ago without a word. His heavy footsteps echoed on the hallway tile.

I held up a finger. "Do. Not. Mess. With me, Audrey. I might not have Brad's clout anymore, but I've got plenty of fight left in me."

I whirled and wrenched open the glass-paned door that led out to the garden. Heedless of the damage to my shoes, I scurried down the gravel path and around the side of the house, out of sight of the conservatory windows.

Tessa waited for me in her SUV. When I yanked open the passenger-side door, my middle fingernail snapped, shooting pain up my hand, but I didn't pause as I hopped into the seat. "Floor it!"

Even though we'd been friends for only about six weeks, Tessa trusted me enough to do what I asked. She whipped the BMW into reverse. I missed the roar of a gas-powered engine, but the whisper-quiet electric motor did the job. Seconds later, we flew down the hill, away from Audrey's house and the peril her son represented.

"So, how'd it go?" She flicked her auburn hair over her shoulder and swerved around a corner.

"Not like I planned." I checked the rearview mirror. "You can slow down now. I think we got away."

She decelerated only slightly as we merged onto California Street.

"What about the shock and awe?" she asked.

"Fizzled into turn-tail-and-run. *He* showed up."

"Andrew?"

"Shh!"

She rolled her green eyes. "We're alone in my car. No one can hear us."

"I'm trying to forget it ever happened."

"Carly. He's thirty-something years old—"

"Thirty-two."

"Old enough to make his own decisions. You're consenting adults. There's nothing wrong with it."

"Nothing wrong?" I plucked my blouse from my sweaty chest. Stabbing at the switch, I lowered the window to let cool air blow over me. "His mother can destroy my career. In fact, she may have already started. Do you think she knows? Is that why Bianca canceled on me?"

Tessa shrugged. "Fuck them both. You don't need those bitches to be successful or happy."

"Don't I?" Women like Bianca and Audrey could afford my services, and I was comfortable styling them after years as their peer. In fact, that gala would be a perfect opportunity to prove it.

"Turn here," I said. "We're making a stop."

She jerked the wheel and flew around the corner onto a side street. "Is it a revenge plot? I'll work out your alibi. I'm an excellent accomplice."

"Not that kind of revenge. Park here."

She parallel parked the car in three moves. "What kind of revenge are we getting at a boutique? Are you going to hide a stiletto in your, um, stilettos?"

"No! It's the kind where I show up to a gala I can't afford." Maybe this wasn't a great idea.

"Ah, and you look like a million bucks and everyone wants to hire you so they can look fabulous too."

"That's the plan." I got out of the car, and she met me in front of the boutique.

"Find me a dress, too, and I'll go with you. And to pay for your styling services, I'll buy your outfit too."

"You don't have to do that," I protested.

"But I want to." Linking her arm with mine, she walked toward the store.

I blinked away the sudden moisture in my eyes. Tessa was worth a hundred Audrey Hayeses. And this afternoon, I wasn't going to worry about my dangerously-close-to-the-limit credit cards or what my frenemy would do if she found out I'd slept with her son.

———

Frenemies and Lovers is available in paperback from your favorite retailer.

ACKNOWLEDGMENTS

This book has been a long time coming, and first, I have to thank all the Jamila fans for your patience as I worked to improve my craft until I felt I was ready to write her story. I hope I've treated her with the sensitivity and respect she—and all of you—deserve.

I wrote and published *Tempt Me* during a personally difficult time, and I thank all my friends, coworkers, and family who supported me and encouraged me to keep going even when I'd rather write about burning things down than bringing people together. Your care and affection helped me reconnect with my love of romance.

Thanks to my fabulous beta reader, Carla Luna, who always inspires me to be a better writer. (Read her books, too, y'all!)

And thanks to my advance reader team who help get the word out about my books. Y'all are the best!

CREDITS

Edits and Proofreading

E&A Editing Services

Cover Design

Qamber Designs

ABOUT MICHELLE

Michelle McCraw loves reading kissing books and working in tech. One day, she decided to combine her two interests, and now she writes steamy, nerdy contemporary romance that just might make you laugh. Her books feature characters who unashamedly love science, engineering, and technology.

A native Texan, Michelle has shoveled snow during nor'easters and knows the proper response when someone yells, "O-H." She now calls Georgia home, where she doesn't miss snow AT ALL. She enjoys reading, travel, drinking bourbon, and spoiling her extraordinarily ill-behaved but adorable dogs. She has been a finalist in the RWA Vivian Contest, the Contemporary Romance Writers' Stiletto Contest, and the Windy City Romance Writers' Four Seasons Contest.

For updates about upcoming books and more free reads—plus guaranteed puppy pics—subscribe to Michelle's newsletter at michellemccraw.com. You can also follow the author on Facebook and Instagram.

facebook.com/MichelleMcCrawAuthor

instagram.com/MMOWriter

amazon.com/author/michellemccraw

goodreads.com/MichelleMcCraw

bookbub.com/authors/michelle-mccraw

BOOKS IN THE SYNERGY SERIES
CAN BE READ IN ANY ORDER

Work with Me

She's got a checklist for every occasion. He's never met a bad decision he didn't make. Can straitlaced single mom Alicia find a way to work with billionaire tech genius Jackson and save her business—without falling for him first?

"Slow burn magic!" (5-star review)

Friend Me

Romance-obsessed executive assistant Marlee has a plan to woo her crush, icy and aloof San Francisco tech executive Cooper Fallon. But it all goes wrong when her fake date, instead of making her crush jealous, sparks more-than-friends feelings. Kissing the wrong guy? Not in her plan. Neither is falling for her best friend.

"Un-put-down-able" (5-star review)

Trip Me Up

Nerdy computer scientist Samantha Jones didn't mean to end up on a book tour trying to pass off her artificial intelligence-written novel as one written the old-fashioned way. And she certainly didn't mean to fall for her flannel-wearing, poetic tour partner. Opposites attract in this road-trip romance.

"This book had me hooked right from the start and up until the wee hours devouring their story!" (5-star review)

Boss Me

Frosty billionaire philanthropist Cooper Fallon would never start a fling with his off-limits assistant, Ben…or would he?

"OMG…If you like forbidden romance this is the book for you!!!" (5-star review)

Forget Me

She doesn't remember their night together. He can't forget it. When Mimi's prospective boss mistakes Mateo for her boyfriend, she's shocked when he rolls with it. But when their fake romance becomes real, will buttoned-up Mimi let down her guard for love?

"I absolutely love this twist on the grumpy sunshine trope." (5-star review)

Tempt Me

When a gaffe caught on camera threatens her company, a no-nonsense tech CEO calls on her bestie's little sister for help. But falling for her sunshiny public relations assistant could get her into even more hot water.

"THIS WAS FUN!!" (5-star review)

BOOKS IN THE 40 AND FABULOUS SERIES

Fashion and Passion

After a disastrous self-help seminar, Carly finds friendship, empowerment, and maybe love with a younger admirer. Get swept away by sparkling banter, new besties, and spicy seduction, perfect for a bubbly escape.

Frenemies and Lovers

When Carly needs a date to her ex's wedding, she agrees to a deal with Andrew, a devilishly handsome younger man. Her frenemy's son. Who happens to be her one-night stand. What could go wrong? Who says you can't be fabulous over forty?

"Total catnip" (5-star review)

Books and Hookups

Writer Lucie's life is looking up: she has a new book deal, fabulous friends, and a bar where everyone knows her name. The last thing she needs is a surprise (geriatric?) pregnancy with her much-younger neighbor.

Conspiracies and Chemistry

Secretive billionaire Tessa seeks redemption from the biggest mistake of her life by betting it all on a groundbreaking biotechnology company, which happens to be run by her younger nemesis. And who knew lab coats were so sexy?

9 781961 373006